Green Goes Forth

Bob Gilbert

CALUMET EDITIONS

Minneapolis

**CALUMET
EDITIONS**

Minneapolis

SECOND EDITION DECEMBER 2022
GREEN GOES FORTH
Copyright © 2018 by Bob Gilbert.
All rights reserved.

10 9 8 7 6 5 4 3 2

ISBN: 978-1-960250-15-5

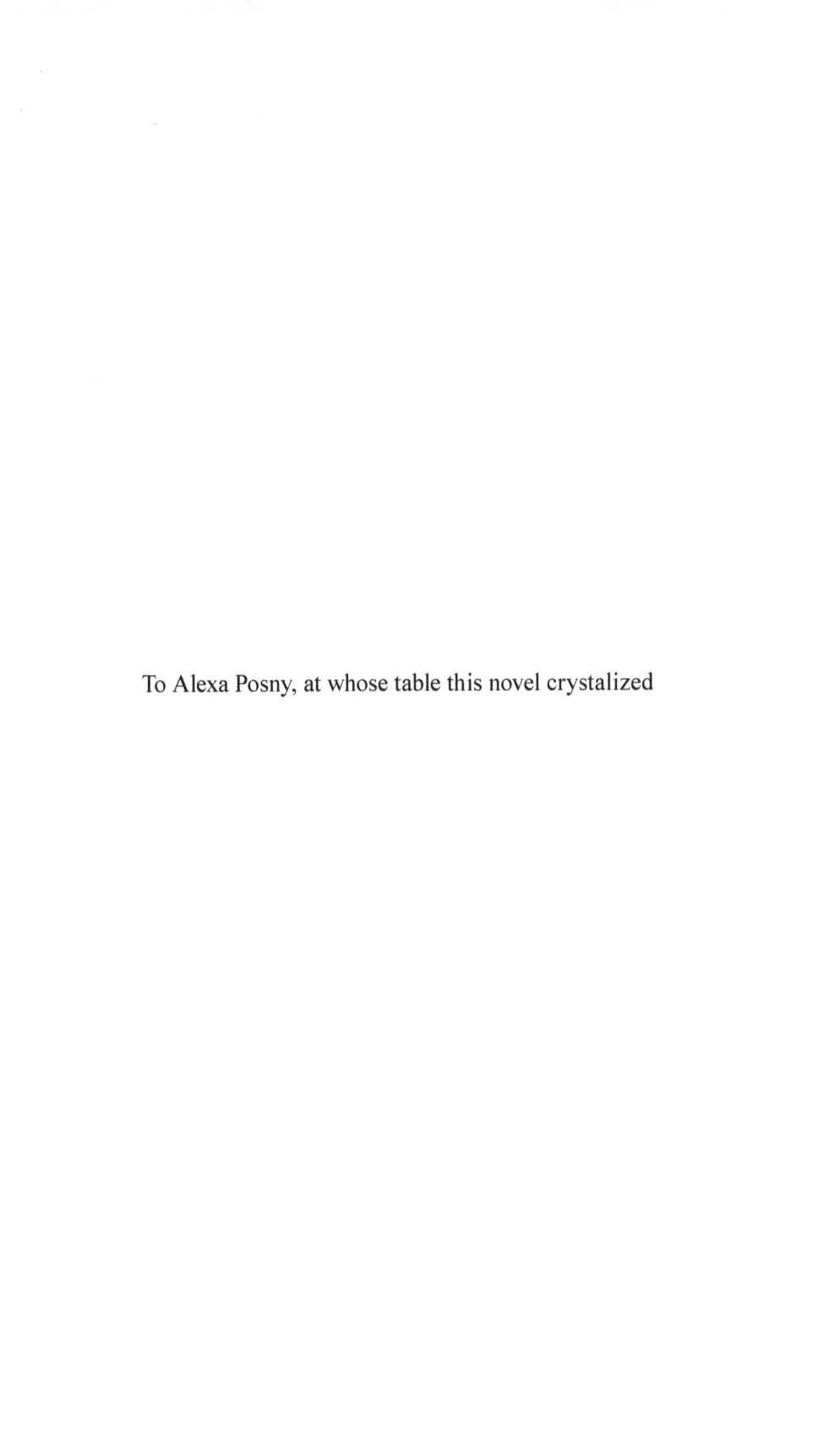

To Alexa Posny, at whose table this novel crystalized

Also by Bob Gilbert

Mintwood Place
The Shady Elders of Zion

Green Goes Forth

Bob Gilbert

Author's Note

I began writing Green Goes Forth in the 1980s when marijuana back-lash was in full swing against the idealism of the 1960s and 1970s. Though discredited as a gateway drug to heroine and a drug promoting indolence, I believe in its positive effects which promote transcendence, creativity and equanimity. Marijuana was the charm of the counter-culture. Over the years, this book evolved the way accept perceptions of marijuana have evolved. Today, it is legal in six progressive American states. The list is growing. It's my belief that marijuana will grease the wheels of globalization and help create a new consciousness for the digital age that rises above religion, anger and the shrill politics separating American blue states from the red.

Chapter 1

Though unbeknownst to me at the time, my hegira started with a sneeze. That's right; it's a simple "ah-choo" that's launching this confession.

Now, I've listened to the fairy-tale about the man who sneezed upon hearing his own truth. It turned out to be a psychic sign portending a sudden change in fortune. And that's just what happened to me. As a result of that short, spontaneous sneeze, I became a fugitive, a runaway sent into exile thousands of miles from home and longing for return.

That sneeze was met with a benevolent response. "God bless you, Joseph." The words were uttered by my Uncle Harry's friend, lawyer and business partner, Winn X. Epstein. The three of us, Harry, Winn, and I, were sitting on Winn's backyard patio before dinner at his Washington, DC home. Pollen blew across his backyard like a tsunami that evening and accosted my sinuses.

As it turned out, Winn's response was no blessing at all. The calling out of my name put me on an audio tape recorded by a federal law enforcement agency eavesdropping on our conversation. That evidence put me on the run as dramatically as it had Mohammed when he fled Mecca for his life to the safe haven of Medina in 622 AD.

Harry and Winn were two fifty-six-year-old Jewish men. They'd grown up together in Newark, New Jersey and were classmates at Barringer High School. Harry was about six feet tall, with brown eyes, a muscular build, a bald head and a moustache. Winn was a few inches shorter. He had thick silver hair, blue eyes and was a little chubby. They came to Washington, DC in the late 1950s and went into business together. They had a variety of lucrative enterprises, some legal, some not.

It was no coincidence that Winn's big beautiful home was on Newark Street, a half block up the hill from Connecticut Avenue in the Cleveland Park neighborhood. He liked the irony. While his hometown in those years was black ghetto, his tony spot on Newark Street reflected the success he had achieved in life.

There was an elegance to the old stucco house with its large front porch and second floor oriels on each side of its broad spacious front. The red oak door was flanked by two large picture windows, each topped with two red and blue stained glass floral designs. Inside was a well-lit, well-decorated home that Winn's wife, Ruth, kept immaculately clean.

The couple believed in the Old World European Bildung culture so prominent among the Jewish upper middle class. There was a painting by Pablo Picasso, one by Jean Miro and another by Ferdinand Leger hanging in their living room. There were two stone sculptures. A reclining female nude was on a living room table, and Moses holding the Ten Commandments was on a pedestal by the front door. Ruth taught fine art at George Washington University and had sculpted them both.

Persian carpets covered the hardwood floors. The furniture was so big it enveloped you when you sat down. But I have to admit I didn't care for the plastic that covered the couch and the adjoining chairs. It crackled beneath your weight and stuck to your skin on warm days.

Friday night dinner at Winn's home was a ritual that had started when I was a high school junior, the year I left New Jersey and went to live with Harry Green, my Washington, DC uncle, and continued on through my senior year at American University.

The host and hostess's weekly welcome allowed me to believe that I had transcended my ambiguous roots. Theirs was an elegant order broader than the one in which I'd been raised. Plus, besides Harry, they were the only family I had in town, and DC can be a lonely place to live. So to be welcomed into Winn and Ruth's home was something I looked forward to at the end of each week. We lit Sabbath candles, drank wine and shared stories.

Ruth was someone's kid sister from the old neighborhood. She was in her late forties. Her bleached blonde hair reached the middle of her back. It was often in a ponytail. She was tall with broad shoulders, broad hips and ample breasts. Large blue eyes, thick lips and a nose that might have been fixed back in the day were the features of her face.

She took a maternal interest in me since my mother was back in New Jersey, and we rarely spoke. Knowing Harry's relationship with women, Ruth made a concerted effort to present herself in a good light, so I might use her as a role model and marry a nice girl like Winn had instead of becoming a middle-aged rake like Harry. There was a hug and a kiss every time we met and every time we parted.

Each Friday night she sent me home with leftovers that were often the only thing in my refrigerator. The Epsteins had a daughter named Lynda who, like her father, had a law degree. She worked for a big Boston law firm. For them, I suppose, I was the surrogate son they never had.

I always arrived at Winn's before Harry. American University was close by, and my Friday afternoon classes ended at four. Harry, driving up from downtown, usually got there at six.

My favorite room in Winn's house was his library. It featured a rolltop desk—the top was always closed and locked. Big oak book-shelves covered two entire walls. Sometimes a book that glows at the bookstore loses its lumen when the reading starts. So there was usually a small box beside his desk earmarked for the used book store. Ruth refused to let him add another bookshelf, and so when a new title was prized, an old title had to go. He referred to it as the "literary Darwinism" of his library.

In addition to his adherence to the law, Winn was also a Jewish scholar who had spent two years at rabbinical school. He decided that jurisprudence held more appeal than the Talmud and later graduated from the law school at New York University.

He had lost several members of his Hungarian family to the Holocaust. His collection included rows of old books about European Jewish culture before Hitler. "It's the way I honor my dead relatives," he said.

And while I wasn't a very avid reader, since I had grown up in a house with three televisions and no books, I loved to roam around the room and fantasize about what wisdom lay buried inside those gilded titles because I lacked the concentration to read them myself.

Seeing how tentative I felt around books, despite my college syllabus and the fact that I was finishing my last semester, Winn liked to give me tours of his library and point out significant tomes that had impacted his life in positive ways. And in those days, I longed for intelligent opinions to help guide my own.

Two soft chairs separated by a small table in the corner of the room became a classroom where Winn shared his enthusiasm. He idolized Walt Whitman, William Carlos Williams, William Blake, W.B. Yeats, Homer, Ralph Waldo Emerson, Vergil, Johann Wolfgang von Goethe and Friedrich Nietzsche. He hated Dante, Ezra Pound, T.S. Elliot, and Arthur Schopenhauer.

"It's a great mistake to think that old men no longer need mentors," Winn said. "Navigating a successful life requires constant guidance, and this is where I find it, in old books like these."

Sometimes we'd play a game called stump the scholar. I'd walk around his library shopping the shelves until I discovered a book with a compelling title. Handing it to him, he'd open it and study the first page. That's where he always signed his name and dated it. He'd thumb through the pages to remind himself of its content. Mentally, he'd take himself back to the time and place he read it. Then he'd place the book on the table between us and offer up his insights about what struck him about the narrative. Sitting at that table, cups of coffee between us, we'd have long conversations while Ruth cooked dinner and Harry was on his way.

"Tell me about this book," I said. It was *Memoirs of an Anti-Semite*, by Gregor von Rizzori. "Doesn't seem right that you'd have a Nazi confession on your shelf."

A smile creased his full lips as he ran his hands through his thick silver hair. His face lit up.

"No, it's not a Nazi story at all. It's a romance," he said. "Von Rizzori was Romanian by birth. He moved to Germany just before the war and worked in radio. He writes beautiful stories about the Jewish community of his youth. Their individual lives, their hearts, their minds, their sorrows are all accounted for. The beautiful Jewesses he took as lovers are revealed in an erotic way. You'd like him too, Joseph. He was quite the wag and could probably teach you a few things about women."

Being that I was raised in a small New Jersey backwater that didn't have a library or a downtown, these conversations lightened the chip on my shoulder. My education had several missing parts, and no one was more aware of it than me. I thirsted for Winn's knowledge. Our conversations were a boost that helped me close the gap on my better educated and more cultured peers at American University. There I was, sitting with my own private tutor, one on one. I learned more at that table than I did in the classroom.

"Look at these beautiful books," Winn had said. "To own so many was once a mark of culture and intellectual standing. Today, they mark me out as a dinosaur."

"Why's that?"

"Television. It will be the death of reading. It's now the most popular medium in the world. Unfortunately, it's got too few words. It's glib, not profound. It spoon-feeds your imagination instead of stoking it. I know that your curriculum is so demanding that you don't want to read on your own. But when you finish college and set out on your way in the world, I want you to borrow some of these books and start developing your own taste for literature. It will help define you as a man."

"There's so many books everybody else on campus read in high school and I didn't," I said. "It's embarrassing. When I was growing up, I never saw anybody reading. We were all watching television. Today, after a week of classes, the last thing I want is to read some more. I'd much rather listen to rock music and hang out. Reading is not something I'm good at."

And yet I accompanied him to literary events around Washington. We listened to the presentations of writers and political reformers at the various cultural venues around DC like the Folger Shakespeare Library, different Smithsonian Museums, the National Press Club, and of course our favorite, the Library of Congress, where we attended several readings by American poets inside the Coolidge Auditorium.

"Allen Ginsberg is reading at the Library of Congress next week... want to go?" Winn asked. "He's a Jewish pot smoking hippie from New Jersey like you. You might find him interesting."

"I know who he is," I answered. "My friend has a poster of him in his dorm room. He's carrying a sign that reads 'Pot is Fun.'"

I still remember that Ginsberg reading. He had a long beard, a bald head and thick black glasses. That he was so openly homosexual made me think that he must be the bravest man in America, because every other gay person was still in the closet. In his hands that night was a squeeze box, a small accordion. He sang out short tunes with lyrics like "Jimmy Berman, Jimmy Berman, laying on the bed. Jimmy Berman drop your pants, and I'll give you some real good head."

"Oy, such a fagela," Winn muttered.

But one poem Ginsberg recited that night hit me right in the sternum. It was a story about his dying father, Louis Ginsberg, who was also a New Jersey poet. It was during his last days before he fell victim to a malignant tumor. Imitating his old man's rasping voice, which sounded as if a boa constrictor was strangling the last traces of life out of him, he repeated his father's dying words... "Don't grow old."

There was a grimace on Ginsberg's face every time he uttered "Don't grow old." It might have been theatrics or an actual imitation of the dying man's last words. Regardless, it was my belief that it also reflected Ginsberg's own anguish at watching a man he revered waste away. I envied him for writing a poetic testament to his late father. For my father was also dead, but I had no idea how to address the event in any creative way.

Winn had brought along two of Ginsberg's books, *The Fall of America* and *Howl*. He made a habit of sending me up to the stage following a reading to get the books autographed while he stayed behind nursing his bum leg.

Winn was an old acquaintance of the southern writer and poet Robert Penn Warren, who had written *All the King's Men*. He also did a turn as America's poet laureate. To Warren's Library of Congress reading Winn brought along a copy of *World Enough and Time*. The book sat balanced on the armrest between us while waiting for him to begin.

"What's the book about?" I asked.

"It's a novel that takes place in Kentucky in the 1800s," said Winn. "It's about a young lawyer who stands trial for murder."

Warren read his poems and talked about the literary mentors who inspired him on his literary journey. When the reading was over, Winn said, "Joseph, let's go down and I'll introduce you. I want him to sign my book too."

I carried it to the stage. We waited in line with about sixty others waiting to meet the man. When it was our turn the poet looked up and shouted, "Winn, you old dog. How are you?" He stood to shake his hand.

"Nice to see you, Red," Winn answered. Then Winn put his hand on my shoulder and presented me. "Let me introduce you to a young scholar here, Joseph Green."

"Nice to meet you, Joseph." Warren held out his hand, and I shook it.

"Can you sign this?"

He took the book from my hand and stared at it.

"I took the title *World Enough and Time* from a poem written by the English poet Andrew Marvell. It's an optimist's idea perfect for a young man like you. And yet in a following line he writes, 'But at my back I always hear, time's winged chariot hurrying near.' I think about that sometimes since time is a component part of life we often take for granted, especially now that I am old."

Though I appreciated the sentiment, I didn't have an intelligent response. The best I could offer was a smile. He opened the book and signed it.

People were standing in line behind us, so we couldn't talk too long. But from their conversation, which everybody wanted to eavesdrop upon, I learned that the two men were active in the Civil Rights Movement back in the 1950s. In addition, the poet had a crush on Ruth.

I handed the book back to Winn as we walked off the stage. He opened it. Both of us noticed it at the same time. His inscription had my name on it. Winn returned it to my hands. "This book is yours now," he said. "Keep it as a memento of our evening. And remember the title."

If Winn was all light, Harry was all heat. He didn't read books. In his Adams-Morgan apartment he had two televisions, one stacked on top of the other in the living room. From his couch with his two clickers, he could watch the Baltimore Colts and the Washington Redskins at the same time. He usually bet on both games. While Ruth kept Winn on a short leash, Harry, the bachelor, had no one editing his action.

Harry wasn't movie star handsome. Yet his emotional presence was striking. It was an aura steeped in testosterone that men and women respected. It soon became my benchmark on how to comport myself in the inner city.

As exotic as he seemed to me, Harry was a creature of habit. While treasuring his freedom, he had a predictable schedule. I usually knew exactly where to find him. Sunday nights he had a long-standing card game that took place at his restaurant, Harry's Bistro. His cronies gathered at a long table in the private dining room where they played poker, sometimes until dawn.

It included Mookie Saperstein, a gray headed chain smoker who made his living playing the stock market. Mort Middlebottom was a dentist who worked on Harry's teeth. Vinnie Romano, a fat New York Italian who sat behind the counter of his liquor store, shilled for the mob and made book on the side. And of course there was Winn.

On Wednesday nights Harry could be found tending bar at Boopsie's. He owned the dive bar which was located in Petworth, a black neighborhood. The clientele was poor, but Harry said the conversations he had on Wednesday nights were sometimes the most interesting of his week. The place never made money. But it was on the corner of a block that some said was going to be along the yellow line, a proposed Metro subway route. Harry hung onto it, hoping one day the property he bought for a song might allow him to hit the cash register and hear its bell.

On Saturday night he was at the Club Saratoga, the strip club he and Winn owned. He'd sit at the back of the bar and watch the action flanked by the Hogs, two former Washington Redskin offensive linemen who were bouncers. They were so big that only an idiot would fuck with them. In addition, each wore a Super Bowl ring. When they rolled their hands up into a fist and hit somebody, it really hurt.

I think you could legitimately call Harry a playboy. He had a habit of dating a variety of women all at the same time. He usually slept with each one after the third date. Then would come the relationship hand wringing. It was a conversation I heard him have with Winn who was always setting him up.

"How much of my freedom am I going to have to give up with this one?" Harry complained.

"Give me a break already," Winn answered. "It's Ruth's second cousin. She's a doctor."

"Doctor-schmoctor. What do I care? She doesn't make as much money as me. Besides, I care more about how she looks than I care about what she does."

For Harry, dating women was a dilemma. If she was poor and had children, how much money was it going to cost him? If she was a rich society gal, how many stiffs did he have to hang out with? If she was a moralist, how much gambling and carousing would he have to curb? If she was a drunk, how much caretaking was required?

These elements weighed heavily on Harry's mind. Considering the nature of his business, they were legitimate concerns. Ultimately, he preferred the freedom of his couch and his TV clickers to a domestic relationship.

"You have no respect for women, Harry. You're just a dog," Winn said.

"Some guys like being led around by their nose," said Harry. "Some guys don't."

"What are you talking about? You haven't been in an honest relationship since Miriam Jacobs back in 1961. That's fifteen years ago. What kind of role model are you for your nephew?"

"Joseph, pay no attention to Winn," Harry said. "Don't ever be honest with women. You start out looking for the love of your life, and you end up in the battle of the sexes."

"What do you mean?" I asked.

"Here's what I mean. If your girlfriend comes home and finds you with your face between another woman's legs, don't ever confess. Say, no honey, I wasn't eating her pussy, I was looking for my wristwatch. The reason…"

When Ruth arrived with four glasses of red wine on a tray, Harry stopped. She had heard the last part of his speech. She raised her eyebrows and said, "Pay no attention to either of them, Joseph. At their age they're lucky if they can still get it up."

"Hey!" Winn protested. "What kind of talk is that? Cut it out."

"The sun's going down," Ruth said. "Let's have a glass of wine and welcome the Sabbath."

Ruth was one of those older women who possessed beauty her whole life. She was very comfortable with the men who stared at her on the street. Winn adored that beauty, and his identity of being loved by a beautiful woman was a large part of him. Yet as an old friend from the neighborhood, Harry would scold Winn right to his face. "What the fuck do you know? You been swimming in pussy juice your whole life."

Ruth loved Harry for their ties to Sanford Avenue and his many years of friendship. Yet she was wary of his habits. Her fear was that Harry's recklessness might entangle her husband. So many of their activities were a secret to her.

We lit the Friday night candles at sundown and chanted the Hebrew blessing welcoming the Sabbath before devouring Ruth's standing rib roast.

Dinner conversation was domestic in Ruth's presence. She wanted to hear all about my relationship with Patti, the girl I sat beside in history class and finally found the courage to ask out. Yes, I kissed her once, I confessed. It was at the end of our second date.

"How's Mike Matelsky?" she asked.

Matelsky was my best friend growing up in New Jersey. After I moved here, he followed me to attend George Washington University where Ruth taught. So I told her about Matelsky flunking out of college and how, after cooking at Clyde's in Georgetown, he had saved enough money to start a new life out in California.

"Good riddance," Harry said in disgust.

That surprised Ruth. She questioned Harry's comment. But he wormed his way out of it. "He's a nudnik." That's all Harry would confess. I knew the real reason but stayed silent.

Winn and Harry liked to tease me about my long hair, the hippie culture I was wedded to, my idealism, the loud cacophony that was my music and my college curriculum of political science and European history.

Studying political science was demanded by the times. Things were a mess in America. And I was no different from anybody else. I just wanted to figure it out for myself. The presidency, the military and the economy were disgraced by Watergate, the Vietnam War, and the Arab oil embargo. It was a reckoning that cast a pall over the American exceptionalism I'd been taught to believe in.

Society was polarized by the Civil Rights Movement, the Vietnam War, Women's lib, drugs, recession, abortion and Watergate. The assassinations of John F. Kennedy, Robert F. Kennedy, Martin Luther King, and Malcolm X tainted all idealism.

The generation gap, a divergence of values between my baby boomer peers and its World War Two-Great Depression era elders, was so palpable you could feel it everywhere. It manifested itself in hair styles and attitudes regarding sex and race. Marijuana and rock and roll pushed my age group down a path that Harry and Winn felt uncomfortable following.

My interest in history was inspired by my late paternal grandfather, Louis Green, an immigrant. He was a corporal in the Russian army when it went to war against the Central Powers in World War

One. He saw the demise of the Czar's army firsthand and witnessed the Communist revolution and the early years of the Soviet state. Collectively, he thought the Russian proletariat and peasantry were dolts, so he split the scene and came to America in 1920.

Whenever I tried to discuss the current situation in Soviet Russia and how far it had come since my grandfather's time, Harry teased me.

"Yeah, yeah, yeah," he muttered cynically. "My father told me about the old days in Russia. Even under the Reds they sucked. And while anti-Semitism declined, deep down even the communists hated Jews."

"That's not what I learned in college."

"Your professors are all dopes. You know that, right?"

"So what did you learn in class this week, Joseph?" Winn asked, trying to change the subject.

"I'm learning about the relationship between the Senate and the House of Representatives."

"Five hundred and thirty-five clowns all there to line their pockets," Harry said.

"Harry, should we tell him what government is really about?" Winn asked.

"Let's not shake the boy's faith," Harry answered.

"I'm sorry. I still believe in America," I said.

"You want a job on Capitol Hill when you graduate?" Winn asked. "We can get you a job, no problem. Although I don't know why you'd want to be part of it."

"To be a part of government at that level would be exciting," I said.

"Restaurateurs have a longer shelf life than politicians in this town," Harry said.

"We can get you in the door," said Winn. "After that it's up to you."

And a little light beamed on my face because I was weeks away from graduating college, and a career path might be opening for me.

But then they'd start reciting stories about their political wrangling with the movers and shakers. None of it conformed to my college curriculum. That's because they did not deal with legislation or appropriations but with the individual appetites of elected representatives and their ilk.

Winn and Harry were good story tellers, and the tales they told were sung out with strong Jersey accents, Jewish irony and full orchestration aided by their hands. The confidential nature of their business was something they were hesitant to share at first. But over the months it became clear that not only was I family, I already was a member of their team. On those Friday nights, they seemed eager to express their verve to the young man who was hanging on their every word.

They had definitive roles in their business relationship. Harry was the front man. Winn, his attorney, stayed in the background, in part because of Ruth. Winn watched Harry's back, curbed his recklessness and made sure that when he crossed the line there was a legal defense he could hide behind should the law come down on him.

Winn lobbied elected representatives privately on behalf of individuals that politicians couldn't be seen with in public. Some were Mafia-types, some were representatives from governments unfriendly to the current administration. Others were well bankrolled businessmen in need of a favor or a government contract.

Winn and Harry bribed everybody—beat cops, politicians, judges, bureaucrats, even people in the press. At Winn's Sabbath gatherings they'd tell tall tales that sometimes were suspenseful, other times hilarious.

When Congressman Wilber Mills, Chairman of the House Ways and Means Committee, was arrested for frolicking drunk in a DC fountain with a DC stripper, whose stage name was Fanny Fox, the Argentine Firecracker, I heard about it firsthand because she was one of Harry's girls.

The two men also owned a few parking lots, three liquor stores and a three-story apartment building with six units near Dupont Circle. A Chinese restaurant was on the first floor. I lived on the second floor for free in return for caretaker duties. The building was their biggest money-maker because two of their units were love nests.

Harry and Winn were no street hustling pimps searching for Johns along the 14th Street corridor. They catered to congressmen, senators and their visiting out of town guests. Their clientele found their way to my building where a clean room, the drugs of their choice and their female fantasy awaited them. Each night, gentlemen, looking for a little something they couldn't get at home, knocked on my door.

I'd give the men, usually well dressed and sophisticated, the key and escort them to their rendezvous. The Johns never failed to tip me, in part to ensure my discretion, in part out of gratitude. And since I read the *Washington Post* daily, I actually recognized some of them from the front page. Most were Republicans from the South and the Midwest.

I had back-up. Frank Lancaster, a white, twenty-year veteran of the DC police department lived on the second floor too. His rent was dirt cheap, and if any trouble transpired between the Johns and the girls, Frank was the guy I called.

I'd been living in that building for two years and was not only the caretaker, but as time went on I became part of the business. There was a stable of women who worked the upstairs apartments, and like many DC businesses it was seasonal, depending on whether Congress was in or out of session.

There was a lockbox near the downstairs mailboxes where men slipped in their cash sealed in white envelopes. Harry was the only man with a key. It was based on the honor system and no one ever failed to pay.

Sometimes the girls met their dates at Harry's restaurant where a big meal was consumed. Then there'd be a trip to the strip club to get the guy excited. Then they'd come back to the apartment. For Harry, it was a trifecta he cashed in on each time.

There were four who worked the apartments regularly. The women were wary of Harry who wasn't above smacking them around when they screwed up. Still, it was a good job, and the risk of losing it for not being submissive or attentive or for showing up drunk or stoned to a tryst could get them in trouble. They got paid every Friday, and I handed out the cash.

Each woman cultivated a relationship with me. They knew I was watching, and they used me as a bulwark against Harry's potential violence. But I wasn't allowed to touch them or let them touch me. Harry insisted and we all obeyed.

Galina Petrovich was an east European blonde whose long bangs nearly covered her pale blue eyes. She had large breasts and a big butt. She loved to wear black, fish-net stockings. She spoke with a heavy accent and had a goofy smile that was always on her face. She loved to laugh and talk dirty, especially when she drank, which was all the time. She treated me like her little brother, especially since I was nineteen years old when we met, and she was probably thirty-four. She loved gaudy, expensive jewelry. Men looking to win her favor lavished it upon her. When money was tight, she pawned it.

Adele Carsden was a Wisconsin gal and a former Capitol Hill staffer. She was well into her forties when I met her. She was a natural blonde with a tight body, political alacrity, and a big libido. Her wheelhouse was young career types who came to Washington to work for the establishment.

She started her career working for a Milwaukee congressman and worked her way up to positions with Senators James Thomas Williams of Illinois and Stanford Perryman of South Carolina. While she never confessed, it was rumored that she slept with both of them.

Young ambitious men looking to further their careers flocked to her. For them, she was an Egeria. She could talk Capitol Hill politics, offer up interesting anecdotes about famous politicians and give them legitimate career advice before bringing them to orgasm.

Myra Urquicho was a petite Filipina with small breasts and smooth brown skin. She came to America for college but ran out of money her sophomore year. She turned to hustling at strip clubs and the apartment to pay her tuition.

One night she knocked on my door. "Joe, that guy, he's from Cincinnati and he snores like a bull. Let me sleep with you tonight. I've got class in the morning."

She spooned with me all night. I must admit that I adored her but was cautioned by Harry's warning, "Don't touch the girls."

Harry's grudge against my friend Mike Matelsky was the result of a visit to my apartment. There he met Myra and fell in love. She went missing for two weeks.

When Harry found out that Myra was living in a Foggy Bottom basement with Matelsky, he was furious. Matelsky was a college student and had no means to support her. So when she ran out of money, Harry lured her back into the fold. He forbad Matelsky to ever visit my apartment again and instructed Frank Lancaster to arrest him if he did. That's why he called Matelsky a nudnik, which means pest in Yiddish.

Minnie Battle was a sexy black dominatrix with a bad attitude and a penchant for S and M. She reminded me of the naked woman on the cover of Santana's second album, *Abraxas*. Harry doled her out carefully. She was earmarked for those with deep libidinal urges promulgated by shame and abuse.

Last winter Minnie almost lost her job. The apartment she was working was just above mine. When I heard furniture crashing to the floor, cursing and screams of anger, I banged on Frank's door. He was watching television. He quickly put on his uniform and rushed upstairs. I followed him inside.

The man, a thirtyish white guy, was happy to see a uniformed policeman. He had a bloody nose because Minnie had smacked him in the face with an empty vodka bottle. He was in his boxer shorts, drunk and high on cocaine. Minnie was in a bikini. "Good, I'm glad you're here, officer. Arrest this bitch, she assaulted me!" he shouted.

"Get dressed. The both of you."

They complied.

"What's your name, sir?" Lancaster asked.

"Rockland McMorrow."

"Mr. McMorrow, you're under arrest."

"For what? She hit *me*!"

"There's cocaine all over your nostrils, sir."

Cuffs were put on him. Looking down in shame, the man suddenly noticed Frank's feet. "Hey! Where are your socks?"

"None of your fucking business!" Frank shouted. Then Harry came in. He was pissed off to be called out so late in the evening.

He nodded his head to Lancaster, a signal to get the John out. As he walked by, the man, all jacked, stared me in the face and shouted in anger, "What are you looking at, punk?"

"I'm looking at a man in handcuffs," I answered.

Once they were gone, Harry slapped Minnie's face. "What the fuck is wrong with you?"

He signaled me to leave the apartment and close the door. A few minutes later, on the street, Frank accepted a bribe and let McMorrow go.

Later that night, when Minnie finished cleaning up the apartment, I heard her walking down the stairs and invited her in for a drink. She was distraught. "I knew I shouldn't have blown that cocaine up his ass with a straw," she said. "But his nostrils were already red, and he was a big shot on Capitol Hill for Christ's sake."

Then I noticed her swollen lip. "Was that from Harry or the John?"

"From Harry. He said I put his whole business at risk."

I grabbed a washcloth from the bathroom. At the refrigerator I wrapped it around ice cubes and handed it to her. She winced when she laid it on the bruise.

I suppose the reason I gravitated to Winn instead of Harry was because he was a better role model. He was more like my late father, Sid Green, Harry's older brother, who suffered a slow, cancerous death I was not allowed to witness.

Men can't choose their biological parents. But when they're teenagers they can choose their surrogates. I chose Winn and took cues from him because he offered me a way forward as a man. He had a working, functional marriage with Ruth, and they were the only healthy husband and wife role models I knew.

After dinner that Friday night we men retired for a brandy and conversation in Winn's backyard. On that warm spring evening, the moon was full, and the sky was clear. I cherished those nights with Harry and Winn. They took me under their wing and offered up a world view I never heard anywhere else.

***

Neither Harry, Winn nor I knew it at the time, but Winn's house was bugged. By saying my name in reference to that sneeze, I was put on the hot seat. I can imagine how it all came about too. Some guy is listening to our conversation on headphones, and upon hearing that ill wind, "God bless you, Joseph," I see him turning to his partner asking, "Joseph? Who is Joseph?"

That's how I became a person of interest to a federal agency investigating my elders. True, I only knew the highlights of their business, but I was no fool. I knew that Harry and Winn were connected to organized crime. But I had no idea that Harry was about to be indicted for tax evasion, prostitution, extortion, racketeering and conspiracy.

That night, when I was about to leave, Winn asked a favor that got me in deeper. "I have a briefcase for Vinnie Romano. Any chance you can drop it off on your way home?"

"I hate that fuck," I said. "He's mean and he's stupid."

"I know," said Winn. "But this is business."

"His liquor store is only a block from the apartment," I said. "Parking is so bad that by the time I find a space for my car, I'll probably end up walking by his place anyway, so let me have it."

Before I went home for the evening, I stopped at his corner liquor store and delivered the briefcase to Vinnie Romano. He was a neighborhood bookie who could be found behind a counter sitting on a stool that seemed much too small for his fat ass.

He had dark wavy hair and a pencil thin moustache. He was in his late thirties and always had his shirt unbuttoned to show off his undershirt. When Harry and Winn did business with the Italians, it was always done through Vinnie.

"Hey, Vinnie, what's up? Winn asked me to drop this off."

He was surprised to find the briefcase unlocked. When he opened it up, I saw for the first time that it was filled with cash. "How much of this did you help yourself to?"

"Piss off," I said. "I didn't take a dollar."

"I know all about you Jews and money. You better hope none of it is missing."

"Oh yeah, what are you going to do, chase me down the block? You'd have a coronary before you reached the curb."

He opened up his shirt and revealed a pistol. "You might be able to outrun me, but you can't outrun a bullet, asshole."

"This is the thanks I get for doing you a favor? You threaten to shoot me?"

"Fuckin' A, I'll shoot you. Take my money? I don't think so."

"Why don't you just call Winn and ask him how much money is supposed to be in there? Then count it. You can count, right?"

"You'll be hearing from me if there's any missing."

"So glad I stopped by," I said.

He put his thumb behind his two front teeth and in a quick motion flicked it forward. It made a small noise. In Jersey, it was Italian for *fuck you*. I turned around and walked home.

Chapter 2

Later that week I reckoned with the sneeze. Winn and Ruth showed up on American University's campus on Wednesday morning. I walked out onto the quad with Patti beside me following our morning class to find the two of them waiting for me. From Winn's stiff body language, I knew something was wrong.

Ruth stepped forward and said, "You must be Patti. I'm Ruth. Joseph has told me all about you. Aren't you a beauty. Yes, absolutely lovely." She shook Patti's hand and smiled. "I don't mean to be rude, dear, but we need to kidnap Joseph for a while. I'm sorry, will you please excuse us?"

"Sure," Patti said. "I'll call you later, Joe. Nice to meet you, Ruth."

"Come along," Winn said.

His Cadillac was parked on Nebraska Avenue. I sat in the front seat with Winn. Ruth sat in the back. That's when he told me the story. That sneeze had brought me to the attention of the US Department of Justice which was building a case against Harry. A warrant had been issued for my arrest. How Winn got wind of it was beyond me, but then they paid off a lot of people.

"Listen to me, and listen carefully," Winn said. "I just drove by your apartment. There are two cars of federal agents outside your door. They are waiting to arrest you."

"I didn't do anything."

"Of course you didn't, but you've heard things that we've told you. You can corroborate evidence. It's our fault for being so open about our business."

"I've got to go home and let my dog out."

"No. You can't."

"Can't go home? What are you talking about?"

"Do you love your uncle?" Winn asked.

"Of course, I do."

"Then you can't go home."

"You know I'd never squeal on Harry."

"No, I don't know that. They have ways of applying pressure."

"I promise to keep my mouth shut, Winn."

"Your promise is not good enough."

"Well, it's going to have to do."

"Listen, kid, some New Jersey senator was being blackmailed. The senator's fucked and Harry's been dragged into it. Now, there's a chance we can beat this rap but only if you're not around."

"What can they do to me?"

"They can lock you up and keep you."

"Why would they do that?"

"You're Harry's Achilles heel and they know it. How do you think he'd feel knowing that you were in jail and it was all his fault? It's the only way they can break him."

"Winn, I promise not to talk."

"That's not good enough. You have to go away. I'll be defending Harry in court. I don't know what they know, haven't a clue how they are going to build a case against Harry, and until I do I can't have you here. We won't have a trial date set until September, and you can't be found until it's over, which may take a year or two."

"Are you out of your mind? I'm scheduled to graduate college in six weeks. I have a life here."

"Either way, stay or go, your life here as you know it is over."

"No, it's not."

"Yes, it is."

"But I didn't do anything wrong!" I shouted.

"What the hell does that have to do with anything? Your father didn't do anything wrong either. But he took three years to die of colon cancer. It was hell for him, and it will be a similar hell for you unless you scram. They have the power to hold you in jail, and later, if you don't cooperate, they can convict you of conspiracy. Forget those ideas about the Bill of Rights and the Constitution they taught you in political science class. The Justice Department plays hardball with young marks like you."

"Don't call me a mark. And there's no way I'd betray Harry."

"Listen, kid. Harry promised your father on his death bed that he wouldn't let you go into the rackets. He promised him. Do you want to make a liar out of him?"

"It's a little late for that now, isn't it?"

"We both know Harry. He's got this meshuggana sense of honor, and he won't let you rot in jail. He'll confess everything just to get you out. Then he'll spend the rest of his life behind bars. Is that what you want?"

"I need to talk to Harry about this."

"Don't you dare. You have to leave right now."

"Why isn't Harry here telling me all this?"

"Guilt, I suppose," Winn said.

I held my breath.

"You know how hard it is to keep a secret," Winn said. "The feds will boss you. They'll boss you real hard until you give up your uncle. Come on, kid, you have to do this. Just 'til the trial's over. I'll take care of the dog, I promise. But the only way this is going to work is if you leave right now." I turned my eyes to Ruth in the back seat hoping she would offer support, some sympathy. But she sat stone-faced.

"I'm sorry, Winn," I said, "this all sounds like bullshit."

"Bullshit? Okay, I'll show you the bullshit."

We drove his Cadillac to Massachusetts Avenue and parked. We got out and entered another car, a Chevy.

"Isn't this Jimmy Luther's car?"

"Yes."

Jimmy was a few years older than me. He had a port wine stain on his left temple. As a result, his friends called him Kool-Aid. He had the enviable job of being the manager of Club Saratoga, their M Street strip joint. While Mike and I fantasized about what it was like to be surrounded by beautiful naked women, I noticed the makeup on the shoulder of Jimmy's suit coat from time to time left there by the weepy, neurotic women of his troubled harem whom he dealt with on a daily basis.

Winn stopped at a phone booth and made a call. Then he gave me a baseball cap and a pair of sunglasses to wear. We drove past my apartment building. Sure enough, just as he said, two black sedans were illegally parked in front of my building's front door. And as we drove around the corner, we spied another car in the alley. Winn found a parking spot down the block.

"What are we waiting for?" I asked.

"Something is going to happen."

"Here he comes," said Ruth.

Jimmy was also wearing a baseball hat and sunglasses. He walked by his own car which we were sitting in. His knuckles knocked against the side of it twice. Winn, his hand hanging out the window, knocked twice in return.

Jimmy was walking my Brittany spaniel, China. She must have caught scent of me because she turned to the car and started barking. It was only with a hard tug on her leash that he got her looking forward.

Jimmy wore an American University T-shirt and a small backpack. When he tried to enter my building, he was surrounded by five men who piled out of two black sedans. They threw him up against the apartment wall.

"I knew you wouldn't believe me," Winn said. "So there it is, proof."

They were giving Jimmy a rough time until he produced his own ID. But even after that they bullied him.

"Okay, Winn, I believe you," I said.

"Duck down for a minute." Driving down the street, Winn honked his horn twice and flashed the G-men his middle finger before speeding off around the corner. We headed back uptown.

"Listen, kid, I'm grateful for the sacrifices you're making. I truly am."

"Where am I going to go?"

"You got to figure it out for yourself," Winn said. "Look in the glove box."

Inside was a big white envelope stuffed with fifty-dollar bills. A white card had a phone number written on it.

"Call that number and let me know where you end up," Winn said.

He handed me another envelope from inside his jacket pocket. "Take this too. It's from Harry." I held it in my hands but didn't open it.

"Here's one more thing," Winn said. "You've had enough of college. You're wasting your time and money. What they're teaching you is a bunch of bullshit. Ruth, hand him that book."

Ruth passed it up front.

"This is my favorite book," Winn said. "Study it. Perhaps all of this will make sense one day."

"What is it?"

"Homer's *Odyssey*."

"Why is it suddenly so important?"

"It's about a guy trying to find his way home and the crooked path that takes him there."

"I've already got a home. You're kicking me out of it!"

"Return it to me when you come back."

"When will that be?" I asked.

"After the trial," said Winn. "If Harry's convicted they'll have no need of you. If we're acquitted they can't put us on trial for the same crime twice so they'll still have no need of you."

Winn drove Jimmy's car back to his own. We all got out. Ruth opened the trunk of Jimmy's car and took out a small suitcase. She put it in the back seat of the Cadillac. Then she got into the driver's seat. I slipped in beside her. Winn was standing on the curb.

"I'll be at my mother's in Morristown," Ruth said to Winn. "I'll call you tomorrow."

"Winn—" I started, but he interrupted me.

"Ruth is going to drive you out of the city. There you can pick up a bus or a train and be on your way."

"Winn," I said, just before the car pulled away, "fuck Harry and fuck you too."

On her way out of town Ruth drove down Connecticut Avenue, stopping frequently at the endless stop lights at the intersections along the way. I looked at the stores, wondering when I was going to see them again. As she entered the Route 270 ramp for points west, she put her foot down on the gas pedal to meet the traffic flow. As the car increased its speed, my breathing unconsciously marked time with the speedometer.

When the car hit seventy, she touched my hand. "Slow down, Joseph. You're hyperventilating. Stop it. You'll make yourself sick."

We drove to a small hotel in downtown Hagerstown, Maryland. She rented a room. All I had was a backpack, a set of keys, two college textbooks, Winn's book and the clothes on my back.

Upstairs, Ruth unbuttoned the blue Oxford shirt I was wearing and looked at the label for the size. "Open your pants," she said. She stared at the label above my butt and and got that size too. "You'll need new clothes. Wait here. I'll be back soon. And Joseph, please don't run away. I know this is a terrible situation. But it's really the only way."

"While you're at it, buy a bottle of Scotch," I said.

When she left, I sat staring at my reflection in the mirror. "What the fuck just happened to me?"

I felt like I just got tossed aside by two guys who were supposed to have my back. The more I thought about it the angrier I got. Twenty minutes in the hotel room went by, and I had enough.

"Fuck this. I'm not waiting here." I walked across the street to a bar, sat down on a stool and ordered a Scotch. I didn't know how paranoid I should be. But my anger was so pitched that I didn't give a damn if I got caught or not.

I had Harry's envelope in my pants pocket. I took it out and held it my hand wondering what was inside. Some lame excuse for him being an asshole? A promise to call my mother in New Jersey to explain my predicament? A promise to make it up to me? I threw it on the bar floor and stepped on it.

The Baltimore Orioles were playing an afternoon game against the Cleveland Indians on television. Four innings and three drinks later, I watched them lose to a ninth inning Indian rally. When the bartender came by to refill my glass, I asked, "Hey, is there a bus to DC?"

"Yes," he said. "You missed the last one. The next one will be at six a.m. tomorrow."

"You can bet I'm going to be on it."

I sat drinking for another half hour. And I didn't talk to anybody. "Fuck those guys… Harry, Winn, the feds," I muttered to myself. "I'm not about to pushed around by those clowns. I'm going back home in the morning. I got my own life to live. I can't be bothered with this nonsense."

A pretty blonde waitress walked by. Seeing the envelope on the floor she bent down and handed it to me. "Hey, you must have dropped this."

I took it more out of respect for the guy who had to sweep the floor than for Harry and stuffed it back in my pocket.

The six o'clock news from Washington came on. The lead story was about a Capitol Hill firestorm that had erupted that afternoon. Authorities arrested seven men in connection with an extortion ring. In addition, a senator and three congressmen were about to be indicted for corruption. Who did I see being stuffed into the back seat of a black sedan surrounded by plain clothes cops and reporters? My uncle, Harry Green. Bail was set at half a million dollars.

I reached for Harry's envelope and opened it. Inside was my birth certificate and a note that read "Joseph, you lucky bastard. Go find yourself!"

When I returned to the hotel room Ruth was waiting. She was angry, but she did not reprimand me. She poured me a Scotch and one for herself. We drank sitting on chairs at a small table beside the bed. She tried to make it seem that everything was all right. But it wasn't all right.

"Spare me the smooth talk, Ruth. We both know you're giving me the bum's rush. Don't insult me by saying you're not."

"Winn didn't tell you the whole story," she said.

"I know. I just watched the six o'clock news. Harry's been arrested."

"No, not that."

"You mean it gets worse?"

"Yes."

"How could it get worse?"

"Vinnie Romano and the Jersey mob are involved. The politicians the feds indicted are in their pocket. They stand to lose a lot if they go to jail. They don't trust Harry to keep his mouth shut. Unless Winn can broker a deal, they're coming after you to ensure Harry's silence."

My anger evaporated. I exhaled everything in my lungs and slumped in my chair.

"What the hell are you doing here, Ruth?"

"You're in trouble, Joseph, and I want to make sure that you understand the gravity of your predicament."

"So why you? Why not Winn? Why not Harry?"

"Harry's in jail. Winn can't help you either. There's a warrant for your arrest. Aiding a fugitive could get him disbarred. So you see, there's only me."

She handed me a ticket.

I stared at it.

"This is a thirty-day train pass," she said. "Go wherever you want."

"But I want to go home."

"I'm sorry, you can't."

"Ruth, I have a girlfriend. If I turn up missing she may call the police."

"Write her a note. I'll see that she gets it."

"What do I say?"

"Do you love her?"

"I think so."

"Ask her to wait for you."

"Can I call my mother?"

"No, I'll pay her a visit in New Jersey."

"My professors?"

"That's not a good idea."

"What about my degree?"

"You can straighten it out when you return."

"And when will that be?"

"I don't know."

Then something important dawned on me. "I need a favor," I said. "The police may have a warrant to search my place. There are a few letters and some other papers in the top drawer of my desk. Any chance you can ask Frank to go and grab them for me? It's important."

"Don't worry," she said. "I'll take care of it."

She turned her attention to the two bags on the bed. The smaller bag contained a toothbrush, toothpaste, deodorant, soap and a roll of cinnamon Lifesavers. Examining the assorted sundries inside, I said, "Looks as if you've catered these 'get out of town in a hurry' excursions before."

"I have," she said, in a voice that sounded like a confession. "For myself."

"But you always came back."

"Yes, I always came back. So will you."

"God, I hope so."

"Here, try this on. I bought it at the army-navy surplus store down the street." Inside the bag were pants and shirts, Vietnam war surplus. The clothes fit.

"They have photos of you," Ruth said. "We'll need to cut your hair."

"Are you kidding me?"

"Would you rather be arrested? Know this, you won't be safe in jail if Vinnie finds out where you are."

Ruth poured us both another drink. Then she led me to the bathroom and commanded that I sit on a chair in the bathtub. She had a pair of clippers, the kind a barber uses. My shoulder length hair came off while I sat with my drink in hand and my shirt off. It had taken me almost two years to grow that ponytail. Now it was in the bottom of the tub. The moustache came off too. When I finally stood and looked in the mirror I blanched. I looked like G.I. Joe. She collected the hair and put it in a bag. She threw me a towel and told me to shower off.

It was the longest shower I ever took. I toweled myself off in front of the mirror. No long hair and no moustache, which was part of my identity since it signaled me as a supporter of the counter-culture. Now I looked like one of the feds waiting outside my apartment. I realized that Ruth had taken my clothes. I walked out of the bathroom with a towel around my waist.

She was lying in bed with the covers pulled up to her chin. "It's cold in here, close the window."

"What are you doing in bed?"

"I drank too much. I can't drive."

"Shouldn't you call Winn and tell him you're okay?"

"I'm afraid someone might trace the call."

She pulled back the covers and exposed her breasts. She patted the spot next to her, beckoning me to join her. I stood beside the bed.

"Ruth, I can't do this."

Then she watched me stiffen underneath the towel.

"Obviously, you can, Joseph."

She reached for the towel and pulled it off.

"What are you doing?" I asked.

"What do you think I am doing?"

"What about Winn?"

"What about him?"

"Don't you think this will be a little awkward?"

"If he walks in on us, I'll just tell him, no darling I wasn't giving Joseph a blowjob, I was looking for my watch."

I laughed, and it put me at ease.

"Ruth, I…"

"Come on, Joseph, don't be that way. I need this."

"Truth is, I think I need it too," I said.

"Don't ever deny the virtue of sexual healing, especially when you hurt."

Knees on the mattress, she positioned herself in front of me. She took hold of me with her hand and kissed my mouth. And so we began.

She was the best lover I ever had. And somehow, following her lead, I was my best too. I got it in my mind that if I fucked her very hard, very good, all this might go away, and I could begin tomorrow as I had this morning. As I climaxed it was with the hope that every ounce of anxiety, anger and fear would shoot out of me too.

When I finished there was nothing left of me. I fell into a deep sleep.

Chapter 3

When life's vicissitudes overwhelm me, I know just what to do—sleep like the dead and figure it out in the morning. And that's just what I did. When the chambermaid knocked on my door it was eleven a.m. I might have slept even longer if she hadn't awakened me.

Ruth was gone. So were my street clothes and my backpack. She seemed bent on making me impersonate a soldier. All that was left were the army surplus clothes stuffed in a duffle bag, an envelope filled with cash and a thirty-day Amtrak railroad ticket good for anywhere in America. On the bathroom mirror, written in red lipstick, she had printed one word… "Endure."

I opened up Winn's envelope and counted out two thousand in cash. There in a Hagerstown hotel room I plotted out my next move. There was no way I was going to let the police cage me like a zoo animal. So I was going on the lam. With that decision my whole sense of self shifted. My college days were over. All my fantasies of working on Capitol Hill vanished. The future was a mystery. With an envelope full of cash and freedom from responsibility, I was about to embark on a grand adventure. There was only one place to run to—Mike Matelsky in a California town called Cotati.

I realized it yesterday. His letter was in my desk drawer and that's why I wanted Frank to grab it. It was the only clue to where I was headed. But, I wasn't sure where he was working. Rifles and Tits? It was a bar whose name sounded something like that. I was hoping the town was small enough that once there I'd be able to find him.

***

On my way to the train station, I walked in front of a police car stopped at a traffic light. The cop gave me the once over through his aviator sunglasses. He nodded his head in a tacit greeting. And I smiled because yesterday, with my ponytail and moustache, he'd have had the urge to search me for drugs.

The Amtrak was heading west, and I took a window seat. I tried to read *The Odyssey*, the book Winn had given me, but I couldn't. The meter was too complicated, and I couldn't focus. Somewhere in the canon of western literature, in a book unknown to me, there must be a hero who was suffering an exile just like mine... some story I could draw strength from. Perhaps my plight was echoed in the Old Testament, or in a novel written by Leo Tolstoy or Fyodor Dostoyevsky or Joseph Conrad. But I never read any of those authors.

However, I did remember an essay I had once read in a history class by the British historian Arnold J. Toynbee. It was from his twelve-volume book *A Study of History*. The essay was called "Withdraw and Return." In it he described a historical archetype that ran through history. He cited as examples Mohammed's escape to Medina, Moses going up Mount Sinai and Lenin's escape to Switzerland. There in exile, the protagonist regroups and figures things out for his eventual return. I was feeling the first part of that drama.

So there I was betwixt and between, staring out the window as the train made its way west through the poor neighborhoods of small towns across Maryland and Pennsylvania. There was a stretch of track where we kept passing cemeteries. And I got spooked because I feared the train car was really a coffin, and I was just some poor dead stiff on his way to the grave.

I thought about Ruth and the intimacy we had shared last night. And despite my anger at Harry and Winn, I felt guilty. But not for the reasons you might think. It seemed that my pliable nature made me the co-conspirator of another middle-aged woman's betrayal of her husband. Ruth was the second; my mother was the first.

I didn't speak to my mother, Lois Green. That's because there wasn't very much to say. The lingering fallout of my father's cancerous death was still too raw. And I felt as if I had betrayed my father with my mother's collusion. Here's how.

It was a Thursday night around eleven. I was in bed, but I couldn't sleep because my father was coughing in his bedroom. It was so loud and annoying that it kept me awake. I went to the bathroom and found some cough syrup. I was about to knock on his closed door when he suddenly stopped. Shit, it must be those damn Camel cigarettes he smokes. I went back to bed but no more than fifteen minutes later it started again. The light was on in the kitchen, so I went downstairs to complain to my mother who was washing a pan in the sink.

"Hey, I'm trying to sleep. Can't you make him stop coughing?"

My mother turned and faced me. "How much of a man are you?"

It wasn't the response I had expected. But it was a question I'd been pondering myself. "I don't know. Why?"

"Your father has cancer."

"He's going to be all right, isn't he?"

"His spleen is so swollen that it's pushing against his diaphragm. That's why he is coughing."

"Well… what…?"

"He's got six months to live."

"So why are you telling me?"

"Because I have to tell someone or I'll burst."

"You mean he doesn't know?" I asked.

"Correct. He doesn't know."

"Do you want me to tell him?"

"No, this is a secret we have to share. Your sisters don't know either. The doctors think it's better this way. If he finds out they're afraid he'll die sooner, and there's too many things to take care of before he passes. Promise me you'll keep this secret."

I was too shocked to respond.

"Joseph, promise me you'll keep this a secret."

"Okay, I promise."

I felt like I got punched in the gut. I didn't cry or hug my mother. I calmly returned to my room. I purposely sat listening to him cough from my bed with the light off until I finally dozed off.

And I obeyed. I didn't tell anyone. But the secret was too much to bear. In the house, I no longer saw him as my father. I saw him as a dead man. I couldn't look him in the eye or stand fast for a conversation lest I break down and tell him the secret he deserved to hear.

Actually, I stopped talking altogether. So distracting was the drama that I was barely able to function. I felt so vulnerable, so unprepared for life that I shut down and fell into a depression. My mother's confession was a careless whisper that altered me forever. So I withdrew to my room and stared at a television wishing the days would pass as fast as the shows I watched.

My teachers noticed. That month three of them pulled me aside. "What's the matter? Why are you acting so morose?" Yes, that's the word one of them used, morose. "Are you on drugs?"

I feared that if I told anyone, Sid Green would die instantly, and I'd be to blame. So I clammed up, trying my hardest to become invisible. It got so bad that the principal called my mother into school. But even then she refused to divulge the secret.

The man most frustrated with my behavior was my father. He was furious at these developments. And in typical Sid Green fashion, he screamed at me for my inadequacies and then gave me the silent treatment which to me was far worse. I was living with a walking corpse who didn't even know it. I felt an incredible contempt for both parents. But it paled to the contempt I felt for myself. Someone had to tell my father he was doomed, but I'd be goddamned if it was going be me.

Three months later, Dr. Tony Marasca told my father the truth. His cancer was inoperable. It was going to kill him. When he realized that I'd been keeping this secret from him he was full of rage. He couldn't even look at me. But he must have known he was dying. He was losing weight rapidly, and his skin took on a yellow tinge.

The physical humiliation of his death, coupled by his son's complicity, made him a bitter man. He never forgave me, and I never received his blessing. A father's blessing, I once heard, is an inesti-mable thing. Yet it was something denied me. Instead, my father had become like a distant deity, a dismissive God, a bearded old judge who, with me standing before him, hat in hand, refused to grant me absolution from his perch in the clouds.

But now sitting on this train, which with every minute took me farther and farther from home, I was forced to confront the unresolved truth. I had sold out my father, and I didn't even know what I had sold him out to.

There was no letting go of it. It was a tragic situation for one important reason—I truly loved him. Lamentable events ruined our relationship, events that would never be transcended. For how can a son heal such a relationship when his father is carried beyond the veil separating the mortal world from the spiritual?

I remembered one afternoon back in the 1960s before his cancer. We were walking the streets of Newark in his old neighborhood. He bought us both a hot dog from a street corner vender who knew his name. I had mustard and sauerkraut; he had peppers and onions. We sat on a brick wall eating our lunch when a long-haired hippie walked by. Under his breath, with a chuckle, he said, "Get a load of this guy."

"He's probably laughing at you too, Dad." For some reason, I now regret saying that.

One night he followed me down to the basement, and in the dim light we had a conversation. It was our last. I was so on the verge of tears I couldn't look him in the eye. He tried to say the right words, but the right words were missing. I don't remember much of what he told me except for one thing that he made quite clear. "Corporate life-style? Don't do it. Promise me you won't fall into the trap that I did."

He was a corporate accountant for a large manufacturer. When he found out his end was near, he regretted that his whole life was spent doing someone else's bidding instead of his own. To add em-phasis to his stern warning, he grabbed my elbow to make sure I was paying attention and said it again. "Don't do it."

When Harry found out about the cancer, he drove up to Jersey. My father was having a bad day and was bedridden. Harry walked in the door to pay his last respects to his older brother and walked out the door with his only son so I didn't have to watch him die.

When I moved to DC my father's warning against the corporate lifestyle seemed like easy advice. Harry never gave a damn for middle class values. For him such conformity was the same kiss of death that laid a wet one on my father's lips. I was more than happy to follow Harry's lead. Being an amiable rogue was so much more interesting than keeping corporate ledgers. Who cares if he's a pimp?

Against the odds, my father stayed alive for one more year. It was a painful, demoralizing, anxiety-ridden wasting away I wasn't allowed to see. One week after my eighteenth birthday he died, and they put him in the ground.

When it was over, my mother, my two sisters and I opted not to speak of it. By not speaking of it we stopped speaking entirely. That's where my family was today, stuck in some sort of emotional limbo waiting for the raw wound to bind.

And then there was Ruth. I had once asked Harry about her following a Friday night dinner. "She had a miscarriage," he said. "The child was four months away from delivery. It was a boy. When she lost the child, she had a breakdown. It was a burden for Winn who held the family together for the sake of their daughter, Lynda."

"What do you mean had a breakdown?" I asked.

"The grief was too much," Harry said. "She became a drunk who fucked anyone who made eyes at her. It humiliated Winn. She somehow blamed him for it. She said it was proof that their marriage was a lie. But he put up with it because he loved her."

That conversation with Harry, no more than a twenty second exchange, now came back to me. Maybe my connection to Ruth stemmed from the feeling of loss—me for my father, Ruth for her son—and our bond was the search for some holy ghost who might offer up some meaning for a pain we both felt so deeply.

Yet the fact that two good women betrayed their husbands with me as their willing accomplice was an irony I could not shake. What was it all about? Searching for my own complicity in the drama made me feel guilty. I vowed not to let it happen again.

A funny thing happened on the train. My short hair and govern-ment issue attire prompted a conversation with a guy named Bruce Jo-seph Wolpin. He was about three years older than me. He was a GI who befriended me somewhere near Sioux Falls, South Dakota. He'd done a tour of duty in Vietnam and afterward was stationed in Thailand. He had just returned from southeast Asia and was on leave before reporting for his next assignment at Fort Bliss in El Paso, Texas. A Peoria, Illi-nois native, he was on his way to San Francisco to visit his high school sweetheart. He had an olive complexion and gentle, big brown eyes. I was glad to meet him because I hadn't spoken to anyone in two days.

"Do you get high?" he asked.

"Yes."

"Can you roll a good joint?"

"Yes."

"Good, because I'm terrible at it. Roll a couple in the bathroom, and at the next stop we'll get out and smoke."

I went to the bathroom and looked at his bag. There was about an ounce of pot in it. The weed was green with purple highlights. It had red hairs and crystals surrounding the buds. The seeds were shaped like baby cherry pits, grey-brown in color with a touch of green vis-ible along the seam. When the train stopped to pick up passengers in Bozeman, Montana, we stepped off the train and smoked behind a tin shed.

"Wow, this is amazing stuff," I said.

"I got it in Pat Pong, the red-light district in Bangkok. But it isn't native to those parts. According to the guy I bought it from it's from Afghanistan. The tribesmen grow it side by side with their opium. Strongest stuff I've ever had."

"Wow, I'm really loaded."

"We smoke pot in order to go places we're not supposed to go, but actually should go," said Bruce. "It's like undiscovered country."

"You're right, it is undiscovered country, but I'm honor bound to explore it."

When I went to return his bag, he said, "No, you keep it, Joe. My girlfriend doesn't smoke, and she gets mad when I do."

"Thanks." I opened the zipper of my duffle bag and put it inside.

The pot allowed me to rethink my problem, as if I had left my body entirely and could look down upon myself sitting in the train's window seat.

Okay, so I was fucked. I knew that much. I'd just wasted a semester's worth of money for classes I'd never get credit for. The monthly survivor's benefits I received from Social Security to stay in college would now cease because I dropped out. There was a woman I had just started with, a buxom Jewish beauty named Patti. Kiss that relationship goodbye. I had a large coterie of friends from work and school and a life that I loved. All gone now. Worst of all, I missed my dog, China.

I didn't want to think about any of it. Fortunately, Wolpin was a talker, especially when he was high. I listened to story after story about his life. There was one story he was keen to tell.

"We were trying to flush out the Viet Cong from a village in the Mekong Delta," he said. "It was dawn. I positioned myself in a ditch at the north end of the village. My sergeant gave me explicit instructions—'we're going in from the south side. If anybody comes running toward you, they're probably the enemy. Shoot them.'

"So I sat by myself, one of three snipers surrounding the area," Wolpin said. "Then I heard gunfire. My sergeant was shouting instructions to the others above the blasts. When three people ran out of the village straight for me, I did what he said. I gunned them down."

"Who were they?" I asked.

"Two men and a woman," he said. "When the rest of the platoon found me, I was standing over the three dead bodies oozing blood. We found maps on their bodies that proved they were Viet Cong. The sergeant clapped me on the back and said, 'Good job, Bruce.'"

"How do you feel about it now?" I asked.

"Actually, I don't feel anything at all. They were the enemy. I followed orders. But now I have a real problem."

"What's that?" I asked.

"I have to face my girlfriend."

"What's her name?"

"Amy," he said. "She was an anti-war protester. She says I served my country but betrayed myself. And feeling nothing about the incident is not going to cut it with her. She's going to demand more. So now I don't know how I should feel about it. All I know is, if I tell her what I did I won't be getting laid anytime soon."

There was a minute of silence between us. "Come on, Bruce, let's go to the club car. I'm buying."

We were together for two days, sneaking outside to smoke pot at stops along the way. No one suspected that the two short-haired men, one in uniform, one in surplus, were potheads.

There's a true camaraderie among marijuana smokers. When you find a brother to share a joint with, he's immediately your soul mate, a friend for life. I began to believe that marijuana was going to grease the wheels of globalization, since when I smoked it with my black, Asian and Hispanic friends in the neighborhood, we all opened up to each other, and the ethnocentrism we secretly held in our breasts didn't matter. Plus, it never stoked rage like alcohol. Instead it stoked, in most cases, laughter.

I bought three rounds of drinks in the club car. An older man, dressed like a cowboy, bought us another round on his way out with his wife. At the end of the evening, right before I was ready to sleep, high on pot, drunk on Scotch, I thought to confess my story about being on the run. My predicament was ridiculous, I knew that. But if I could hold onto the secret of my father's cancerous doom, I didn't see any reason to spill over the side with my current drama. When he asked where I was going I told him this story.

"I have a friend named Mike. He's actually a pal of mine from New Jersey. His mom's sick. No one can find him. I've been sent out west to bring him home."

It was a bullshit story. But we were stoned, and Bruce didn't question it.

"Where does he live?"

"Last I heard, Sonoma County. A small town called Cotati. But that was four months ago."

Then I was reminded that the only letter he had ever sent me was in my top drawer. It had a return address. And I got scared that whoever was looking for me, be it federal agents or Vinnie Romano, might find it. I hoped Ruth had retrieved it.

"So you're going cross country to visit a guy who doesn't even know you're coming?" Bruce asked.

"Yes."

"What are you going to do if you can't find him?"

"Not sure."

He pulled out a scrap of paper and began scribbling on it. Here's Amy's address. She lives in Oakland. If you don't find him, come hang out with us."

I put it in my wallet. When he stood up to go to the bathroom, he accidentally knocked over a small pack that held his personal belongings. The zipper was open, and papers spilled on the floor, including his military ID, an Illinois driver's license, and a letter from Amy. He picked them up and put them back in the pack before leaving the train car. The driver's license picture featured a face with short hair. It was close enough to my own visage. When he was out of sight, I stole his driver's license and put it in my pocket.

Next morning the train arrived in San Francisco. There on the platform, we shook hands and parted as brothers.

Chapter 4

I hopped a bus from San Francisco north to Sonoma County looking for a place I'd never been. Mike had landed in Cotati on the advice of his cousin, Cary Frank, who attended Sonoma State University and had stayed on after graduation. Last Fourth of July in New Jersey, Cary regaled Mike with stories of beautiful long-haired hippie chicks, excellent marijuana and blue California skies. A week later Mike received a letter from George Washington University saying he would not be readmitted because of bad grades. So he worked in a Georgetown restaurant, saved his money and hitchhiked out to California, arriving there on New Year's Day.

Except for that one letter I hadn't heard from him. I couldn't remember his address or his phone number. I knew finding him might be a long shot, but truth is, I didn't have many options.

So there I was, sitting in the front seat of a Greyhound bus admiring the golden hills of California, which in the flickering twilight resembled a naked Mexican woman laying on her side revealing voluptuous curves. The bus driver struck up a conversation.

"You in the military?"

"Why do you ask?"

"Men around these parts don't usually wear their hair so short."

"No, it's not that. It's something else," I answered.

"I was in the army back in 1962. Did twelve months in Germany driving tanks and raising hell. Some of the best days of my life."

"Maybe I should wear a hat."

"Nah, let all them hippies think you're just a good ole' boy."

The driver had a big cowboy belt buckle, cowboy boots and long black sideburns. He was probably fifteen years older than me, a man who came of age when Elvis Presley was king. As for me, the Beatles were my musical lodestar.

Somehow the energy had changed in the early 1960s. Red blooded American boys were conquered by four lads from Liverpool. Elvis and the Beatles represented a line of demarcation between a single generation with regard to consciousness. One drank, the other smoked pot. One wore short hair, the other long. And sometimes that division could even be found among siblings just a few years apart in age. The older brother for Elvis, the younger brother for the Beatles. The bus driver was an Elvis guy.

"This sure is beautiful country," I said.

"First time here?"

"Yes."

"It's a part of California that you don't hear too much about. It's wine country. Some of the best bottles in the world come out of this soil. They're saying that it's a good time to buy land too. It's predicted that in the next twenty years the urban sprawl from San Francisco is going to push its way up as far north as the Alexander Valley. Yep, everybody wants to live in California."

"Ever hear of a place called Rifles and Tits?" I asked.

"No, I been living in this county for thirty years, and I've never heard of the place. That's a strange name for a gun store."

"Actually, I think it's a bar," I said.

"And that's the name, Rifles and Tits? Are you sure?"

"No, I'm not sure. My buddy wrote me a letter saying he's a cook at a place that I think is called Rifles and Tits."

"Sorry, I never heard of it."

I went back to looking at the scenery when suddenly the driver shouted out, "Elfie and Toots?"

"Yes, that's it! Elfie and Toots."

"Oh sure, it's a roadhouse bar right on the Old Redwood Highway. The food's pretty good. On weekends it's a college hangout. I'm going to pass right by it. I'll drop you off."

"Thanks," I said.

"Kind of sad though. Elfie and Toots were an old Italian couple who ran the place for years. Elfie tended bar while his wife, Toots, cooked in the kitchen. She made the best tomato sauce in the county. One night about two years ago Elfie committed suicide in the basement. They say his ghost still haunts the place."

"Oh, I'm sorry to hear that."

I pulled Bruce Joseph Wolpin's driver's license out of my pocket. I studied his face and tried to imitate his expression in case some cop asked for my ID. Except for the short hair, we didn't look much alike. But I hoped that with a little luck I might get away with stealing his identity. I committed his address to memory. Then I put his license in my wallet and hid my own in the duffle bag.

Not more than forty minutes later the driver pulled to the side of the road. I shook his hand and walked off the bus. I was standing in the parking lot of Elfie and Toots. The bar was a long one-story building all by itself. The big picture window had neon signs advertising the different beer brands inside. The gravel parking lot had a few cars and a few motorcycles too.

I walked into the cool dark saloon, found a seat at the short end of the L-shaped bar and dropped my bag. The bartender was a big man with long hair parted in the middle and a handlebar moustache. After ordering beer, I took a deep breath and crossed my fingers. "You got a guy named Mike Matelsky working here?"

"Mr. Slowpoke? Yeah, he's in the kitchen. He's supposed to be cooking steaks for those three guys over there. So don't interrupt him. They've been waiting a half hour and they're pissed off." He turned and walked away. Despite his hostility, it was the best news I'd heard in days.

The three long-haired men he referred to were in their early thirties. They sat at the bar about fifteen stools away. They didn't seem impatient to me. Instead they were laughing loudly and flirting with a waitress. The biggest one of the three was banging his fist beside the cigarette strewn ashtray screaming rhetorical questions with his bass voice.

"Now look at this fine piece of womanhood," he said as he held her arm so she wouldn't walk away. "Why isn't screwing the girl next door good enough anymore? Say what you will about the 1960s, at least it had an organic purity to it. Not anymore. Homosexuals have taken over San Francisco. Can you believe it? And I'll tell you why I'm pissed off. Status anxiety. Yes, that's right, status anxiety. My liberalism has been eclipsed. Just because I refuse to let a man's cock enter any of my orifices I am suddenly a reactionary."

"This whole country is going to hell," said the guy on his left. "Those fuckers in Washington are ruining everything."

I almost shouted "Right on, brother." But I held my tongue.

Then the third man spoke. "All I can say is let's stay high and wait for the good times to return."

"Fun place, huh?" The guy next to me folded his newspaper and was attempting conversation. "This must be your first time here," he said. "I'm the local rummy. I come in here every night, and I've never seen you before."

"You're right, this is my first time."

"Rednecks and rebels. The place is filled to the gills with them. He bent his head down low and raised his shoulders around it like a turtle recoiling in its shell. "When you got to listen to that crap every day it gets on your nerves."

"Who are those guys?" I asked.

"That's Jerome Mercuri, and his sidekicks are Dr. Clear and Matt Cornfoot. They're the local drug kingpins. They call themselves the Yippie Rats."

"Yippie Rats?"

"Yeah, I know. Sounds stupid, doesn't it."

I shrugged my shoulders.

"My name is Mark Anderson. What's yours?"

"Joe."

"Nice to meet you, Joe," Mark said.

Suddenly, Matelsky appeared at the service bar holding three plates. Each was piled with steak, asparagus and mashed potatoes. Mike handed two plates to the bartender who delivered them to his customers while he waited with the third. Because Mike was unaware of my presence I got a good look at him in his new environment.

Mike was a Jersey roughneck. He was handsome but over-weight, big hearted but conniving. It showed in the way he narrowed his eyes when sizing up a situation. He'd deliberately delay answering a question just to create some tension. The answer he responded with was never the one you expected. Because of his barrel chest and vocal roar, friends called him "the Bear."

And what a talker. He'd strike up conversations with sales clerks, waitresses and any attractive woman that happened by. If they snubbed him, or walked by in silence, he didn't care. There were plenty more women walking the streets, and he played the law of averages. Sooner or later he'd connect.

Back in high school, his garrulous nature was the perfect counterweight to my quietude, especially when burdened with my father's secret. Many were repulsed by his loud, rapid speech, his love of sensation and his tendency to rank people. Hanging out with him was a lesson in assertiveness training. He bowed to no law, custom or convention. And yet he had a remarkable concrete sequential mind that made him efficient at every task he undertook.

Driving down the wrong side of the road at eighty miles per hour with Mike at the wheel while he reaches for a beer in the back seat. Sitting in a dark, crowded movie theater when you suddenly take an elbow in the ribs. He's handing you a joint, ridiculing middle class businessmen in suits for their conformity and bullying them eye to eye when they talked back.

That's what hanging around with Mike was like. Sometimes it was embarrassing. Yet, he stood six feet two and weighed two-twenty. No one was ever as truculent, not even the black toughs on DC streets. He warded off danger like an automatic rifle. I used to think he would succeed in life by running over everybody in his way like some muscle-bound fullback.

But there was another side of him that few people saw—the knight in shining armor. One night we were at the Sunshine Inn in Asbury Park for a Jerry Jeff Walker concert. The place was packed. Jimmy and Johnny O'Toole, twins from high school were at the bar with us doing shots of Jameson. As the concert got good, Mike and I pushed our way to the front.

To the right of us, we watched a pretty young girl in a halter top and tight jeans dancing wildly to Jerry Jeff's guitar riffs. A group of guys were feeding her drinks. She danced with one and then another. Her moves were alluring, and her friends were all in. Several songs later, she saw Mike staring at her and remembering herself, threw her arms around his neck. She whispered in his ear... "Please don't let these guys take me home."

That's all she said. When the next song started one of them grabbed her by the hand, and she started dancing again. Four guys surrounded her like sharks circling a shipwreck. When that song ended, she put herself behind Mike's shoulder. When the biggest of the four reached for her arm, Mike slapped it away. "She's had enough."

"Mind your own business, pal."

"This *is* my business."

Now the four of them surrounded Mike. Seconds later I returned with the O'Toole boys, two drunken Irish sots ready for mayhem. Jimmy looked me in the face and shouted out loud, "Which one of these douchebags do I get to beat up?"

When security saw it, three big black guys arrived. The man in charge spoke. "Okay fellas, let's not do this inside. Break it up before someone gets hurt."

Mike looked at him and said, "Hey man, this girl has had too much to drink. She said she has a sister around here someplace. Can you help find her?"

"Sure," he said.

The four predators, pissed because their gang bang plans had been thwarted, walked away, but not before trash talk poured out of each one of them.

When my father's secret sent me into shock, Mike was the first guy to figure it out. I confessed, but only to him. From then on, he had my back. He gave me space to talk about it, made sure I had plenty of pot and defended me from the gossip of others until the day they told my father his truth.

Seeing him standing across the bar, waiting for the bartender to retrieve the third plate, was a relief. I pushed my beer aside, and I waved my hand up in the air to get his attention. The bartender blocked his line of sight, yet everyone else at the bar seemed to see. They looked at me like I was a flake. When the bartender fetched the third plate he gave Matelsky a dirty look.

"Hey, what's your problem, Tuffy?" Mike growled.

"My customers shouldn't have to wait a half hour for their dinner."

"They do when they order it well done. Tell them to order it medium rare like normal people, and they'll get it in half the time."

"Hey, Matelsky, I'll eat my steak any way I want," said Dr. Clear.

"Oh yeah, only a moron eats a rib eye steak well done," Mike shouted back. He returned to the kitchen.

When Tuffy delivered the last plate, he gave the three guys an apologetic look and said, "That fucker just exasperates me."

"No sweat, Tuffy," said Jerome. "Bring us a round of brandy, the good stuff."

Mark, sitting next to me, grunted. Then he confided in me. "Those guys are responsible for half the marijuana cultivation in the county. Then they trade it in the city for cocaine. They snort that speedy white powder, and it turns them into Superman."

"Well, people like to change their consciousness," I said.

"If you're looking for drugs those are the guys to see."

He spoke too loud. The hand I waved at Mike drew attention to me, and the tough guy, Jerome, walked behind our bar stools. I don't think he liked the idea of the loquacious rummy speaking so openly about his business to a short haired stranger. I turned to face him. Mark did not.

Jerome poked him in the back. "You talk too much, Mark. Shut the hell up."

Mark cringed. Then looking at me he said, "And who the fuck are you?"

A shout came from across the bar. "Joe! What the hell are you doing here?"

Matelsky came marching around the bar throwing his apron to the floor in the process and gave me a big hug.

"You know this guy?" asked Jerome.

"Know him? He's my best friend. Jerome, meet Joe. He's from my hometown back in Jersey."

Though I stuck out my hand, Jerome never touched it. Instead he muttered, "Great, just what we need around here, another Jersey boy in Sonoma County. Don't you people have somewhere else to go?"

"Hey, it's a free country," Mike answered. The two big men stared at each other. Jerome was the first to break eye contact. "I might have some work for you next week if you're interested," he said.

"You know me. I'm always interested," Mike replied.

"Okay then," said the big man.

"Go rats." Mike said.

"Go rats," Jerome repeated and returned to his steak. Then Mike called to the bartender.

"Tuffy, two bourbons if you please."

"Is he still talking to you?" I asked. "After that exchange I thought you two were going to throw hands."

"We go through this routine several times a week. He's always pissed off about something. But he's not a bad guy."

Tuffy delivered two rail bourbons on the rocks. Matelsky offered him a high five but was rebuffed. "Hey, I'm still mad, okay?" He turned and walked to the other end of the bar.

"Let's go sit over there," said Mike, with a big smile. We moved to a table in the corner. "Look at that haircut... you look like a marine. What the hell are you doing here? Why aren't you at school?"

"Mike," I said. "I'm in trouble."

His smile gave way. He swallowed his drink in one long gulp. "Of course you're in trouble. Why else would you be here unannounced and looking like that. I get off in a half hour. Stick around."

"Where am I going to go?"

I returned to the bar beside Mark, but he didn't talk. He took Jerome's threat seriously. Jerome ate his steak in haste and left because a cop, dressed in uniform, came in and sat at the bar.

"Chief McCurdy, how are you this evening?"

"Living the dream, Tuffy," he answered.

"Want to see a menu?"

"No just give me the rib eye."

"How do you want it cooked?" The bartender was relieved when the cop ordered it medium rare.

It was the last order of the night. Mike finished work. We jumped into his car, a 1963 Volkswagen Beetle. It had no tail lights, no radio and no heater, which was an issue now that the sun was down. Conversation was useless because there was no muffler either, so I just enjoyed the landscape as the moon rose.

Mike lived by himself in a small house that once housed Mexican farm workers. The two acres were surrounded on three sides by vineyards that were just starting to green in the spring sun. The house was built on a small horizontal area near the top of a hillside that looked like it had been leveled by a bulldozer. It had a lordly view of the valley and a long dirt road, called Limerick Lane, that connected it to civilization.

Since it was the very last house on the road, cars coming to visit could be seen a mile away. There were higher hills behind the house that acted like a barrier. Two big, barking dogs met us when he pulled up.

"Who do those dogs belong to?"

"Those are Cary's dogs," Mike said. "The German shepherd is named Bo, and the big mutt's named Bess. I'm watching them for him."

The dogs jumped all over Mike when he got out of the car. But they growled at me and inched their way forward. "Hey, knock it off!" Mike shouted. The two hounds recoiled just like Mark had when Jerome poked him in the back.

"Go over to that garbage can," Mike said. "It's filled with dog food. If you feed them, they'll like you."

I filled their dog bowls which were located next to a homemade dog house big enough for both of them.

"Wouldn't I like to have their life," Mike said. "They spend their lives roaming free around the area outside. But they're great watch dogs. They stay close enough to the house in case somebody comes along."

"Do they bite?"

"Hell yes, they bite. That's why I have to march a mile down the road to pick up the mail. The mailman won't come anywhere near this place."

Once inside he grabbed two beers.

"So sit down already. What the hell are you doing here? What happened to college? Did you drop out to join the army?"

I told him my story... how Epstein had demanded that I leave school for my Uncle Harry's sake and probably for my own.

"Who's taking care of China?"

"Winn promised to take the dog in," I said.

"Damn, I love that dog. Any chance he could ship her out here?"

"I don't know... I'm afraid to contact him."

"You won't have to. I'll call the son of a bitch. Making you leave school and your home is one thing, but your dog? I mean what the fuck! What kind of guy asks you to give up your dog?"

"An asshole."

"A gigantic asshole," Mike said.

"How long you been living here?" I asked, looking around his small house.

"Since January. I really like it here. There's no winter. It's always sunny. There's lots of loose hippie chicks around, and the guys are cool."

"Sounds like you're doing well."

"Not as well as I'd like," Mike said. "I started out strong. Cary and I were roommates. He introduced me to all his friends, and I bought that car. I was getting lots of hours at Elfie and Toots. But Cary took a job in San Francisco. He lives there now, and I'm here by myself. Business is slow at the bar, so they cut my hours. Without Jerome's work I'd really be fucked."

"What do you do for him?"

"He grows marijuana in small warehouses around the county. He brings in these large crops of pot every few weeks. You won't believe how advanced Californians are about marijuana compared to the east coast. They grow these giant buds of really strong stuff. He gets a lot of money per pound too. But to get that price they have to be perfect. No stems, no seeds, no leaves, just those big buds. The pot has to be taken off the stems, clipped, bagged and weighed. It's a lot of work. Once they leave his secret farms he has to move fast."

"Why?"

"It's all about cops and robbers, Joe… cops and robbers. Both want his weed. One wants to arrest him, the other wants to rob him. Guys are getting shot over pot around here. Can you believe that? It's big business. Jerome pays me twenty an hour. Because I'm an outsider he kind of trusts me because I don't know many people here. Plus, I'm one of the few guys who stands up to him. He's a bad motherfucker by local standards. But by Jersey standards he's just average."

"Sounds like good work."

"It is, but it's not enough to support me."

Why don't you look for another job?"

"I thought I had something last week. It was an entry level position working for a winery. They called me back for a second interview. At end of the interview the boss laid it right on the line. Look," he said, "I think you have a lot to offer an employer. It's come down to you and another applicant. He's not as smart as you, but he is going to get the job and I'll tell you why. I'm afraid to take a chance on you. I'm nervous that I am going to give you all my time and energy and that you'll get bored with California, that you'll long for your family in New Jersey and take everything I taught you back home. The other guy is from these parts. If he quits at least I know the skills I give him will stay in the community. With you I can't be sure."

"You mean he just blew you off?" I asked.

"That's it exactly… he just blew me off."

"That sucks."

"I didn't know what to say. I thought maybe he knew something about me that I didn't. The problem is that they all think I'm just a transient, a Jersey boy put here to get on their nerves. But for me, this is paradise. I don't know how, but I'm going to make a life for myself here."

"Well, I'm on the lam and don't know where to go," I said.

"Why not hang out here with me?"

"Too dangerous. The FBI is looking for me and so is the mafia. One wants me to to testify against Harry, the other wants to hold me hostage to make sure Harry keeps his mouth shut. Either way, I'm fucked. You don't need that kind of trouble."

"They'll never find you out here. It's the middle of nowhere. And nobody at the Elfie and Toots knows where I live."

"Are you sure?" I asked.

"Absolutely."

Matelsky was my high school savior. That he had my back again was exactly what I needed.

"I could use a roommate," he said. "Can't pay for this space on my own."

That's when I pulled Epstein's envelope out of my duffle bag and threw it on his lap. He picked it up and looked inside.

"Ulysses S. Grant. My favorite president," Mike said.

"Looks like you got a roommate."

"How long do you have to lay low?"

"Six months, maybe a year, maybe more. At least until the trial is over."

"Two Jersey boys like us, well financed, could do a lot of damage in Sonoma County," he said.

Chapter 5

I drove Mike to work for his dinner shift a few nights later so I could use his car. After a beer at the bar, I embarked on a thirty-mile trip west to the Pacific Ocean. On the way, I smoked half a joint from Wolpin's bag. For me, the virtue of marijuana was that emotionally it helped me rise above my drama. It promoted a spiritual understanding that made religious dogma and political orthodoxy seem stupid. Instead of slavishly obeying the revelation of some prophet or politician, I got to discover my own.

Near a place called Stoney Point I perched on a palisade and watched the sun slip into the ocean. Only with concentration can the descending motion be apprehended. The last light was best. Red, orange and purple rays shot skyward when the orb dipped beneath the horizon. Then over my shoulder, like death, came the night. I couldn't follow the sun, so there I remained, left behind to negotiate with the darkness.

Mike and I grew up at the Jersey Shore, but I never liked the Atlantic. It was a violent ocean, and the fact that it could swallow me up like some Leviathan and never even know, made me fearful of it. But this west coast ocean was different. It was calmer. Ironically, even the water's name seemed therapeutic, pacific—putting an end to all conflict.

The marijuana and the beer simulated a kind of death I explored with my imagination and imitated with my still body. The moon rose over my shoulder, glimmering on the tide before me. Its gravitational push seemed to soften the incoming tide.

There I sat at the very end of America. It was as far away from home as I could get, the very last yards of terra firma before the watery depth encompassed everything. There I sat with my back to the east coast. There was no going back there now. The situation demanded exile. So I stared west as if my future lay there exclusively. Somewhere beneath the roiling tide lay the answers to all the questions troubling me. But no answers would come forth anytime soon.

After an hour of meditation, I took a long walk along the shore line. I removed my sneakers, tied the laces together and threw them over my shoulder. I splashed along the shallows walking south. The water was cold, and goose bumps appeared on my arm.

That's when I saw something strange up ahead. Someone had taken a piece of driftwood and just beyond the shoreline where the tide was now retreating drawn a large Jewish star in the wet sand and surrounded it with a circle. The lines were artistically drawn. As I came up upon it, it gave me pause. After a minute, I stepped inside the star as if it were ritual space. Standing up straight, feet planted right in the middle of it, wind blowing in my face, I began screaming insults at a God I did not see, hear or smell or touch. And in the presence of that tidal roar I also screamed at my father, at my mother, at Winn, at Harry and especially at myself for getting myself into this predicament.

"What is it with the goddamn Greens? Some family curse? A father in a casket, an uncle in a jail cell? Fuck all of you! I won't be following in either of your footsteps. I'll find a way that goes past you both!"

My tirade went on for several minutes. I might still be screaming except that my back straightened when I suddenly realized I wasn't alone. Someone was watching me. Turning slowly, not more than twenty yards away, a big black and brown Rottweiler was staring at me. He was down on all fours, amused at the spectacle of a young man standing inside a Jewish star trying to outshout the tide.

I wasn't sure if I should be afraid of attack or if he would let me pet him. The stick that drew the star was ten feet away. One eye was on the stick, the other on the dog.

He stood and seemed ready to attack. I ran for the stick and pre-pared to strike him. He was full speed at me, and I pulled it back like a batter waiting for a fastball, but wait, that wasn't it.

Ten feet away he stopped, juked to the left and then juked to the right, his short tail wagging. I got it. I tossed the stick down the beach, and he chased after it. Grabbing it in his mouth, he shook it like prey and then returning, dropped it at my feet.

A whistle blew. It was shrill enough to hear above the surf. A woman called out, "Ari. Ari. Come on, boy."

In the distance, I saw her. She wore a blue denim jacket and a white wool hat. She was standing beside an old red Volvo in the pale moon-light. The dog ran to her and jumped into the back seat when she opened the door. She stared at me for a few seconds before climbing inside and driving off. I watched the taillights until the car drove over the hill.

I didn't care that the sand was wet and cold. I zipped up my jacket, and I sat right in the middle of the Jewish star. That night on the beach, I vowed not to follow my father's bourgeois path. I vowed not to follow Harry's reprobate path either. But that begged the ques-tion… how should a young man like me go forth? I hadn't a clue.

I drove back to Elfie and Toots to pick up Mike. I was a little ear-ly. I sat at the bar where I found Mark Anderson in his usual place. He was sitting beside a guy named Gene Gagnon. When I arrived, Gene was showing Mark pictures of these big beautiful marijuana plants he had taken with a Polaroid.

"Holy shit," Mark exclaimed, "they're beautiful."

"You have no idea," Gene said, brimming with pride. "They're not only beautiful on the outside, they're beautiful on the inside too. Here… taste this, and you'll see what I mean."

When Gene handed Mark a joint, he put it in his pocket. They both shut up when I sat down and ordered a beer.

When Mike finished work we jumped into his car. I drove. There was half a joint of Wolpin's pot in the ash tray. Mike smoked it on the way home.

"Wait a minute. This isn't my pot," he said. "Where did you get this?"

"From a guy I met on the train. He said it comes from Afghanistan. The farmers grow it in the same soil as their opium."

"Good shit," he said. "Got any more?"

"About half an ounce."

When we got home he asked to see the bag. He rummaged through it for a seed. He held it up to a light to determine its size and color. He squeezed it. It didn't crack. Then he popped it in his mouth and chewed on it a bit. He pulled it out of his mouth and stared at its guts. I had no idea what he was measuring, but he seemed to know exactly what he was doing. His eyes lit up like a hundred-watt bulb, and he began to giggle.

"Holy shit, these seeds are enormous. Joe, don't you dare tell anybody about this."

"Who am I going to tell?"

The phone rang. Mike picked it up and listened to very explicit instructions. "I'm on my way," he said. "Go rats."

He grabbed his jacket, wallet and keys. "I'll be home tomorrow afternoon."

Chapter 6

One morning at the breakfast table, Harry, the D C businessman, gave me what he considered valuable advice. With his reading glasses casually resting at the bottom of his nose, he peered over his sports page and said, "Start a business, make a lot of money and then you can tell the whole world to go to hell."

This was not misanthropy my uncle was proposing. He placed no moral value on money, unlike so many of his philistine cronies. For him, money was freedom, the ability to feel ease, the option to try something new with your life and not to be chained to the comings and goings of another man's whim. Harry's words came back to me when Mike presented his get rich scheme.

"We're going to become what? Farmers? What are you crazy? Hey, I'm a city boy."

"Don't worry about a thing. I know just what to do," Mike said.

"Geez, you're not going to get all Abe Weisman on me, are you?"

He laughed. "Yeah, I'm going all in with Abe."

Abe was Mike's maternal grandfather who came to America in the early 1900s from Warsaw, Poland. After several years of struggling in New York City he had saved some money and bought a chicken farm in Jackson Township, New Jersey. Land was cheap. Two of the biggest metropolitan areas in the country, New York and Philadelphia, were within one hour's drive and everybody ate eggs.

So Abe, like so many other immigrant Jews, raised chickens. Can't remember exactly how many birds he had but there were thousands of them. During the summer, Mike was his grandfather's slave. In return for his hard work, he paid him off with weekly trips to the Point Pleasant Beach boardwalk.

His grandfather made a good living. Not only from the eggs, but he also sold fryers and the liquid gold of the whole operation… chicken manure that Mike shoveled from the coops and piled outside. It fertilized Abe's field of Jersey sweet corn and his apple orchard. So when Mike started detailing his plan, I was confident he knew what he was talking about.

Turns out the biggest cash crop in Sonoma County was not wine grapes at all, it was marijuana. We were about to become farmers. Mike's faith in Wolpin's seeds, chicken manure, the hot California sun and our secluded spot at the end of Limerick Lane, convinced him that we had a winning combination. Plus, we had Bo and Bess as guard dogs.

That night we took Wolpin's seeds and put them in wet napkins and stored them in a closet. A few days later the seeds opened, and frail green stems emerged. We marveled at the sight of these newborn, living plants that with proper care might make us rich young men. We buried them in little flower pots. Several days later they emerged.

We jumped into his VW and went into Healdsburg. In the course of an afternoon we went to a home and garden store to purchase such items as a hundred yards of hose, nozzles, amphetamine plant food, work gloves, rakes, shovels, wire ties, plastic bags, rose clippers in assorted sizes, a wheel barrow, flower pots and three hundred pounds of chicken manure.

The bill that day came to over four hundred dollars. I paid. But hell, I didn't care, it wasn't my money. Yet the investment legitimized the endeavor. Things were now looking up. Not only did I now have a place to live, I also had a job.

"You're the key to the whole operation," Mike said. "The plants need to be watered twice a day. Without the water the sun will burn them up. I got to work so I can't do it. Since you'll be hanging out here anyway that will be your job. In a few months when the plants get big, we'll also need you to stand guard over them."

"How did you learn about all this?"

"Working for Jerome. Cary used to work for him and recommended me when I arrived. When a crop is ready he calls on guys like me. Ten guys will show up at an hour's notice. We'll get there in the afternoon and clip pot, weigh it and bag it all night. Sometimes we're at it for fifteen hours straight. The next morning a truck pulls up, and an Iranian guy named Mo pays Jerome thousands and takes it to San Francisco for sale. Jerome pays us twenty dollars an hour and all we can smoke, and when he's not looking, whatever we can steal.

"Most of the growers are idiots," Mike said. "I pressed them for how it's all done, and now I understand their technique. This year I'm going to show them all up. You trust me, Joe. Those seeds you brought are going to make us rich."

"You think we can really pull this off?" I asked.

"I know we can. Jerome's got a big business going, but he's sloppy with the details and he's a lousy farmer. Abe Weisman would have laughed at him. I know a secret that none of them know."

"What's that?"

"Chicken manure slurry. The pot plants are going to love it."

Mike took the chicken manure and piled it in three giant plastic garbage cans. He filled the remaining space with water, stirring it once every morning.

Behind the house was a hill, and we decided that was where the plants would go. It was a safe spot because no one ever ventured back there, and the plants would be out of sight to any random visitor who might drop by unannounced. With shovels we started to dig.

"How deep do we have to dig?"

"The holes have to be big enough to fit a refrigerator in," Mike said.

"You're kidding, right?"

"No, I'm not kidding."

"We're starting them out as seedlings."

"Forget that urban life you've been living. Start thinking like a farmer. It's not about you. It's about what the plants need to thrive."

Soon I was standing in a hole up to my waist and it still wasn't enough. I thought it was a ridiculous gesture on Mike's part. But there he was digging right beside me, shovelful after shovelful, assuring me that this was more than a pipe dream. I put my head down and continued digging.

"You're homesick, aren't you?"

"Yes, unbelievably so," I answered.

"Come on, talk to me. Time would pass a lot quicker if we could have some conversation."

"I guess I'm just blown away by what just happened to me. I mean there I was weeks away from a college degree. I had a girl-friend, friends and a life I loved. Now instead I'm hiding out here in the hills. I feel like a paranoid draft dodger looking over my shoulder for federal agents and Vinnie Romano. And Winn was right. I probably would have eventually broken down and told the feds everything they wanted to know. So I'm glad I ran away."

He laughed at me. "Kind of funny that you were able to keep your father's secret but maybe not the one about Harry. It should have been the opposite."

"To tell you the truth, I'm more troubled by what happened with my dad than I am about what happened with Harry. I look back at those days in high school and wonder what the hell was I thinking."

"Why did you keep that secret from your dad? Why didn't you just tell him?"

"I suppose because my mother told me not to."

"Do you know how lame that sounds?"

"Yes. I'm more aware of that than you can imagine. And it's something I'm going to carry around with me for the rest of my life because there's no way to fix it."

"It's your karma. Own it, dude."

"You know my father never liked you. He said you were a bad influence, and he didn't want me following in your footsteps."

"That's okay, he never liked you either," said Mike.

At the end, he had that right.

***

The next day Mike sent me alone to an agronomist named Rupert. Mike worried that if word got out that he had made a big purchase of Rupert's "cannabis candy," it might get back to Jerome and endanger our plan. So I went by myself in a pickup truck Mike borrowed from Tuffy. I bought several hundred pounds. It was a homemade potting soil concoction consisting of high concentrations of ash, potassium, nitrogen and believe it or not, Styrofoam, which yielded to expanding roots. Add the mother's milk of chicken manure slurry, and Mike felt he was feeding the plants a diet of haute cuisine.

Unfortunately, I ran into Gene Gagnon at Rupert's, the Elfie and Toots regular I had seen the other night. He was going out and I was going in. He flinched when he saw me, but we ignored each other. Then an angry look came over his face, because if I put two and two together I'd understand that he too was growing weed.

Later that week we filled twelve gigantic holes with the cannabis candy and topsoil and let the plants drink the chicken manure slurry. The plants were six inches high. I watered twice a day. We didn't want anyone seeing a hose going off in an unknown location, so we dug a trench, put the hose in it and piled a mound on top of it. On the far side of the hill it emerged from our trench with lots of hose to water all the plants.

Mike could be a cruel taskmaster, especially when things were not done according to his instructions. When a hole was too shallow, when a plant wasn't given enough water, or when I went to the store and didn't buy the giant economy size I'd catch hell for it and we'd fight.

He abandoned the casual attitude marking other aspects of his life. He knew what had to be done and demanded that everything be right. And though I was his lackey, I was learning so much that I willingly carried out his directions.

But a week after putting them in the ground, Mike returned from a Jerome clipping marathon and drove up to the house mad as hell.

"We've got a problem," he said. "There is a rise in the road about a half mile back where I saw you watering the plants. When they grow big, and they will grow big, they'll be visible from that spot. It's going to jeopardize everything."

"Don't tell me we have to dig new holes and transfer the plants somewhere else," I said.

"We might have no choice."

But there was another choice. The next morning Mike went out and bought cherry tomato plants, sunflower seeds and a thin, white wooden trellis six feet high and wide. They got the same concoction of slurry, cannabis candy and vitamins. We put them in the ground to act as a curtain from that one spot in the road.

We were running out of cannabis candy and still had two small plants left so we took a risk and put them in the ravine between our house and the house on the next hill. The best soil from the two hillsides had washed down there over the years, and the brush that grew around the ravine would give them some cover.

Our young plants luxuriated in the hot California sun, and I hydrated them with lots of water. Once in the morning and once at dusk I'd turn on the spigot connected to the house, walk over the hill and give them a long drink. Each plant got five minutes of water, and I kept track on my wristwatch. As their branches reached up to touch the sun, their roots reached down like fingers for the cannabis candy and the chicken manure slurry containing the nutrients to enrich them.

We groomed them so they grew wide, not tall, pinching the end of stalks reaching for sunlight. And following the pinch, two small stalks grew from one, reaching out in opposite directions. We tied the plants to green sticks for support against the strong gusts of wind, fed them vitamins and nutrients and carried on long conversations with them about how they needed to grow big and strong.

And so, my initial weeks passed by. I had a safe place to hide and an enterprise that even Harry might admire. I began to notice, in the eyes of Mike, and certainly in my own when I'd catch myself musing in unguarded moments, a paternal pride that delighted in our crop's progress.

"What are we going to call this pot?" Mike asked. "If we get lucky enough to sell some, we have to have a name."

"How about Ghani Purp? Wolpin said it comes from Afghanistan and the color's purple. I don't know much about marketing, but it sounds like a cool name."

"Okay, Ghani Purp it is," said Mike.

"Great. We can even sell it to Jerome."

"Not so fast," said Mike. "Jerome hates competition, and if he finds out we're growing he might turn on us."

"Will he call the cops?" I asked.

"Worse, he'll come in the middle of the night and rip us off. We can't trust him."

Jerome and Mike were beginning to become friends but because each had an illegal marijuana business they were bent on protecting, neither trusted the other. Whenever I showed up at Elfie and Toots with Mike to drink, I was persona non grata. I knew Jerome had secrets to keep, but he had no idea how good I was at holding them. Despite my subtle attempts to ingratiate myself into his good graces, Jerome ignored me even though much of his swagger seemed intended to impress me.

The big man dressed himself in a black leather motorcycle jacket with a skull and crossbones on the back. He drank and did drugs to excess and prided himself on his ability to hold his load. He laughed loudly at inside jokes with his buddies as if they had the exclusive bead on the value of life's commodities.

The sacred cows of his generation were brought out every time I saw him. He'd carry on about 1967 in Haight-Ashbury, "the summer of love," Grateful Dead music, Osley acid, women of easy virtue, giant bongs, and reckless abandon. And while I did not doubt that the era was avant-garde, to me they were just words reminiscent of a time long past.

"Of course we have sympathy for you younger guys. You'll never know that side of life like we did," he said to Mike while I stood beside him. "You were just kids at the time and were basically too young to have experienced what we had in abundance."

Jerome called the house once when I was home alone. He had something on his mind, and he needed to speak to Mike. He didn't want to leave a message. When Mike returned I complained.

"What's with Jerome? He treats me like I'm a leper. Fuck him. Does he think he's so much better than me?"

"No, that's not it," Mike replied. "He acts real tough, but as far as I know it's just an act. I told him you lost it in Vietnam and got thrown out of the army with a dishonorable discharge after you tried to murder your commanding officer. I told him you spent twelve months in a psych ward. To a tough guy like him that can be intimidating because you could call him a wimp and get away with it. And he never wants to give you that opportunity. You make him feel insecure."

"You told him what? Damn, Mike, what kind of cock-and-bull story is that?"

"Well, I had to tell him something. He wanted to know why your hair is so short. The question caught me off guard. He said that you looked like a narc. He had it in for you. I told him you were straight out of the military, and that you were a gun nut with a large collection of weapons."

"Who else knows about this?"

"Probably everybody," he said. "This is a small town, Joe. Word travels fast. It's not like a big city where you're anonymous."

"Is that why people look at me like I'm a kook?"

"Yeah, but it has a benefit. People are too scared to come out here. When our plants get big, that will be important."

The bigger the plants got the greater was our excitement. But along with it came fear that the police might find out, arrest us and destroy our little family of green. Fortunately, the sunflowers and the cherry tomato plants grew tall and thick offering a blind from inquisitive eyes at that one rise in the road. But still, the bigger they grew the more fearful I became. I expressed my fear to Mike, but he calmed me.

"No need to get paranoid yet. Anybody who discovers them is going to bide his time. They'll wait until they are as big as Christmas trees and are worth thousands of dollars each. That's when the real stress comes. Thieves will wait for the harvest moon, or what the Yippie Rats call 'the ripper's moon.' It's the big moonlit nights in September. That's when they'll come to our property and steal everything."

"How are they going to know?" I said.

"You know better than most how hard it is to keep a secret. No one can know we're growing pot… no one."

"I get it. When I went to see Rupert for the soil I ran into Gene Gagnon. He recognized me, and he was pissed off about it. I also saw him showing pictures of pot to Mark Anderson."

"That's the way you lose your crop," Mike said. "Someone finds out and steals it when you're not home."

* * *

I had lived with Mike almost a month before I ever saw his neighbors. The first time I met the father of the family from the next hill, he was drunk. He was a lean young man named Rex Bennett. I was with the dogs one afternoon out to fetch the mail. He was standing with a dazed look while reading the front page of the newspaper he had extracted from his mailbox. He wore a white T-shirt and jeans. His disheveled black hair had cowlicks in different directions at the back of his head. He froze when the dogs went up to inspect him. He'd indulged in red wine that day, some of which had stained his shirt and the corner of his mouth.

He struck me as a lost soul. Originally, as I later found out, he was from San Diego. Being from New Jersey, it never occurred to me that there might be a difference in culture between northern and southern California.

Anyway, that was the alibi he used for his hopelessness, according to Mark Anderson, an acquaintance of his. Rex had recently graduated from Sonoma State with a social science degree. But he didn't have a sellable skill and was bewildered by the rigors of the marketplace. He was out of work, and his only assets were a dozen chickens, a cow, food stamps and money from his parents.

Rex spent much of his time drinking wine at the Old Redwood Inn and was suspicious that Matelsky, "an east coast smart ass," was after his woman. This was another bar stool confidence told to me by Mark Anderson, the village gossip, who split his barstool time between Elfie and Toots and the Old Redwood Inn.

The woman's name was Rita, a big blue-eyed blonde with a pug nose, big white teeth and an innocent face. She was a tall woman, amply breasted with wide hips due in part to her recent pregnancy. The first time I met her was at the mailbox too. She jutted her hip at a wide angle and rested her newborn baby on it while she sorted through her mail.

Mike told me that he sometimes visited her. He did handyman chores for her that Rex was incapable of. But after some ugly arguments between the two men, he stopped.

Rita made money as a potter. A few of her pieces were in the house. A raku dish with red slashes was a resting place for Matelsky's wallet, keys and spare change. A brown clay vessel kept his pot, papers, screens and pipe.

Rita had her potter's wheel secured in a little makeshift wooden hut in their backyard. It was a three-sided structure without a door that Matelsky had built. It had a shingled roof allowing her to do her pottery outside during the day and be protected from the sun and the occasional rain.

My first notion that there might be something between Mike and Rita came one morning while Mike was cooking lunch at Elfie and Toots. I went looking for the sports page and found it in his bedroom. He had a comfortable chair beside his bed, and I plopped down onto it to read. Looking up, I found myself looking out Mike's window and right into Rita's outdoor pottery studio in the distance. There inside the structure Mike built was the blonde, nudging her potter's wheel with her foot and building up shapes with her hands. More than once I saw her staring across the far ravine into Mike's window.

Now that I had come to live with Mike he was less in need of the Bennett's company. Because of our pot crop, he acted rudely toward them in order to keep them away. Rex seemed quite content with the arrangement, but I wasn't sure about Rita. Whatever their feelings were for each other, it was secret. A week later when I casually mentioned that the Bennett family looked as if they had gone for the weekend, Matelsky muttered, somewhat irritated, "Wells… her name is Wells, not Bennett. They're not married."

Chapter 7

Thomas Jefferson's ideal of the good life consisted of reading in the morning, exercising in the afternoon, and socializing in the evening. Since the operation now only required watering the plants twice a day and the patience to let nature take its course, I sought to discipline my life in a similar way.

By the standards of my family I felt like a failure. I was a college dropout. It was awful to do eight semesters and have no degree to show for it. So I decided to take responsibility for my own education. Winn was my role model. I took cues from his literary preferences. This was a switch for me because throughout my life I had always read what my teachers told me to read and never took the initiative to choose my own books.

Try as I might, I wasn't making progress with Homer. However, I did understand one thing. The first part was about the hero's father-less son, Telemachus, and his struggle to go forth in a life that was marred by his missing father and a collection of adult men all trying to fuck his mother, Queen Penelope.

But where was I going to find books to read? I attempted to get a library card in Santa Rosa. But without a local ID they wouldn't let me. I was still too paranoid to get a local driver's license, so I looked in the yellow pages for bookstores.

Someone once wrote "East is east and west is west and never the twain shall meet." I don't think the origin of that quote referred to the bookstore scene of the two coasts when it was uttered, but it was true. What people read in Sonoma County was different from the DC literary diet where congress, the presidency, the military, foreign policy and history dominated.

So one late afternoon after dropping Mike off at work I went book hunting. There were two stores in the area. One was a used bookstore, Yesterday's Books. When I walked in, the man behind the counter, a big Irishman with a red face, said, "Welcome, can I help you find anything?"

"No, but you can help me find *something.*"

He gave me a puzzled look. So I explained. "I just moved here from the east. I dropped out of college, and I'm feeling pretty rotten about it. Since I can no longer afford tuition I figure I need to take control of my own education."

"So, what are you interested in?"

"History, politics, literature. A friend gave me a copy of Homer's *Odyssey,* but to tell you the truth I'm not smart enough to read it."

"That's probably because it's written in iambic pentameter. It's not an easy read, but if you can master the story it's certainly worth the time."

"So I've been told."

"I think I have it in a prose narrative of the story which would make it easier. I also have a few books written about the book that explains what it's really all about."

I walked out of the store with a prose version of *The Odyssey* and another written about Homer by an Oxford don.

The second store I visited was kind of a psychic new age book and gift shop. The teenage girl behind the counter was gabbing on the phone the whole time and paid no attention to me. It had a lot of new age texts, self-help and psychology. The owner was big on Christmas Humphreys, Alice Miller, George Gurdjieff and Carl Jung. Those were authors I had heard of but did not really know much about.

But before I left, something caught my eye. It was a dog's water bowl on the floor beside the counter. The red plastic dish had a name printed on it—"Ari."

Then from a backroom, two Chinese women emerged. One was middle aged. The other was my age. The older woman had the younger one by the hand, and they were saying their goodbyes.

I wasn't sure but perhaps she was the woman I had seen at Stony Point. So I stared at her from behind. She had a slim frame. Her long black hair was twisted into a thick braid that reached the middle of her back. At one point she tilted her head upward, and her chin rose away from her neck. I saw a glint in her eye. I didn't know if it was a reflection of the overhead light or if its origin was from inside her. I walked out of the store empty-handed.

Mike's hideaway was the perfect setting for a book man. Long distraction-free hours were in abundance. I sought to set up my own university. Fuck college. I'll get smart the same way my professors got smart. I'll read. But for me that was no mean feat. That's because I never read as a kid, and I lacked the necessary concentration.

Matelsky's house had a big porch above the walk-out basement that surrounded half the house. I pulled an old table out of a storage shed, and that became my desk. A vinyl lawn chair was where I sat. An old lamp became my reading light in case I wanted to study past sunset. I walked to a pile of old rocks we had dug up and found a flat rock. I put it on the table so my book would be at a forty-five-degree angle to make reading it more convenient for my hands and eyes.

The next morning, I was ready to begin. But mentally, I wasn't ready. I could find a million excuses for standing up and walking away from the book. Go and get coffee, take a crap, ask Mike a question, check the newspaper etc. Reading requires the flexing of intellectual muscles I didn't have. In frustration, I'd smoke pot and space out, especially when Mike went to work and left me alone.

It was Matelsky's pot, filched from Jerome when he wasn't looking. Had we this much in New Jersey we'd have been considered rich. Sitting there stoned in the living room, I returned to the safe haven of television. One day I was monitoring the screen changes of the TV show I was watching. I'd snap my fingers every time the picture changed. Sometimes, it was more than thirty times a minute. And it dawned on me that a reason I was unable to concentrate was because I was conditioned by the rapid eye movement of flashing TV images. No wonder I couldn't focus. The more I thought about it the angrier I got. TV felt like manipulation.

But one morning I smoked some of Wolpin's Ghani Purp instead. The difference hit me like a lightning flash. I was ready to read. The purple pot opened me up to books. Little by little, concentration increased until I was able to focus my attention for hours. I found books to be exciting. That's right... I said it... maybe for the first time ever, books were exciting.

I became the willing disciple of any writer who could hold my attention. Certainly my problems didn't go away, but it was pleasant to alleviate them with someone else's ideas. Barefoot and shirtless I tackled difficult texts with a pen, a notebook and a dictionary at my side. I looked up every word I didn't recognize.

The linguist Noam Chomsky suggested that words and thoughts are synonymous, that the possibilities of thought increased with an enlarged vocabulary. That the nuances, degrees and the variations in sight, sound, smell, and taste could be more acutely discerned with a greater awareness of words. So I cleaved close to the dictionary because I wanted to become wise to the ways of the world and began believing that the tools for achieving it lay with improved language skills.

Each afternoon I'd take a long walk down the dirt road to get the mail and the newspaper. The afternoon sun bleached my hair and tanned my arms. The dogs joined me. They'd follow the scent of rabbits with mouths open and tails wagging. The energy I spent on those walks paled compared to their sprints up and down hillsides.

One day while returning to the house, mail in hand, I came upon Rita planting flowers in her front yard. Russell was on a blanket beside her. Bess and Bo were at my side, and upon seeing the two of them they ran off at full speed. I had never seen them dash after anyone like that before. What if they attack? One bite of that little boy could be fatal. I shouted at the dogs, but they ignored me. So I ran as fast as I could, which compared to them wasn't very fast at all, screaming at the top of my lungs and waving my hands to warn Rita.

The dogs pranced around her. She got down on one knee with the baby in her arm to scratch them behind the ears and accept their tongues on her cheek. By now I had caught up and realized how foolish I must have looked. "I guess I overreacted," I said trying to catch my breath.

"No worries," Rita said. "Bess and Bo are good friends of mine."

"How old is your son?"

"Almost two months."

"Getting any sleep?"

"Not much. He wakes up two or three times a night."

I took a closer look at the kid. Then I did a double take. He had a bald head, blue eyes like his mom and a dimple in his chin, just like Matelsky. The dimple in the chin got me. Neither Rita nor Rex had one. Studying the shoulders and the ears made me realize that the kid did not resemble his father at all. The child was Matelsky's. Why was I the only one who saw it? This new revelation embarrassed me, and I walked away lest my poker face fail.

That night when Mike came home from work I thought to broach the subject. But there was a more important matter.

"We got a problem," Mike said. "A guy came into the bar and started showing your picture around. In it you have long hair and a moustache. Nobody you know was there. When he showed it to Tuffy, he admitted he recognized you."

"What did he say?"

"He said you came in with some gay guys on a three-day vineyard tour. He told the guy that he thinks he overheard you say that you were heading down to Australia to do gay porn."

"Tuffy said that?"

Mike laughed. "Tuffy had to say something. That's the first thing that came to mind."

"That fucker."

"Relax, Joe."

"Did the guy say who he was?"

"No. But at least we know what he looks like. He'll probably come back."

"He might have been sent by Winn looking to make sure I was okay. It might have been the law looking for my whereabouts in order to arrest me. Or it might have been Vinnie Romano looking to hold me hostage to make sure Harry keeps his mouth shut. Hard to say."

"I've been at Elfie and Toots for a while now. If anybody suspicious comes in, I'll know right away," Mike said. "Since Jerome and his posse of pot growers are regulars there, they're suspicious too. Every new guy is immediately singled out."

"I remember that from my first night."

"How did they trace you here?"

"Probably from that letter you sent me back in January. It had your name and where you were working in California. It was in my desk drawer. I asked Ruth to get it before anyone else did."

"Not sure you should trust her."

"Why not?"

"Don't forget I went to George Washington University where she taught. On campus, everybody gossiped about her. I knew business majors who took her art classes because every semester she slept with one of her students. Everybody wanted to be that guy. Word is that she's great in bed."

"She is."

"How do you know?"

"She seduced me the night before I left."

"Is she as good as they say?"

"Better."

"This could be a problem," Mike said. "If I were you, I'd have an escape plan. You can see cars in the distance. It takes about five minutes from the time you get off Old Redwood Highway to get here. That five minutes might be all that separates you from trouble."

"You're right. I better figure something out."

The next morning, I loaded my duffle bag with cash, food, clothes, a blanket, and a flashlight. I even had coins for the phone booth. I stashed it beneath a tarp that protected it from the hot sun and occasional rain. Later that week, I bought a little Honda motorcycle for two hundred fifty dollars that would carry me through the hills where cars could not follow. I practiced my escape. I found that I could be out of the house and away on the dirt bike in ninety seconds.

Each afternoon after reading, I took a walk into the barren hills behind the house. Since we were the last house on Limerick Lane the land behind us was undeveloped. Fortunately, there was only one way in, but there were many ways out. The hills and the deep ravines offered a good place to hide should the necessity arise. I walked the area every day until I knew it well.

My walks ended each day on a high knoll. The hill overlooked our property, and I could see all the way to the Old Redwood Highway in the distance.

From that perch, the marijuana plants were in full view. Beside them were the giant cherry tomato and sunflower hedge hiding them from the eyes of anyone driving to our place.

The valley below was so quiet I could even hear the squeak of Rita's wheel inside the pottery shed when she worked. It was also my favorite place, short of Stony Point, to watch the sunset.

The next night Mike was playing lowball at a card room. During one hand, on which he folded, he watched a confrontation between two players, an old black man and a young white kid that Mike befriended in the course of the game. They drew their cards and both of them continued to raise believing they had a winning hand. When the black guy raised the stakes, the white kid ran out of chips.

"Come on man, spot me the a hundred," the white kid said. "I got a pistol in my trunk that's worth twice that much. If I lose I'll walk right outside and give it to you."

"No way," said the black man. "Meet the bet or fold."

Mike threw a hundred dollars' worth of chips at the kid so he could keep the hand. "If you lose, you'll give that gun to me, right?"

The kid grabbed the chips. He tossed them into the pot. "Absolutely, but don't worry. I'm not losing this hand."

The black guy didn't object. When the kid laid down his cards he had a full house with three kings and a pair of eights. The black man beat him with a straight flush. "A deal's a deal," said Mike. "Give me that gun." They walked out to his car. The kid opened his trunk and handed it over.

When Mike showed me his prize, it was with a sense of pride. "Listen, if the cops bust in the door, we'll surrender. But if Vinnie Romano and his gang come, they won't be interested in the due process of law. We'll have to shoot it out with them. After all, I'd rather be judged by twelve than carried by six."

Chapter 8

Mike looked out the window one morning and saw a low flying helicopter about a mile north of the house. He called out for me to come and see. "That right there is our biggest worry," he said.

As it flew out of sight he was rubbing his hands so hard that little black worms of sweat and dead skin formed on the heel of his palm. He flicked it away with his finger nails.

"That's how they caught Jerry Kloby," Mike said. "Cops flew over his property, saw his plants and came the next day. They confiscated his plants and arrested him."

"The power lines are out in that direction… maybe they were just inspecting them," I said, hoping to reassure him. But he didn't believe me and was quiet the rest of the day.

Later that night following work, Mike returned with two shopping bags filled with plastic roses. Half were red, half were yellow. While the plants drank water, Mike started tying the flowers onto the marijuana branches with clear fishing line.

"Do you really think that this is going to fool the police, Mike?"

"I know a florist in Petaluma who'd know they're fakes in a minute. But I'm willing to bet that flowers aren't something your average cop knows much about, especially viewing them from a helicopter. Besides, it's the only thing I can think of."

I began attaching the plastic flowers to the plants, but he interrupted me.

"Damn Joe, what the hell? Have you ever seen red and yellow roses growing on the same plant? Not even Sonoma County cops are that stupid."

"Oh, sorry," I said. I removed the yellow roses I'd tied on. "I never knew cannabis sativa was so beautiful."

"Take a good look because they are not going to be cannabis sativa for long."

"What do you mean?"

"I mean we are going to manipulate mother nature and change them into cannabis indica."

"How are we going to do that?" I asked.

"When the days get shorter, the plants want to procreate. The females secrete resin on their pistils to catch the pollen. But we're going to identify all the male plants and eliminate them. The female plants think that their inability to catch pollen is from a lack of resin on its pistil so they produce resin with a passion to get the pistil sticky enough to catch pollen and reproduce. But there is no pollen because the male plants are gone. The resin is filled with THC, and that's what's going to give us more money than we've ever had before."

By late July the plants had revealed their sex. The females sent out little white hairs while the male plants sent out shoots that would become pollen bags. It was manslaughter time. We singled out the males and uprooted them. We took cuttings from the female plants and planted them in the male plots. We burned the male stalks in a fire pit with a pile of garbage.

Later that afternoon, Mike's cousin Cary visited. "I had my car window open, and I could smell pot burning a mile down the road. I didn't know you guys were advertising," he said in a mocking tone.

Mike suddenly stiffened. He ran to the window to see if any cars were coming. Then he ran outside to see if anyone was lurking outside. "Goddamn it. I'm such an idiot," he said. He stamped out the coals immediately.

Cary had come up from the city to hang out with his dogs. He was the only other person who knew of our operation. He wanted to see our plants, so Mike gave him a tour of the garden. When he noticed a beautiful little bud growing on a plant the two men examined it closely.

"Look at the crystals on it," Mike said. "And the red hairs and the color of the bud. I've never seen anything like it before."

"Snip it," said Cary. "Let's see if it's any good."

We put the bud in the sun and let it dry out while Cary took his dogs for a long walk behind the house. After dinner we rolled it into a joint and started smoking it. Before long, each of us was looking into each other's eyes and giggling.

"Damn, Mike, you've hit a home run with this stuff. Jerome would be so jealous," Cary said.

"Don't you dare tell him," Mike said. "If he finds out he could come here and steal it late one night."

"Why would he do that?" I asked.

They both looked at me like I was a rube. "Because that's what he does," said Mike. Cary reached for his car keys. He wanted to go to the bar.

"You guys go," said Mike. "I'm staying home with the plants."

"Come on Mike, we haven't been off the property together in weeks. We deserve a little fun. Besides I thought I was in charge of paranoia," I said.

"You are. But you're too calm about this. I get the feeling that I have to worry for the both of us."

"Look, let's go out tonight. I promise to fret the whole time we're away."

"If I drive, your car will still be in the driveway," Cary said. "Leave the lights on too."

"I'll leave the radio on and even take the phone off the hook, so anyone will think we're here," I added.

It took five more minutes of persuasion and the promise to be home early to get him to come along. But once inside the car, Mike lightened up and got excited by the prospect of reckless abandon.

We went drinking at Elfie and Toots. The place was packed, and we found the last parking spot in the lot. Because Mike worked there they only charged us for half of what we drank. It was fun too because we knew many of the regulars. While Mike and Cary challenged two others to darts, I sat with Mark Anderson. He was an avid reader, and we gave each other a book report on our latest.

"I just picked up a book about the history of Vietnam," I said. "What a heroic nation!"

"Heroic? Your ass is purple. No one will ever convince me that mass psychosis is heroic. They tried to free their nation. They should have freed their minds instead."

"Hey, they won an important war. Not only against us but against the French and the Japanese too. They're formidable, damn it, and they deserve respect. We're talking about an historical event involving millions of men and women. They set out to rid their country of foreigners, and they did it. You can sit there and disparage that passion, but in my opinion the deed will always be more important than the thought."

Mark paused and became pensive. "And in my opinion the microcosm will always be more important than the macrocosm."

"I've been thinking," I said. "I'm going to try and read three books a month for the next twenty years. Damn it, by the time I'm forty-three years old I'll be one smart motherfucker. There's no telling what I might do, or who I could be."

"You read garbage," Mark said. "Those history and political books are worthless. You're going to spend the next twenty years making yourself agreeable to society. Big deal, you'll be the smartest buffalo in the herd. You should try and develop your personality instead by reading guys like Carl Jung. He gives you stuff you can really use in your life."

"Not that interested in my personal issues," I said. "I'm reaching for a better grasp of the world."

"But that's the point. If the goal of knowledge is a greater grasp of reality, then you'll never grasp it without a better knowledge of yourself. The way you see it, you're cutting yourself out of the equation. That makes no sense." Then he guzzled his beer, triumphant over my boozy idealism.

Jerome came to the bar and ordered a drink. He laughed at our conversation. "You guys don't know shit about anything," he said.

"What do you know that we don't, smart guy?" I asked.

"Lots," said Mark in an expression of deference. "Jerome here is a professor at Sonoma State."

"What do you teach, gym?" I asked.

"No, I teach the ancient classics."

"Classics, like Latin and Greek books written by dead white guys with hillbilly names like Homer and Vergil?"

"Yes, that's it," Jerome said. "If you had any knowledge about either one of them you wouldn't be so flip about what they've written."

"I think I have a little idea," I said.

"A little idea suggests that you really don't have any idea."

"About what?"

"Like the big questions that have puzzled men for centuries," Jerome said. "A man doesn't have to reinvent the wheel when it comes to life's quandaries. It's all there in Homer and Vergil, who despite their hillbilly names are more sophisticated than anything the Christians, Muslims or the Jews have put forth over the centuries."

He stared at us for a minute, cognizant of the fact that he had the last word on the subject. Then he walked back to his table to join his friends.

When I went to the bathroom to recycle my beer, an older man followed me in. He stopped at the mirror and ran a comb through his dark hair. He had a swarthy, well kempt Italian look to him. His clothes were top shelf, and he seemed a little out of place in a country bar like Elfie and Toots.

"It sure is crowded out there tonight."

"Yes," I answered. "I haven't seen it this busy in a long time."

"Is that an east coast accent I'm hearing?"

"Maybe," I said.

"I love the east coast. I once had a government contract in Washington, DC… lived there for five years. It was during the Kennedy years. America had a greater sense of itself back then."

The last thing I wanted was to be confessing facts about myself to a stranger. "That's a little before my time," I said. I checked my look in the mirror and returned to my seat beside Mark Anderson.

Then Gene Gagnon entered the bar. He was drunk and angry. When he saw me, he took in a large breath, and that seemed to expand his chest.

"You, you fucker," he said to me. "I'll bet you were in on it, weren't you?"

"In on what?"

Now we were face to face and, as we were the same size, eye to eye as well. "My pot plants, somebody ripped them off. Somebody came in the middle of the night and cut them down and walked away with them. There were twenty beauties, and I think you had something to do with it, you fucking bastard."

"You're out of your mind," I said, as calm as if he'd accused me of being Vietcong. "Find yourself somebody else to blame."

Mark was sitting behind Gene. During the exchange I noticed him flinch. He turned his head to the side so he didn't have to see. Then Gagnon grabbed my shirt. I grabbed him in return and we started wrestling around the bar. Three glasses broke when they hit the floor. Two stools fell as well.

Gagnon knocked me to the ground. He was towering over me, so I went low for his legs. I wrapped my arms around them, pushing him backward. When he reached for me, a space opened between his arm and body. I grabbed his elbow with my hand and pulled it close to my body and gave him the under-arm spin. I flipped him right on his back and made ready to punch his face. The whole bar gathered round to watch.

Tuffy ran from behind the bar and grabbed me by the back of my collar, pulling me off. Chief McCurdy, sitting at a nearby table, came too. He blew his whistle. We both startled. "Break it up!" the cop shouted.

We both stood. Gagnon looked at me and said, "You fucking fuck."

"If you got a problem, go tell him," I said, nodding at the cop.

"I'll get you back, bitch."

McCurdy, who was bigger than both of us, nightstick in hand, commanded us to step outside into the dark parking lot. He asked for our IDs. When I showed him mine he studied it carefully. "I thought your name was Joe," he said.

"No, it's Bruce, Joe's my middle name. My name is Bruce Joseph Wolpin."

"Why then do you go by Joe?"

"Because I was named after my grandfather who was a dirty old man. He beat my mother and was a no-good drunk, that's why." He seemed satisfied.

"And you Gagnon, what the hell was all this about?"

Gagnon lowered his eyes. What choice did he have? He couldn't tell the truth. "Sorry, Chief. It was just a misunderstanding."

He handcuffed both of us and put us in the police car, me in the front seat, Gagnon in the back. "Now, if you assholes don't mind, I'm going back inside and finish my dinner. Then we'll go to jail."

Matelsky came out to see if I was all right. When he saw me in the front seat with my hands behind my back, he grimaced. I gave him the wink and nodded for him to go back inside. McCurdy walked out of the bar ten minutes later but was interrupted by an older man, the one I had met in the bathroom. He pulled McCurdy aside to a place I could not see and had a short chat with the chief.

When the cop opened the doors, he told us to both get out. He undid our handcuffs and threatened us with a beating should he ever have to deal with us again.

"It wasn't me, Gene."

"Yeah, bullshit." He walked to his car and drove off.

When I walked back inside, Mike met me. "Are you okay?"

"It's all good," I answered. A young brunette was sitting in my place. She was Asian with long black hair and a pretty face. She looked surprised when she saw me. I reached for my Scotch that had been pushed to the side.

"I thought you'd be spending the night in jail," she said with a touch of sarcasm.

"So did I."

"You wrestled in high school, didn't you?"

"How did you know?"

"I recognized the move."

"You have a big dog named Ari, don't you?"

"Yes, how do you know?"

"I met him one night at Stony Point. I was screaming at the ocean, and your dog snuck up behind me. He scared the hell out of me."

"Do you make a habit of screaming at the ocean?"

"Actually, I'd rather howl at the moon."

"I remember you now. You were throwing a stick for him."

"He just wanted someone to play with."

"From your accent I'd guess you're from the east coast."

"It doesn't sound very Californian, does it?"

"No," she said. "How did you end up here?"

"I sneezed at the wrong time."

She raised her eyebrows.

"Do you work at Present Moment Bookstore?"

Her back straightened. "Are you stalking me?"

"No, not at all. I saw that water dish at the store. It had Ari's name in it. I just put two and two together."

"Well, aren't you clever… you can actually add."

"Learned it in high school."

"I actually own the store," she said. "I also do psychic readings on the side."

"Do you go to Stony Point often?" I asked.

"Sometimes."

"I like hanging out there too. Maybe we could meet there sometime."

"I don't think so," she said. "I don't date guys who get in barroom brawls when they drink."

"Are you Chinese?"

"Yes, I'm Chinese. My grandfather came from Hong Kong. But actually, I am Chinese-American, or are you one of those guys who think that only white people are American?"

"I wasn't thinking that at all."

"Just to save you from asking, I do not have an opinion about Mao Tse Tung and no, my pussy is not horizontal. So don't bore me with redneck jokes. I've them heard them all before."

"Actually, I do know a Chinese joke," I said. "It's kind of funny too."

She pressed her lips together, and since she didn't object I began.

"Mr. and Mrs. Wong own the Chinese restaurant downtown. It was a busy Saturday night, and they worked their asses off. At the end of the night they realized that they had a made a lot of money. So after closing up the restaurant they drove home and showered, opened up a bottle of expensive wine and found their places on the couch. Suddenly, Mr. Wong reaches for his wife and starts making out with her. Then the clothes start coming off, and he's touching her all over and she's touching him all over. Suddenly, he breaks away from her lips and says, 'honey, let's sixty-nine.' She looks at him in disbelief and says, 'beef and broccoli at a time like this?'"

She didn't laugh. And I silently scolded myself for being such a dope.

"I'm new in town and I'm lonely."

"Sounds like a predicament."

"Can I take you out?"

"Why would I want to go out with a Vietnam veteran who probably hates Asians? I've dated guys like you before. It doesn't work."

"You have beautiful smooth skin," I said.

"It's my makeup."

"Your smile lights up a room."

"It's the orthodontics."

"You smell really good."

"With a nose like yours, I'll bet you don't miss much."

She was about to walk away when I grabbed her arm.

"You call yourself a psychic and that's all you see?"

"I'm sure you're very deep."

"I got an A in Buddhist philosophy."

"Where? Trade school?"

"No, American University in Washington, DC."

"That school is way overrated."

"Where did you go?"

"Stanford."

She made some sort of subtle Tai Chi move. Now she had control of my hand. I did not resist. She placed her thumb on my wrist as if she were taking my pulse. She felt a dozen beats, all the time looking into my eyes. "You're not who you say you are," she said softly.

"Who of us is?" I answered.

"Me."

But I was undaunted. I reached out my right hand. "My name is Joe."

Two of her friends interrupted. They all came together. Now they were ready to leave. She grabbed her purse. "By the way, your lip is bleeding."

As they made for the door, one of her friends said, "Who's the greaser?" She shrugged her shoulders.

I looked at Mark sitting on his stool. "I should buy a hat."

"That might help you fit in a little bit better."

"You know that girl?"

"The spooky one? Yeah, her name is Iris."

"Why do you call her spooky?"

"She's a shaman."

"Yeah, but she's cute."

Cary, Mike, and I weren't home ten minutes when the phone rang. Mike took the call. He gave Cary the wink and turning to me said, "Hey, we got to go. See you tomorrow afternoon."

Chapter 9

Mike got home the next morning after being up all night with the Yippie Rats. He went right to sleep. I grabbed his car keys and started out the door. But they were so gooey from pot resin that they stuck to my fingers. Fearing that they might gum up the ignition, I wiped them clean with an alcohol soaked rag.

I went book hunting. Mark's conversation at the bar stuck with me. Deep down I realized my reading was not about compensating for my lost college degree or the urge to become some sort of educated smarty-pants. It was an exercise in self-help to address blind spots in my personality.

What I knew, I knew for sure and it was this—the answers most men accept to the questions of what to do with their lives were too shallow for me. I'd been pushed by outrageous fortune into a predicament I could never have foreseen. The guilt and confusion swirling around in my mind had to be addressed. And yet, I didn't have to reinvent the wheel. Predicaments like mine had happened to young men before. My goal was to find books that articulated that dilemma and read my way out of it.

The first place I went was Present Moment. The first time I went there I walked out empty handed. This time I went looking for a book and for Iris.

Mark Anderson had nothing but praise for his Jungian shrink, Dr. Bell. He thought I might benefit from the Swiss psychologist's work too. In the psychology section, I found a row of books by Carl

Jung. I reached for the smallest one, a ninety-eight pager that I hoped I might be able to get through. It was entitled *The Undiscovered Self.* The clerk put it in a small "Present Moment," bag. I was walking out with it when Iris emerged from a back room with a book in her hand.

"Hello, Iris," I called.

"What are you doing here?"

"Buying a book."

"What are barroom brawlers reading these days?"

"Carl Jung."

"How long have you been into him?"

"This is my first," I said. Staring at her book I asked, "What's that?"

"*The I Ching.*"

"Sounds Chinese."

"It's a Chinese fortune telling oracle. I do psychic readings for a number of the store's clients," she said.

I wasn't listening to her words. My attention focused on the fact that she was really pretty. Just looking at her centered me. I decided not to beat around the bush.

"I was hoping we could have lunch at Stony Point."

"Alone out there with you? I don't think so."

But I was prepared for a tough sell. "Come on, it will be fun."

"You're not really my type."

"What is your type?"

"Someone who is smart and gentle and feels some compassion for this world. Someone who likes himself and as a result can participate in a healthy relationship."

"Granted, I'm a work in progress, but..."

"You sound like a lot of work."

"Are your I Ching readings expensive?"

"Yes."

"Good. Mark me down for two."

"You can bullshit me, but you can't bullshit the oracle."

"Good, I don't want to bullshit anyone, least of all myself."

"I think you should read about it first."

We walked to a shelf where three different books on the I Ching stood side by side. She picked the fattest one. "This is the standard translation. It's by Richard Wilhelm. Carl Jung actually wrote the forward. It will be difficult going at first, but if you are really interested in it, I suggest you start here. This way when you get a reading you'll have a context to put the information into."

We walked to the cash register, and I paid for it.

"I've got to go," she said.

"I'll walk you out."

On the way out I noticed an alcove filled with pottery. "Is that Rita's work?"

"Yes," she said, "you know her?"

"Actually, I do."

"She's a great artist," Iris said.

"How good a friend is she?"

"I've known her for years."

"Then you must know that her baby is Mike's, right?"

She turned her head away.

I knew which car was hers and we walked to it in silence. In a tree just above her car, a large raven sat on a branch. He started cawing loudly when I came near. She stared at it and listened to its voice. Then she looked at me.

"Joe, please don't come around anymore. I'm really not interested."

"My loss," I said. No more words passed between us. She got in her car and drove away.

* * *

When I got back to the house, Mike was awake.

"Okay, everything is in order," he said. "The plants are almost ready. Now the real work starts. I'm going to leave Elfie and Toots, but I have a minor problem. I don't know how to quit without raising suspicion. I mean, I can't look Tuffy in the eye and say I'm going to harvest what looks like about seventy grand worth of pot, so I'm quitting next week. I mean McCurdy the cop is a regular there. I got to be real sneaky about this. No one can know, especially Jerome. I don't want to mention a word of it to him until it's chopped, clipped, weighed and bagged. If we blow the secret now we're screwed and all the work we've done will be for nothing."

"I remember when you first arrived here your biggest complaint was that no one took you seriously," I said. "'Oh, that Mike will be back in Jersey before you know it.' Remember? That's what they all said. Why don't you tell them you've had enough of California and you're going home?"

He thought about the suggestion for a minute, and a smile came to his face. He exhaled a big breath, "Huhhhhhh. How was that?"

"I don't know. What was it?"

"A heavy sigh. I sure do miss the Garden State."

When Mike came home from work the next day, he sat down on the couch, opened a beer and stared at me.

"Did you give notice at work?" I asked.

"Not yet. Bringing in this harvest could take two months. I got to figure out how we're going to live before I quit."

"I'm running out of money."

"Do you think Winn might pony up some more?"

"I don't know. Let's call and see."

So Mike called the number Winn gave me from a phone booth at Little Joe's, a North Beach seafood house in San Francisco. "You never know who's listening, so you better let me talk," Mike said.

"Okay, go ahead," I said. We both put our ears to the phone. He dialed the number, and Winn actually picked it up. "Yo, Epstein," Mike said, with just a hint of disrespect, "how's the trial coming?"

"Who is this?"

"A friend of Joe's. He needs more money. He told me to ask you for it."

"How do I know you're telling me the truth?"

"Because you gave him a copy of *The Odyssey*. He's not enjoying the book, it's too hard for him to read. Were it me, I'd use it for toilet paper, but you know how respectful Joe is. And here's another thing, he may have world enough and time, but he can't do it without cash. So come on old man, pony up some pictures of U.S. Grant."

There was a moment of hesitation. "Okay, tell me where to send it."

"There's a Western Union outlet on Haight Street. Send it there and make it snappy. Don't want the feds or Vinnie Romano to be there waiting for us."

"They're going to make you give them a password. What is it?"

Mike looked at me. I heard the question through the phone.

I whispered. "Tell him China."

"China," Mike said. "Like the dog."

"How is Joseph doing?" Winn asked.

And Matelsky, Jersey wiseass, said, "Better than you."

"Harry's out on bail. Tell him we miss him, and we hope he can come home soon."

Matelsky saw the look on my face. He paused to consider the correct response. None came to mind.

"Tell him the trial could last a long time," Winn said. "If we lose, we'll appeal. Is he all right?"

"He's homesick. Other than that he's fine," Mike said.

"Okay, tell him I'll send him two thousand this afternoon."

"No, that's not enough. He's going to need three thousand. Hiding out is expensive." An hour later we picked up three thousand dollars at Western Union. The next day, Mike gave notice at work.

Chapter 10

Autumn's harvest moon came on a cloudless night in September. It was big, round and orange as it rose above the horizon. It lit up the cloudless sky and was so bright that it was hard to see the stars. It was nicknamed the "ripper's moon" by anxious growers who feared that their pot crop would be "ripped off." During that lunar cycle the night was so bright you could see at midnight. Those nights the five of us slept outside beside the plants—me, Mike, Bess, Bo and the Beretta.

Keeping our project secret was difficult because the plants were so magnificent that both of us wanted to shout about it from the rooftops. But keeping our enthusiasm still was part of the discipline. I understood that from Gene Gagnon's fuckup. He bubbled over with plant pride and his need to brag about it had cost him his crop. Being obedient to the rigors of the end game, we stopped going out to bars and socialized less in town. All of our energy, physical and emotional, was sublimated to the needs of our plants.

We were like the Viet Cong—stashed away in an obscure location, a guerrilla cell protecting our turf, wary of strangers and helicopters, keeping a watchful eye on the one dirt road that led to our property. Tense and ascetic, we waited for time to pass as we guarded plants six feet high and six feet wide worth thousands of dollars each.

The isolation was harder on Mike than it was on me. He was an extrovert. He longed for the company of people. Sometimes he'd stalk around the house restlessly and get himself worked up into an emotional frenzy. He'd smoke some Ghani Purp, listen to records, watch television and stare out of his bedroom window. The boredom would become more than he could bear.

As for me, I read. Sitting on the deck in my makeshift class-room, I delved into the *I Ching* book Iris sold me. It's also entitled *The Book of Changes* because just as the earth spins so do the epi-sodes of a man's life. It's a fortune telling oracle written by Confucius and Laozi, two Chinese heavy hitters. It was older than the Bible and offered up an understanding of life that made you a little bit more de-tached and helped you navigate the vicissitudes of life.

To consult it you take three dimes and throw them six times, writ-ing down whether the results are two heads and a tail, three tails, two tails and a head or three heads. It's coded to form a hexagram that ad-dresses your question. The meaningful coincidence existing between your question and its spontaneous answer reinforced a spiritual element in life that's always there though seldom recognized. Yes, it's all very random. But that was okay with me since no logic could explain why I was sitting on a lawn chair at the end of Limerick Lane hiding out from the cops and the mafia, obsessed with the pursuit of book knowledge.

There are sixty-four possible answers to an I Ching question. Number twenty-one is about punishment, number three is about youthful folly, twenty-two is about grace, forty-six is about push-ing upward, thirty-three is about retreat. A long, written explanation comes along with every answer detailing the spiritual principles at stake with your question.

Carl Jung helped introduce it to the west. He studied it for years. When asked in old age why he stopped reading it, he answered, "Be-cause after a while, I always knew what it was going to say."

I liked that because it suggested that the oracle held a consistent point of view, a concrete sequential response to the issues impacting a man's life instead of some random flip that changed with the weather. I felt that if there ever came a time when I always knew what the I Ching was going to say, it would be because I had mastered the spiri-tual principles it was based upon.

It was a lot to read and even more to think about. A man could spend weeks with it. Since I had so much time on my hands, I did just that. The new world it opened for me was not based on cause and effect, logic, middle class values, physics or constitutional law. It was based on an eastern spirituality that was as deep as scripture.

I was studying when Mike burst out the door and onto the deck. "I can't stand it anymore. I'm going crazy. I need to see lights, people and women. How much money do you have?"

"Lots."

"Let me have some… c'mon I've got to get out of here. I'm driving down to Oakland to play low ball at The Blue Chip."

As I reached in my pocket, he started giggling. "I love the action!" he screamed. He roared out of the driveway in his VW with the dogs chasing after him. As for me, I watered the plants at dusk, smoked some Ghani Purp and continued with my reading.

Mike came home a few hours later. I was surprised that he was so early because once he got in a card game he could go for as many as ten hours at the table. He returned the money he borrowed and, holding the bottom of a larger wad of cash he had won, waved it in my face.

"I got a new poker plan," he said.

"Really? What is it?"

"I'm a professional quitter."

"Professional quitter? What does that mean?"

"Remember when you used to wait tables at Harry's restaurant?"

"Sure."

"You'd go in and do your shift and on a good night walk out the door with a hundred bucks. I remembered that. So when I go into a card room, I shoot for a hundred-dollar shift. When I make that, I quit. I've done it the past three times, and it works. So from now on whenever I go into a card room I think of it like a restaurant shift at Harry's."

"Look at you with all that self-control."

"I brought home Chinese food. Let's eat."

Then my turn would come. I had one of two choices… society or solitude. I'd pack a lunch on warm days and hang out at the seaside with Bo and Bess. People were friendly there, and if I got lonesome, conversations were not hard to come by. Other times I'd take the bus down to San Francisco and absorb something urban. Just looking at the variety of people walking San Francisco streets was stimulating. Unfortunately, Mike and I could not leave at the same time.

He was always in a good mood when I returned. One day I found a child's pacifier under the couch and began to think that an extra reason for his card room extravaganzas was to afford me a day in the city and him a day with Rita.

* * *

I decided not to broach the topic of Russell. Events have an organic quality to them and sometimes it's best to just let wild things be wild. That idea was summed up in a line from the *I Ching* I was particularly fond of—action takes place in accordance with time.

In late September we started the harvest. The plants were only clipped at dusk. We walked a different route every time so that no path would be created in the ground. Mike carried the pruning shears and I, a bed sheet.

He was the expert, meticulously examining each bud, deciding which ones were ready. We cut the big buds first. The pistils were mutants that grew to the size of donkey dicks. After snipping them off we put them in the bed sheet, and I carried them back to the house over my shoulder like a sack of potatoes.

That's when the hard work started. First, we'd clip the buds from the stalk… we called that process de-wooding. Next job was to manicure the buds so that no leaves were sticking out of them. Then we'd hang them upside down from a clothes line in the basement so they would dry out. Our hands got so sticky that we began wearing plastic gloves. At the end of each shift we'd rub the goo from our gloves and smoke it. Mike called it finger hash.

After a few days of letting them cure, we'd clip them some more. With the big buds taken, Mike would give the plants big doses of vitamins and sure enough, in a few days new buds would appear. It was the gift that kept on giving. We cut each bud with scrupulous care, one by one, grooming them into perfect cylinders. Any bare spots, showing the stalk, were clipped.

After being in the cool fresh California air, the odor, upon entering the poorly ventilated confines of the living room was fragrant, especially on cold nights with the windows closed. It was as overwhelming as a squashed roadside skunk. The buds were covered with a histamine dust that was nasally offensive, yet ultimately lucrative. It made me sneeze. I kept waiting for someone to say "God bless you, Joseph" because surely all this was a blessing.

The house was littered with elements of the plant at different stages of production. Branches were piled high on the bed sheet draping the couch. Sticks and stems were thrown into the kitchen garbage can. Small pieces of the plant clipped by our scissors littered the carpet. The finished product was put in big plastic bags next to the scale on the coffee table. After we weighed them, they were put in big glass jars and stored in an underground tomb we dug away from the house. We covered the hole up with a prickly pear cactus attached to a large chunk of earth.

Door knobs, TV dials, drawer handles, juice glasses, everything we touched was sticky with resin. We worked twelve-hour days and any excuse to escape the property for an errand or shopping was welcomed.

One afternoon at Yesterday's Books I had a breakthrough. There on a shelf behind the cashier, Homer's *Odyssey* was for sale in a box of twelve cassettes. It featured a British actor, Derek Jacobi, narrating the story. I scarfed it up and drove right home. The story became a part of my day that I attended to diligently. Jacobi's voice narrated the gist of the story, its beat and meter, its declamation, its gnosis and finally, I got it.

Winn thought *The Odyssey* should be my lodestar. Now I understood why. It was a road map to manhood. Such secret knowledge should be part of every young man's curriculum because Odysseus is a role model on how to shoulder life's stress and overcome calamity.

The story put a hook in me. I had a boom box, and I listened to it while we were clipping. With headphones in a portable cassette player, I listened to the story during afternoon walks in the hills behind the last house on Limerick Lane.

As the clipping continued I'd go through three tapes a day. It only required my ears and not my eyes which were busy guiding scissors around beautiful green buds tinged with the color purple. At the end of the story, I started again. Just like a TV rerun, you always find something in it that you missed the first time. So I found the time and the concentration to absorb it all. For my effort at clipping buds and mastering *The Odyssey*, Mike estimated I was earning about thirty-five dollars an hour.

And so I found myself engaged in the culmination of two long-term tasks simultaneously. How gracefully they dovetailed the Ghani Purp harvest and the epic harvest of Homer at the same time. We still had five weeks of work ahead of us. And when it was done, if we were lucky, I saw the chance for intellectual and financial success.

Since I now knew Homer's epic tale by ear, I found reading the book easier. It spoke a language as manifold as the Old and New Testaments. What a man walked away with after reading it was individual. But it's one of those tales you read over and over if only to master the material.

With Homer there's a battle of the sexes, and most of the time they fight fair. Ancient warriors talk trash as good as any Jersey tough guy. The orchestration of what constitutes manhood is always on display. But the part that interested me most was the relationship of the hero and the gods who had his back. The presence of divinity is found in all the action. And I recognized that spiritual presence when I was high. Twists and turns confounded the hero trying to find his way home. In Odysseus's case, he was Ithaca bound. But as my metaphor, it was all about finding my way back to Washington.

We had a collection of scissors soaking in alcohol. They were stuck inside a jar that once held Bubbie's Kosher Pickles. It featured a Jewish grandmother on the label. We liked positioning it so her eyes were upon us as we worked. It reminded Mike of his Grandma Sophie who, he confided, was the real brains behind the chicken manure slurry recipe. Each scissor was good for about an hour. After that they got too sticky and wouldn't close. We'd dunk them in Bubbie's jar and reach for a clean pair.

Mike was a seasoned Jerome professional. When clipping, he was faster than me. I understood why Jerome hired him whenever he harvested a load of pot. He groomed the buds with the tip of his scissors. His fingers were like a hummingbird's wing. He'd hone one down and reach for another.

We were immersed, surrounded, inundated with pot. Several joints a day were smoked sitting at the coffee table clipping pot and listening to Homer. We had so much weed we started throwing away half smoked joints and the clipped leaves.

"Mike," I said, "it's not right throwing out all this weed. We need to be like a slaughterhouse that uses every part of the animal."

"You're right," he said. "Remember that Zap Comix character, Fat Freddy of the Fabulous Furry Freak Brothers? He said it best. 'Pot will get you through times without money better than money will get you through times without pot.'"

"I think I better fish out the shake I threw in the garbage," I said.

Clipping clipping clipping clipping clipping clipping clipping clipping clipping clipping clipping. The work seemed endless.

Our least productive days came on Sunday. From ten o'clock to four o'clock, football games rule the airways. Because it required the eye to appreciate the action, those hours never produced much work.

We lost ourselves in thought when conversation was exhausted. I'd ponder what I'd been reading. I think from the longing glances cast across the hillside Mike pondered Rita. Yet he was still the shop foreman, and he monitored my work closely.

"Don't fall in love with the bud," Mike shouted. It was his constant refrain. "You're clipping them too close. Remember we're getting paid by the pound. Plus, hurry up. We've got another thirty pounds to go."

Manicuring those blossoms sometimes made me feel like a sculptor, an artisan molding natural forms into statues of Venus. The buds were thick, deep green arabesques of tight leaves, red hairs, rock crystal resin, tinged with purple from the vineyard soil and its Afghani origins. I'd make their natural beauty commercially perfect when all of a sudden a loud voice would shock me out of my reverie. "Hey! Don't fall in love with the bud!"

Then there was the other extreme.

"Come on Joe, look at that. You're clipping Don King buds!"

"What do you mean?"

He grabbed one from my pile. "Look at this. It looks just like the guy's hair."

"Which guy?"

"The boxing promoter who does the Muhammad Ali fights, Don King. He's got the worst afro ever. Just like this bud. Jerome won't buy Don King buds. Make them pretty."

One day he returned from a flea market with a canvas gazebo which was about twelve feet by twelve feet. We placed it over the garden of pot plants and sat in the shade over the hill and clipped outside protected from the autumn sun.

We began grooming the buds while they were still on the vine so that when we eventually did clip them off they'd be easier to process. That way they were commercially acceptable but continued to grow. The canvas cover protected the plants from the rain that was on its way and the dew at night which contained salt water from the ocean over the hills. Mike was wary of the dew because, he said, it might cause the buds to mold.

"Holy shit, Mike, check this out." We walked close to a branch to examine a bumble bee.

"I noticed him yesterday," he said. "He's been there for two days. Hasn't moved a bit."

"Do you think he's dead?" I asked.

"No, just stoned. I don't think he can move."

"Maybe he doesn't want to move."

"Leave him alone. He'll figure it out in a day or two."

When the big buds were all taken we moved on to the smaller ones. They were harder to clip. We tossed each into a big salad bowl where they sat like little jewels. That took about a week. Then we got to what Mike liked to call the shaggy dog buds. They were the smallest ones sometimes no bigger than a fingernail in width and length. Despite their small size they were really gooey. We'd take the sticky little buggers and squeeze them together with two or three others and throw them into a second salad bowl. But we kept them small because we didn't want to make them look like the pressed Columbian brown pot we smoked in New Jersey.

We rolled the shake into joints. Mike took a few hits and handing it to me said, "Look at the end of that joint. It's not even a quarter of the way done and there's goo oozing out the end of it. That's the mark of quality marijuana."

After we cut off the smaller buds, we fed the plants Miracle Gro and water and then clipped the new emerging buds again three weeks later… and then repeated the process again two weeks later.

Though our love for Ghani Purp put us at odds with the law, we never saw ourselves as criminals. For us it was more like a religious experience, as if we were part of some ancient cult honoring Dionysius, the Greek god of reckless abandon.

But each night, watching the local news channel on TV brought us back to reality. Its nightly broadcast always included news about police busting local pot growers. Such stories compelled and frightened us at the same time. Everybody and their brother was bringing in their crop. The legislature in Sacramento passed a bill that gave more money to law enforcement agencies combating marijuana growers. "No tolerance," was their watchword. Newspaper headlines echoed the same sentiment.

"That's one thing I hate about TV news," I said. "It's all about how somewhere, somehow, somebody had something shitty happen to them. But that's not us, or our karma. I think we should boycott the news. It's got nothing for us."

"I like the drama," Mike said. "For me this is when the game gets interesting. Now is the time to hold our cards close to our chest. All the others got scared and took the fast buck. Each day we wait, our plants grow larger and the supply shrinks."

I wasn't about to doubt my fearless leader now. I felt his passion to succeed was stronger than the policeman's passion to thwart us. So we waited. We let the plants continue to grow and clipped the remaining buds as they became ready. When the end of October came, so did the rain.

Mike got wind of its coming from the weather report. "I think it's time to pull up all the plants. We don't want them to get full of water."

We went out that night with a saw and a bed sheet, and we stared at the plants.

"They sure have been good to us," Mike said.

"I kind of feel like we should say Kaddish over them after we cut them down. I mean, it's a respect thing."

"I haven't heard that prayer since my Bar Mitzvah," Mike said. "Don't know if I remember it."

"I can probably remember the first twenty seconds of it," I said.

"Better than nothing."

So I chanted, "*Yis ca dahl vis ca dalh shimay robo.*" I sang it out loud after we chopped them down. After all, with all the money we were going to get from them, it was the least we could do. We left two plants in the ravine. They weren't as hardy as the ones in the garden. Not sure why Mike left them alive.

One afternoon, while making myself a sandwich in the kitchen, I gazed out the window. Mike was examining the plants in the ravine. Rita saw him there. She marched right down the hill. I saw her slip the overalls from her shoulders and pull off her tee shirt. Her large breasts were exposed. She dropped to her knees, and he wrestled her to the ground behind a mesquite tree. He didn't return for an hour.

Perhaps Rex became aware of their meetings, because soon after I saw them fucking, a big branch was snapped in half on one of the ravine plants. It hung down like a broken bird wing. A foot print that might have been his was in the dirt nearby.

We'd been cooped up for weeks in the living room clipping and upon seeing the branch Mike was furious. He took the Beretta from the closet. Right beside the broken plant, and in plain view of the Bennett's window, he emptied a dozen pistol rounds into a bale of hay he set up as a target. The Bennett household was sufficiently disturbed.

Rex rushed out the door with Russell in his arms. The baby shielded his father like a hostage. The kid was screaming as they charged down the hill. Rita stood at the door with her fists glued to her temples, petrified that her boy was in danger. She pleaded for Rex to come back.

"You woke up my damn baby!" Rex screamed.

Matelsky waved the gun around with one hand and pointed his finger in Rex's face with the other. "Next time you step on my property, I'll use you for target practice."

**

We sat on the living room couch for the next three weeks grooming the buds until each squeeze brought anguished sighs from sore muscles and monotonous minds.

It was time to take inventory. Late one night, with flashlights and shovels, we dug up every jar we had placed in the earth for safe keeping and moved them to our living room couch. There was about fifty-five pounds. Seeing it all at once was a bit overwhelming. What do you do with so much abundance? It made me paranoid. I couldn't help staring out the window every ten minutes to make sure no one was coming down Limerick Lane to nab it.

"It's time to pitch Jerome," Mike said. "If he doesn't go for it then everything we have is at risk. That's why I wanted us to be nearly done before I let him know what we were up to. If he doesn't buy it, we have to worry about the cops or one of the Yippie Rats paying us a visit."

"Is Jerome the guy that robbed Gene Gagnon of his crop?"

Mike looked a little sheepish, especially since he and Cary were at Jerome's that very night processing Gene's pot for market. "Yes, it's what Jerome does."

"What if Jerome won't buy our pot?"

"Then we're fucked."

"So what are you going to do?"

"I'm going to take an ounce of our prettiest buds and drop by his house."

"Let's hear your sales pitch."

So Mike began to speak. "Listen, Jerome, I've been your lackey for a year now, and the only reason I did it was to steal your secrets, which I have. Now I'm as good a grower as anyone you know. I got the stuff and you've got the connections. It's time we hooked up as partners."

"How much are you going to ask per pound?"

"Two thousand."

"Will he pay that much?" I asked.

"No. But we might get him up to seventeen hundred."

"It's all ready to go. He doesn't have to clip one bud."

"True, but he's a cheap fuck," Mike said. "We have to wait and see."

I pumped Mike up with music by The Who, warmed the car up for him, poured him a cup of coffee and sent him on his way the next morning. Two hours later he returned ecstatic, entering the house with fists raised above his head like a boxer who had just won a big fight.

"The big Kahuna. I got him with his nostrils wide open," said Mike. "He saw the size of our buds and nearly shit. And then he smoked some of it. You should have seen him pretending not to be impressed. He pissed and moaned, wasn't sure about the purple color, the taste was different and the effects kind of crept up on him. His old acid-head buddy, Doctor Clear, was drinking a morning beer with him. He looks at Clear and says, 'Well, they're just okay.'"

"Clear looks at him in disbelief as Jerome's beer can slipped right between his fingers and landed on his big toe. He's screaming in pain while his beer is spilling all over the rug. Clear said, 'What are you crazy? Those are the best damn buds I've ever seen. If you don't buy them Jerome, I will.' With his act punctured, Jerome started getting excited too. And I got him to seventeen hundred a pound."

The next day Jerome came over to inspect our harvest. There were scratches on his face. "Dude, what happened to you?" Mike asked.

"I was rough housing with my friend's cat," Jerome said. "He got me with his claws."

"Bummer."

"It doesn't hurt."

"Let me show you the two plants I saved in the ravine," Mike said.

The three of us walked down the hill to examine them. Walking back to the trunk of his car, he pulled out one male plant in a red flower pot. It was a scrawny thing, but it was filled with pollen. Reaching in his pocket he took out a small plastic bag. Putting it around the male stalk, he shook it so some of the pollen fell inside the bag. Then he carried it to our female plants, tied it around the ends of a high stalk, and sealed it with a wire tie.

"There," he said. "You'll have seeds on this branch in a little while that will keep you in business for the next year and not infect the rest of your crop."

He left with twenty pounds and gave us ten thousand dollars in hundred-dollar bills. "It's going to take me a few days to get the rest of the cash," Jerome said. "I'll take the rest of it at the end of the week. If I were you I'd sell the leaves to Denny Lamb. He'll rub them through cheesecloth and make hashish. You won't get a lot of money per pound, but it's better than throwing them out."

We watched in silence as he drove down Limerick Lane and out of sight. And when we could no longer see his BMW, Mike turned to me and said, "Holy shit, we're done."

"Give me five, bro." The crack of our palms echoed across the house.

"Let's roll a bomber," he said.

"I'll open a couple of beers."

Chapter 11

At the end of the week, we threw five boxes filled with jars of Ghani Purp in the back of the VW Beetle and delivered it to Jerome.

It was my first time at his house. It was a large, one-story home with a built-in swimming pool and a large backyard. He lived in the town of Windsor. Each home in his housing development was set on a half-acre of land.

He had colorful art on the walls. Boats were the dominant motif. It made sense that the Homer scholar would identify with boats. After all, Odysseus spent much of his time crossing the wine dark sea. But there were also colorful motorboats splashing through the water under California blue skies. Jerome had a boat on Lake Sonoma and much of his partying on weekends took place aboard it.

The furniture was black leather. The kitchen appliances were top shelf. He reserved his two-car garage for his man cave while his BMW, his motorcycle and the Thunderbird suffered the elements outside. It had a large table with eight chairs, industrial carpet covering the cement, a big TV and a well-stocked wooden bar with four stools. It dawned on me for the first time how rich one could actually become growing pot in Sonoma County.

We popped open some beers, smoked a joint of Ghani Purp and transferred the buds from two-pound jars to the one-pound bags to make ready for Mo, his buyer.

While Mike and Jerome weighed the pot and talked shop, I excused myself to use the toilet. On the way back, I stopped in his living room to examine his library. The classics professor at Sonoma State had a large collection of books that included three whole shelves devoted to the ancient classics. Many were written in ancient Greek, which Jerome could read. There were rare titles I had never seen before… not at Winn's, not at the library, not at the used book store I frequented.

A book from the top shelf caught my eye. It was entitled *The Homeric Gods*. That was an aspect of Homer's poem that excited me most because the Greek gods seemed to have a more intimate relationship with humans than their counterparts in Judaism or Christianity. Their gods also seemed more tolerant of male behavior regarding lust, feasting and violence. I reached for it. When I pulled it down I heard something fall behind the book row that that had been leaning against it. Curious, I stood on my tip toes and reached for it.

I pulled out an envelope full of photos. They included several naked women bound and gagged. An array of sadistic toys lay on the bed beside them.

From the color of the walls and the bedspread it looked like they were taken in his bedroom. The women's faces were not revealed but the bruises and lashes across their bodies were. I wasn't sure what to think, except that Jerome liked to play rough. Realizing I had trespassed on his privacy, I quickly returned his photographs behind the books.

We left soon thereafter, and Jerome promised the remainder of our money that weekend. I did not mention my snooping to Mike. Back home we were too exhausted to celebrate. We both went straight to bed. But when we awoke the next morning, it felt like an enormous weight had been lifted from my shoulders.

Next day, a surprise came. Mike found it in the mailbox and handed it to me. It was a green envelope addressed to Bruce Joseph Wolpin. There was no return address. No stamp either. Someone had put it there by hand. Inside was a note written with red lipstick. There was one word—"Endure."

It was the same word Ruth had written on the bathroom mirror the morning I came west. But I couldn't remember if it looked like

Ruth's handwriting or not. I never erased it so someone else might have seen it. The green color of the envelope, which was also my last name, was a subtle reminder that my location was no longer secret.

Mike had a puzzled look on his face. "What's that all about?"

"They know where I live," I said.

"Who knows?"

"Whoever sent me the envelope. Look at the color."

"Green. Who sends a letter like that?" Mike asked.

"There was no stamp or postmark. Somebody put it in our mailbox, and it wasn't the postman."

"Was it Ruth?"

"That's the logical assumption," I said. "She wrote the same word on the hotel mirror before she snuck out that morning. But it could be just about anybody."

"I don't really trust her. She had a reputation in college. If it wasn't for her lawyer husband threatening to sue the school, they'd have fired her."

"Never heard that story before," I said, and I thought about it for a moment. "God, that must have been incredibly humiliating for Winn."

"That time I went over to the Epstein's with you for dinner there was a real tension between me and Ruth because she knew I knew, and she was afraid I'd tell. That's why I never wanted to go back even though you invited me."

"What do I do now?"

"Finish what we've started. They know where you live. If they wanted to, they could just come and get you. Just lay low. If you stick around for a few more days Jerome will pay us off and you'll have enough money to go anywhere in the world. If you cut and run now the most you'll have is a few thousand. Can't live on that for very long."

"You're right."

Two nights later, unannounced, Jerome showed up to pay us off. I was sitting on the front porch reading a book. Matelsky was reading the sports page in his nightly pose—slouched horizontally on the couch with his favorite snack, eight halves of unbuttered rye bread toast leaning up against each other like four tents on his chest, eating them carefully, one by one so as not to destroy the triangular design. His T-shirt and black beard were now full of crumbs that would soon be on the carpet.

When we heard a car coming toward the house we stood and stared out the window. It was Jerome's Thunderbird. We watched as he pulled up to the house. And just like he promised, he delivered the cash he owed us. He threw it on the couch in bunches of hundred-dollar bills wrapped with rubber bands.

"Those your books?" Jerome was looking at a stack piled vertically on a table. "You ought to buy a bookshelf for them. They deserve that."

"That's a good idea. I'm starting to form a library."

"Homer... I'm surprised," Jerome said. "I figured you for just another Jersey scumbag."

"What do you know about Jersey?"

"My mom grew up in Passaic."

"I find that Homer explains a lot of things about life that you don't hear about on TV and in the movies. Like the relationship between the gods and men and what kind of behavior fosters their good will. Plus, in this day and age, where everything we were taught about America is wrong, it's good to have a standard about what constitutes manhood to set it all straight."

"For Jews, Shema Yisrael is the watchword of their faith," he said. "For the Greeks, Homer was the watchword of their manhood."

"So are you really a classics professor at Sonoma State?"

"Just an adjunct professor right now. I can get tenure in two more years."

"That's funny, I figured you for just another Sonoma County drug dealer."

"Why can't I be both? It's one thing to teach epic literature like Homer and Vergil in an ivy tower. It's another to actually harness those principles and put them in play in real life situations. I make way more money selling weed than I do teaching. But the principles I inspire in my students also reinforce the lessons I've learned in drug dealing."

"Maybe I'm just dull, but I find the two things you do incongruent."

"They're not at all. I'm not selling drugs, I'm selling a conscious-ness, one that will transcend the morass that's overtaken America. It's one of the reasons the powers that be are trying their best to shut us down. But I've watched my business grow every year for five years. The love of pot is not going away, and no government crackdown is going to change that."

He picked up a book I had just finished by Werner Jaeger—*Paideia: The Ideals of Greek Culture, Volume Two.* "I read this book years ago."

"Do you still teach a class on *The Odyssey*?"

"Tuesdays and Thursdays at one p.m."

"Any chance I could sit in on it?" I asked.

"No." With that he walked out the door, got in his car and drove away.

We jumped into the VW shortly after Jerome left. Mike was holding a paper bag filled with the money. We were on our way to the safety deposit box we had at the bank. Just before I put the car in gear, Matelsky looked up the hillside and saw Rita staring from outside her potter's shed. Her arms were folded tightly, and she stood as still as a statue.

Matelsky stared back at her. Bennett's Chevy wasn't in the drive-way. Rita marched down the hill, and suddenly our euphoria faded. "What does she want?" I asked.

"I don't know. Give me a minute."

Mike met Rita in the ravine. I couldn't hear what the two of them said, but Mike was angry with her. After a short conversation he returned to the car distraught.

"Rex knows all about us," Mike said. "Everything from the pot growing to your story from back east."

"How the fuck did he find out?"

"Mark Anderson."

"That rummy fuck. I'll bet he was the guy who told Jerome about Gene Gagnon's pot plants too."

"He was. Mark and Jerome are cousins."

"Cousins? You never told me that."

"I only found out a few days ago from Tuffy."

"But how did he find out about me?"

"Mark ran into the guy who had your picture at the Old Red-wood Inn. Rex is threatening to call the police unless Rita and the baby move to San Diego with him."

"He can't do that. That baby is your baby. There, I finally said it and it's about time. Come on, Mike, admit it. Russell is your son. When are you going to own up to that?"

"I don't know, and I don't want to talk about it right now."

We went to the bank and deposited the money, but there was no joy in it. There were too many unresolved issues in our lives. We both went to sleep early.

The next morning a police car, siren blaring, rushed down the dirt road toward our house. The dust cloud that they kicked up indicated the rapid speed at which they were traveling. Matelsky spotted them first and called me to the living room window. I was frozen to the spot.

"You better get going," Mike said. "We only have those two plants left. I can stand a bust. But you, who knows what they'll do to you."

I ran out the back door, uncovered the little motorcycle, fired it up, grabbed the duffle bag and took off for the hills behind the house. When I made it to the top of the hill I turned and looked down at the valley. My shoulders dropped when they pulled into Bennett's drive-way and rushed into the house. After a few minutes Rex, in handcuffs, was taken away.

I returned home, but not until the cops were driving down the road with Rex in the back seat of the squad car. I suggested Mike go up there and find out what the problem was. I watched him as he walked down our hill and up the other to the Bennett house. He sat down on the back stoop of the house with Rita. She held a cold compress over her eye where Rex had hit her. She was crying and one time she seemed to lose all her strength and fell against Mike's shoulder. I never saw Mike act tenderly before. He sat with her for the better part of an hour. Then they went inside. He was there the rest of the afternoon.

He returned in time for dinner. "You know, I've been sitting here thinking about this whole situation and you know it really sucks. And here's something else. It's all your fault."

"My fault! How do you figure that?"

"It was your idea that when I quit my job I should tell everybody that I was leaving California. Rita found out about it and came into the bar one evening to say goodbye. She said a lot of things I wanted to hear for a long time. She met me after work and we fucked. And then I felt rotten about lying to her about leaving. So I told her the truth. I wasn't really leaving. I was bringing in a pot crop. We decided we should start to see each other again."

"You never wanted to talk about her," I said, "but I knew the two of you had something going."

"It started when I first got here. I came real close to stealing her away from Rex. Just before she was going to dump him, she got pregnant. I told her I wouldn't be party to an abortion. I couldn't take it. And I had just met her, and I was really scared to take responsibility for a kid that wasn't mine. So she decided to stay with Rex, and we broke up. He moved in with her and kicked her sister out. He wanted to get married, 'for the child,' he said. We decided that it would be better not to see each other anymore. His parents owned a business in San Diego, and he had a job waiting for him. They were going to move after he graduated college.

"There wasn't much I could do. I was new in town and just a cook at a bar. But she realized that she didn't love him and kept putting off the move. Watching her turn her wheel up on that hill made me crazy with desire. I couldn't get her out of my mind. The rest you can probably figure out."

"He's your kid, Mike. Only a blind man could miss it."

"When he was born it was impossible to tell. Then I got involved in growing pot and everything just happened so fast. I've got to figure out a way to clean this mess up."

It was the first time he ever admitted his feelings for Rita, and I think he was relieved to finally say the words out loud.

"I think she resisted coming to me because I had no money, no solid prospects," he said. "She didn't think I could support her and her baby. I told her how much money I had in the bank and that she no longer had any excuse."

So the next day, Rita brought Russell up to our house and deposited him in Matelsky's arms. She was worried what Rex might do when she told him the baby wasn't his. She returned home and waited for Rex to make bail.

"He's a chubby little bastard, isn't he," Mike said.

"Chip off the old block," I said.

We googled over him and played stupid baby games like peek-a-boo. A half hour later, he filled his pants. "Damn Mike, do you smell that? He's definitely your kid."

"I never changed a diaper before," he said. "Any advice?"

"Breathe through your mouth."

Russell peed on Mike's arm while his diaper was off, which sent me into hysterics. Mike grunted and said, "Damn, being a father is going to be a lot of work."

Rex returned that afternoon. Mike's eyes focused on the house on the next hill as he paced back and forth across the porch. When Rita came over for the baby, Mike followed her back to the house.

"Fifteen hundred in cash and fix my car," said Rex. That was his price for leaving. Rita chipped in five hundred and Matelsky the rest. He also signed a piece of paper not to ever try and get custody of Russell, since his name was on the boy's birth certificate as the father.

Two days later Matelsky helped Rex load up his car and watched him drive down the dirt road for the last time. He happily headed off for San Diego and a new life.

So Rita traded a moody laconic man for a garrulous impulsive man. Matelsky seemed content. He soon moved into the house on the next hill and assumed all the duties and obligations as head of the household. Rita went on with her pottery, and we made plans for next year's crop.

***

At first, I thought of these changes as the end of our friendship. *Another one bites the dust*. That's the lament of a single man in his twenties watching his friends, one by one, fall by the domestic wayside. Matelsky had struggled here, but now he had roots and he was happy. He was becoming the kind of man he had always hoped his father might be.

The despair I felt about being left behind didn't last long. Though the crop was gone, I had money and free time to enjoy it. Rita had dozens of friends that had stayed away because of Rex. Now they visited frequently, and Mike and Rita actually had parties. One of the guests was Iris Chan.

"Were you really in Vietnam?" Iris asked.

"No."

"Then you're not a shell-shocked psycho with a dishonorable discharge."

"No."

"You were right, I relied on gossip and not my own good sense."

"You believed a deliberate lie that we spread. Can't say I blame you."

"To tell you the truth, you don't seem like the warrior type. I got that idea that morning you were in my bookstore. You're more the adventurer type."

"What's the difference?"

"The warrior believes that the world is a dangerous place and that he has to be strong, disciplined and hyper-alert in order to take arms to defend what is his. The adventurer finds the world an exciting place he wants to explore and enjoy. You do it with your reading. The pot you smoke expands your mind and makes you independent of authority."

"Do you have any books at your store that talk about the difference?"

"I think I do."

"I'd like to read them."

"So what's the real story?" she asked.

I didn't respond. The question passed.

"Rita's taking Mike and the baby home for Christmas," Iris said.

"Mike's never been taken home for Christmas before."

"What are you going to do?"

"Do what Jews all over America do on Christmas Day. Go to a Chinese restaurant."

"Is that true?"

"Sure. It's a Semitic tradition going back a hundred years mostly because on Christmas, it's the only thing that's open."

"Maybe we should go together."

"Aren't you going to celebrate Christmas?"

"No," she said.

"Were you raised Buddhist?"

"We weren't really raised with any religion. And even if I had religion I wouldn't abide by it, especially Christianity."

"Why?"

"Just look at their icon. Two wooden planks at right angles. It represents death. When I think of Christianity I think of a religion going nowhere. Compare that to Judaism. Now there's a religious symbol. It's got six lines instead of two. It's got a big-hearted space right in the middle of it. The lines interact with each other and actually form six little triangles within it. It's got slanted lines like life, instead of perpendicular right-angle points that are two dimensional."

"Okay, it's a date," I said.

"I'll pick you up at noon," she said.

On Christmas day, Iris drove me to Petaluma. She drove her car very fast. Her maneuvering in and out of traffic made me nervous. I felt compelled to talk so she might concentrate on the road.

"Where did you meet Mike?" she asked.

"We were friends in high school."

"He always speaks well of you," Iris said. "At least that's what Rita says. She claims he's always felt safe hanging out with you because you were always willing to hold the pot."

"I suppose that is true."

"Mike told me and Rita a story about the time you all got pulled over by the cops, and you actually told him to give you the pot to hold."

I started to laugh. "That story has been repeated a hundred times. Sometimes I feel like I'm resting on my laurels."

"Mike said it wasn't about courage, it was about luck."

"Well, like he always says, I'd rather be lucky than good."

"Why is that?" she asked.

"Because when you're lucky, you *are* good."

"I'll have to remember that one. But why were you so willing to risk arrest?"

"Because I hated my life and the situation I found myself in."

"What situation was that?"

I said nothing and soon the question passed.

"The west coast suits Mike," I said. "It's sunny and bright, and the people remind him of the ocean county where we grew up. Rural, near the ocean, inexpensive to live in."

Iris pulled her car into the parking lot of a dim sum restaurant. It was Christmas brunch, and the place was crowded. From what I could tell, the majority of customers were evenly split between Chinese and Jews.

While she wanted me to open up about my past, I resisted and instead asked questions about her psychic readings.

"Don't meet many guys interested in it."

"I grew up with hard guys from Jersey. And I trained myself to match them in venom so I was safe on the streets. Then I realized that it was a fool's errand because most of it was based on self-hate."

"There's no future in that except alcoholism and an early death," she said.

"I know. That's why I find the books at your store so compelling."

"When you understand your story, you understand your life."

"That's my goal."

"The urge to confront spiritual issues is usually the result of the death of a loved one."

"That's true," I said.

"Was it somebody close?"

"My father," I said. "He died six years ago."

"Really? Tell me a story about him."

"He had this utopian theory about life," I said. "He thought men should retire 'til they're forty-five and then work 'til they die. It's too bad. If he was allowed to take that route he might have died a happy man. Instead, cancer caught him when he was fifty-two. He died four years later a bitter and broken man."

"How did you take it?"

"I was blown away by it all. I made his death all about me. Somehow looking back, I think it was kind of disrespectful. I mean he was the one who watched as his body wasted away. He lost sixty pounds and his skin turned a shade of yellow. His eyes bulged, and he lost all his strength. Worst of all, he lost his faith in God and was bewildered by the whole experience. I think that's the reason I'm interested in Homer and the I Ching."

"You could spend a lifetime working on that," she said.

"I just might."

"Losing a father is hard on a young man."

"It's an unresolvable issue. That's one reason I smoke pot. I'm not angry at my dad when I'm high. Instead I can almost feel his presence, and that feeling is more precious to me than anything."

"My grandmother used to say that there's only one way to address that kind of wound."

"How's that?" I asked.

"Do a better job than your father did or shut the hell up."

Just as she said that a dumpling slipped off my chopstick and rolled off the table. She laughed.

"Never really got the hang of these things. Would it embarrass you if I asked for a fork?"

"Here, hold it like this." She gave me a practical demonstration on how to use the two wooden sticks to get the food in my mouth instead of on the floor. "I didn't realize you were a lefty."

"I'm ambidextrous."

"That's cool."

"Not really, I was born a lefty. My father was a lefty too. But in New Jersey schools they worried that if you were a lefty you might grow up to be a communist or a homosexual. They made me switch hands when I learned to write in first grade. So I eat, brush my teeth and wipe my butt with my left hand and throw a baseball and write with my right hand."

"Which hand do you masturbate with?" she asked with a sly smile.

"Left," I said.

"Did you stutter?"

"You know something about it?"

"Yes. My college degree is in early childhood development."

"I did stutter. For a year I went to Mrs. Blintz, a short woman with big boobs in the bell tower at Franklin School. I don't remember too much about it. We used to play word games. After a year I didn't have to go anymore."

"That's a fascist thing to do to a kid. Your brain is hardwired in a certain way. When you have to do it in a way that's not natural for you it makes your brain work overtime just to keep abreast of things."

"There was another girl in my class who was a lefty," I said. "They made her switch too. She nearly had a nervous breakdown. One day she refused to use her right hand anymore and broke down crying in class. And she wouldn't stop crying. So they called the school nurse to remove her. And though I felt sorry for her because she certainly was miserable, I remember how relieved I was that I was able to make the switch."

"What they did to you was wrong."

"So is that my excuse?"

"Maybe… it's never good to mess around with a child's developing brain."

"Glad you pointed that out to me."

"It's true. For some people it's no big deal making the switch. For others it's a nightmare. It's like rewiring a whole machine."

"It was hard. I got Ds in writing until third grade. Funny thing is, I was totally unconscious about what it meant."

"There's something else about you I don't get," she said. "I don't think you get it either. There's something about your energy that prevents you from displaying your inner worth. At first, I thought it was that you were one of those Vietnam War veterans asked to do unspeakable things. Then I thought it was you were one of those crass guys from New Jersey. But that's not it either. It's something else that puts you on guard all the time."

"You're right, it's neither of those things. But it's not something I can talk about."

"I can respect that."

"Hey, I know Wednesday is your day off. I've been coming in to your store on that day just so I didn't run into you. Didn't want you to think I was stalking you. Is it okay to browse whenever I want to?"

"Sure, maybe we should do an I Ching reading too."

"That's okay. I've been reading up on it. I can do it myself."

"Which translation do you use?"

"Wilhelm."

"Next time you come in I can recommend a few others as well."

"Why would I need more than one?"

"Because each author brings his own understanding to the oracle. I have over twenty different translations, and sometimes when one rendition doesn't make sense to me another one does. It's like being able to consult a variety of friends on the same issue."

Two fortune cookies came along with the bill.

"That's one of the things I love about Chinese restaurants," I said. "They give you a cookie with a random message inside. Sometimes they're even significant."

We broke open the cookies and grabbed hold of the paper. We both smiled at what we saw.

"What does yours say?" I asked.

"I'm going to keep mine a secret for right now."

"I think I will too." But before I stuck the small note in my pocket, I read it one more time. It said "Life's best when you share it with someone you love."

After lunch, we drove to the ocean. After a walk along the beach, we sat upon the same Stoney Point perch I sat upon the first week I arrived. It was a bright blue day that reflected on the sea. We split a bottle of wine. We talked. We talked about her store, her childhood and one of her life goals, to write her own translation of the I Ching. When she dropped me off at home, it was past ten.

For a Jew, it turned out to be a pretty good Christmas.

Chapter 12

New Year's Eve came on a Friday night. I was glad to see 1976 go. It was America's bi-centennial, its two-hundredth birthday. For me it was a year of surprises, disappointments and self-reliance. Instead of going out to the bar, I spent it with Mike, Rita and little Russell. They came for dinner.

Iris called at 10:30 p.m. She was looking for Rita. I handed her the phone, and the two women wished each other a Happy New Year. When Rita invited her over for a drink I got excited.

She was at a party in Santa Rosa. She said she'd be here in an hour. But the hour passed and then another hour and just after midnight Rita and Mike took the baby home.

At one a.m., I heard a car driving down Limerick Lane. Normally, it might be cause for fear. But when I realized it was a red Audi, I felt a warm rush inside. I had a few minutes to prepare, so I straightened up the living room.

Then I heard the sound of feet climbing the stairs. Iris was here on New Year's Eve. What a great end to a dramatic year. Forget the great conversation between us, I delighted just looking at her. Having her there was like a parting gift offered up by the spirits of 1976, those very bastards who tossed me like a ship on a roiling sea.

Opening the door, I found her with her back against the wall. She was looking down and strands of long black hair fell in front of her face. An unopened bottle of champagne was in her hand. Without even looking at me, she handed it over. "Happy New Year, Mr. ...

whatever your real name is."

"Hey, we didn't think you were coming," I said. "Mike and Rita went home to put the baby to bed. But come in anyway."

"You're going to be nice to me, right?"

"Of course I'm going to be nice to you." I ushered her inside. I found two glasses and popped the cork. "Did you know that champagne corks are the major cause of eye injury in France?"

I poured two glasses full. I handed her one as she stood near the door. I raised mine high in order to make a toast but before I could speak, she repeated, "You're going to be nice to me, right?"

"Yes, Iris, I'm going to be nice to you. Come on, sit down."

We sat on the couch. The celebration I hoped for wasn't going to happen. Her lips were turned down. Her droopy eyes looked askance around the living room as if she was searching for ghosts.

"Iris, you shouldn't have been out driving tonight. You've had a lot to drink. Maybe you should just sleep here."

"Okay, but you're going to be nice to me, right?"

That was the third time. What was this all about? "Okay, Iris, I want to hear about the guy who wasn't nice to you."

She turned her head away.

"Come on, you know you want to talk about it. So don't hold back. Tell me about the guy who wasn't nice to you."

"No, no, no," she said. "Don't worry about me, I'm fine. What do you care? You're not even from here."

"That's baloney. You know you want to talk about it. That's probably why you came over after Rita and Mike left. Tell me. Tell me about the guy who wasn't nice to you. Come on, it's New Year's Eve. It's time to start fresh."

"Hey, are you going to pop that champagne or not? Because if you're not, I'm leaving."

"I already popped the champagne, Iris." I handed her the glass that she had placed on the coffee table.

"I think I should go."

"What are you afraid of? Scared that I'll find out you're damaged goods?"

"You don't even know what you're talking about."

"I absolutely know what I'm talking about."

I recognized that look. I've even seen it in the mirror. And I've seen it on the faces of Galena, Adele, Myra and Minnie on quiet nights in my DC apartment when they confessed dark secrets. I knew all about secrets. And I knew how hard it was to hide them too. I grabbed her car keys from the coffee table and put them in my pocket.

"I think I'm going to be sick."

I pointed her to the bathroom. Once there, she fell to her knees and put her head over the toilet. I stood over her while she hyperventilated, ready to vomit. But she didn't.

"Come on, Iris. Quit jerking me around. Tell me about the guy who wasn't nice to you."

I'm not good at being hard. But by now I'd lost my patience and was yelling at her. "What happened? You know you want to confess, so confess already and stop being so chickenshit."

She started to sob. Then her body gave way and crumbled to the floor. I let her lay for a minute. Then I helped her back to the couch. My patience spent, I shouted, "Come on and talk!"

She stopped crying. Then in a little girl's voice she told me a dark tale about a Friday night date. He drugged her and brought her to his home. He raped her, tied her up and gagged her, spanked her, sodomized her and threw her in a closet. He went out to the bar and returned several hours later. When he discovered that she had pissed herself, he pulled her out of the closet by the rope around her neck and beat her with a belt. Then he fucked her again and threw her back in the closet. It went on all weekend. When he finally let her go on Sunday morning, he threatened to kill her should she ever breathe a word of it.

"Who was the guy?"

"None of your business. You think you're the only one with secrets. If I breathe a word of it he'll burn down my store."

And then she started to weep. Loud wails came from her. Were it not for the hard rain, Rita and Mike might have heard it too.

"Want to know the worst part?" she asked. "My friends didn't even realize I was missing."

"Did you tell any of them?"

"I couldn't. Now every time I see him I start to shake."

"You mean he lives around here?"

She did not answer.

"Iris, who is he?"

Her head shook horizontally. She wouldn't give him up.

I wanted to caress her. But that seemed inappropriate. Instead I listened to her sob for ten minutes. She didn't want to be comforted. She didn't want soothing words. She wanted to wallow in her pain, and she wanted a witness.

When the sobbing stopped, she threw her head down against the arm of the couch and closed her eyes.

"You know about secrets, Joe. Promise me you won't tell anybody, not even Mike. Promise me."

"I promise, Iris. Not a word of it will pass my lips."

I fetched a blanket and a pillow and tucked her in. I kissed her for the first time. It was on the cheek. I watched over her for a few minutes and then went to sleep myself.

She was gone the next morning. The blanket was folded neatly, and the pillow was placed upon it. There was no note.

Chapter 13

The next morning, I walked up to the hill behind the house that over-looked the valley. It was so quiet that you could actually hear the whoosh of hawk wings flying across the wind. The bell of the house phone echoed up the hillside. It rang twice and stopped. That was Mike's signal from Rita's. Someone was coming. Looking up, I saw the car inching its way down Limerick Lane to our location. It was a pink Cadillac convertible. The top was down, and a blonde woman was in the driver's seat. She stopped in the driveway and honked the horn.

Matelsky walked down the hill from Rita's and through the ravine. Rita stood outside her potter's shed and stared at the scene with her hands on her hips. The dogs accompanying Mike barked viciously at the driver. I heard Mike call out to her. It was Ruth Epstein. She and Mike had a conversation while I stayed on the porch watching. Then she turned the car around and drove back to the highway.

I called down from he porch. He looked up and spotted me. He waved, and I waved back. I joined him on the driveway.

"What did she want?" I asked.

"She said she's come to bring you home," Mike said. "I told her I didn't know where you were."

"Is the trial over?"

"She didn't say."

"What did she say?"

"She's staying at the Lotus Flower Hotel in Healdsburg for the next three days. She asked you to come over tomorrow night at five."

"What do I do now?"

"I don't know," Mike said. "But she has your dog."

"Well, I suppose I'll have to see her now."

The next day, late in the afternoon, Jerome pulled up to the house in his Thunderbird. Looking out the window and watching him come up the stairs I turned to Mike. "What's he doing here?"

"He offered to come along."

"What for?"

"One of his students works at that hotel. He called and asked her to keep an eye on Ruth. She called him back this morning to say there's a man with her. It might be a setup. Maybe she's in cahoots with Vinnie Romano. Who knows? All I know is that we're both bringing guns. He pulled up his shirt and showed me the Beretta. We'll sit in the lobby just in case anything goes wrong."

"Look at you, getting all big brother on me."

"Got a problem with that?"

"Not a bit."

We drove to the hotel in Jerome's car. I sat in the back seat like a mafia don with two armed bodyguards in the front seat. When we parked at the hotel, Jerome went to check it out while Mike and I stayed in the car. He met his student, a girl named Josie. She had knocked on Ruth's door and delivered clean towels and found Ruth there by herself. Jerome and Mike went to sit in the lobby, telling me to wait thirty seconds and then proceed to room twenty-four.

"If you see me running down the stairs with somebody chasing me, shoot them," I said.

I knocked on the door. Ruth opened it. Reaching out, she kissed me on the cheek, hugged me and shut the door. I was at a loss as to how I should act. Images of that evening in bed with her in Hagerstown came back to me. So did Friday nights at her dinner table with Winn. But I wasn't sure what she was doing here so I held back.

"Where's China?"

"I didn't bring her. I was afraid you wouldn't come unless I said I did."

"Are you kidding me?" I didn't like that one bit and started for the door.

She grabbed hold of my hand. "Don't go Joseph. We need to talk." She sat on the bed while I stood. "We all feel terrible about what happened. I can only imagine what you've been going through these past months."

Finally, someone said it. What happened to me sucked. The words were said, and I got to wallow in it.

"Harry has been acquitted," she said.

"How did Winn do that?"

"The star witness changed his testimony, and the chief prosecutor was given a federal judgeship in Nevada two weeks before the trial."

I burst out laughing. "Those fucking rascals."

"Please don't laugh. It wasn't that easy. The trial took a toll on both of them. Yes, they won the fight, but Winn had a stroke about three months ago. He lost his speech, and the right side of his body was paralyzed for six weeks. He's recovering now, but he's not the man you once knew. Neither is Harry. This battle turned them both into old men. We need you to come home."

"It's not that easy. I can't just drop everything. Besides, what about Vinnie Romano?"

"Vinnie passed away," said Ruth softly.

"Heart attack?"

"It was at a very difficult time during the preliminary court dates. Vinnie threatened me, claiming I knew where you were. He started stalking me. Every time I turned around there he was watching. He wanted to hold you as a hostage to pressure Harry. He threatened my life. Late one Friday night, a black man pulled a gun on him while he sat at his cash register at his liquor store. When the robber took the money and ran down the block, Vinnie chased him out the door with his gun in hand. He walked into an ambush. Two assailants gunned him down on the sidewalk."

"Did they ever find the killers?"

"Do you think Winn would ever let them find the killers?"

"I suppose not."

"He also saw to it that the warrant against you was dropped."

"So, let me get this straight, I'm supposed to come home and pretend none of this ever happened?"

"That's my first choice. It's Winn and Harry's too."

"What did you tell my mother?"

"I told her the truth. She cried."

"What did you tell my girlfriend?"

"I told her a terrible lie."

"And my dog, China?"

"She lives with me now."

"I need some time to think about it, Ruth."

"I understand."

A key unlocked the hotel room door, and a man came in. He walked right up to Ruth and planted a kiss on her lips.

"Joseph, let me introduce you to Don Mangialardo. Don is a retired FBI agent. He's an old friend of mine."

He reached out his hand, and I shook it.

"Winn and I have separated. I'm with Don now."

I was disappointed that she and Winn were no longer together, but disappointed more by the fact that I wasn't going to be intimate with her. And who was this fucking guy? I looked him over. The bastard was sleeping with Ruth, and my dog.

But then I recognized him. We had met in the bathroom at Elfie and Toots. He had a chat with Chief McCurdy right before I was released from the back of the squad car. He didn't seem surprised to find me in Ruth's room.

"We've met," I said.

"Joseph Green, glad to finally meet you. Last I heard you were doing gay porn down in Australia."

"I didn't know the FBI hired Italians, Don. I thought they only convicted them."

Ruth touched my arm so I would look at her. "See, Joseph, I had your back the whole time."

Maybe she did have my back the whole time, but I didn't feel comfortable around her boyfriend. Sure, as a favor to Ruth he may have saved my ass at the bar, but if the trial proceeded would he have returned me to DC in handcuffs?

Ruth never liked the way Harry and Winn did business. That's why they kept so much of it from her. But now she had gone over to the enemy. And me, a local pot grower, felt paranoid Don might know what I'd been up to. It was too much all at once. I made for the door.

"Send my regards to Winn and Harry. Tell them I love them both."

"Can I see you again before I leave?"

"I don't think so."

"But Joseph…"

"You shouldn't have lied about the dog."

Jerome and Mike stood when I marched into the bar. "Where's your dog?" Mike asked.

"Back in DC."

"She lied?"

"Yes."

"That sucks."

"It does. Well, at least I can grow my hair again."

"What's that mean?" Jerome asked.

"None of your business," I said.

We left immediately. I wanted to tell Mike everything, but Jerome's presence stopped me. It was a lot of dirty laundry to air out all at once. We drove back to the house. When we arrived, I reached out and shook Jerome's hand. "Thanks for coming, man. It meant a lot to me."

In the distance, I saw Iris pull her car into Rita's driveway. I smiled when I saw it. Jerome noticed and just before he drove off, he said, "Be careful with that girl, Joe. You're liable to catch the clap."

When his Thunderbird was gone I asked Mike a question. "Does Iris have a reputation for being promiscuous?"

"Not that I know of."

That's when I figured it out. The scratches on Jerome's face, the photos hidden behind his books, Iris's New Year's Eve confession. It was clear to me. He was the assailant.

I hadn't seen Iris since New Year's Eve. She and Rita were wait-ing in the pottery shed for Mike and me when we arrived.

"Are you okay?" Rita asked.

"Yes, my little ordeal is over."

"Where's your dog?" she asked.

"Ruth lied about it to get me out of hiding."

"Are you going back home?" Iris asked.

"I don't know."

It was clear that Rita had told Iris my story. She was sympathet-ic. "You don't have to figure this out alone," Iris said. "Come home with me. We can throw the I Ching and ask its opinion."

"You've never invited me over before."

"I'm inviting you now," she said. "Except for one thing."

"What's that?"

"I need to know your real name."

"Joseph Green."

"Green, like the color of your eyes," she said.

"Yes."

"Let's go, I'll drive."

There was a seriousness of purpose with Iris. That's what at-tracted me. Intellectually, she rose above the suntan and stupid crowd. She knew things I longed to know, had feelings that I wanted to feel and a point of view I wanted command of. She lived in a ranch style house near Lake Sonoma. It was on five acres and had two bedrooms. She lived there alone with Ari.

"Would you like the tour?" she asked as she unlocked the front door.

"Sure."

Ari barked and pranced around at seeing his mistress home. The three of us walked out the back door. The back part of the property bordered the Russian River. She had a small wooden gazebo on its bank to protect her from the sun on afternoons she sat there.

There was an area in her backyard bordered by big rocks. It act-ed like a fence around the pen where five tortoises lived. There was a cave for them to sleep in at night with a narrow entrance. It was covered by a large clay lid that had a design of the Tao on it. It weighed about ten pounds. To peek inside their den you had to lift it. When she lifted it, I saw five tortoises in a circle, their faces pointing toward the center.

"Did Rita make this for you?"

"Yes, it's beautiful to look at isn't it? It's also sturdy enough to protect the tortoises from raccoons at night and the rain and the cold. They like to sun themselves in the day and retire to their lair at night because I have a heating element in there. During the day, Ari is here to guard them."

She told me their names. Each was named after a different I Ching hexagram. There were three females and two males.

"Why tortoises?"

"In China, at the end of the nineteenth century, they dug up an ancient archeological site at Mawangdui. They discovered writings about the I Ching etched out on tortoise shells. Since it's my oracle of choice I thought it would be appropriate. References to tortoises are written throughout the book. Plus, they're wonderful animals, slow and steady with no anger issues. If cared for right, they can live to be seventy-five years old. Hanging out with them is very calming."

When we moved inside, I saw her study. It reminded me of the Renwick Gallery in DC in that all four walls were covered with art. Most were framed Mandalas. There were a few portraits of nude women and some primitive wooden masks.

"Sure is a lot to look at here."

"I know. I find it stimulating."

There was a table that also served as a desk. Five *I Ching* books were piled upon it. Seven crystals were lined up in a row, four of them orbs, the rest straight from the earth.

"Nice crystals," I said.

"Sit in that chair," she said. She turned on the desk lamp and each crystal reflected back colored light. "I love crystals. For me, it's all about the inclusions. That's their real virtue. It's the little crannies in the quartz that reflect prism light. Unless I see the pinks, reds, purples and the greens refracted back, they're no good to me."

"Why's that?"

"Because those colors are the same color as spiritual light. Staring at them is inspiring."

"Inspiring?"

"I give psychic readings here."

"I could use some spiritual direction."

"Perhaps we should consult the spirits."

She took out three Mercury dimes from 1954.

"That's the year I was born," I said.

"I know. I bought them especially for you."

"How did you know?"

"Rita told me you were the same age as Mike."

"That was nice of you. How long have you been studying the I Ching?"

"Since I was about ten. My grandmother taught it to me. She's a neighborhood shaman who everyone brought their problems to. But she never uses coins, she uses yarrow sticks because she said it gave her a better bead on reality."

"Do you ever use yarrow sticks?"

"When I read for myself, yes, but not when I read for other people. Put them in your hands and let them get a sense of who you are."

I picked the dimes up and squeezed them. At the same time, Ari walked into the room, slumped down before me and rested his head on my feet beneath the desk.

"You can ask the oracle anything you want. But recognize this. The I Ching is the book of changes. It will give you an answer to your question, but it is not the end all and be all of it. It's just the beginning of your procession."

"I guess I should figure out what question to ask it."

"There's no question about it."

"How do you know?"

"Mike tells Rita, Rita tells me. It's the way news travels around here. I think I understand your predicament."

I shook the dimes in my hand and threw them on the table. It was two heads and a tail which was a solid line. But the next five were broken.

She wrote down the coin toss indicators on a piece of paper in a notebook that she had dated and put my name upon. She looked at the hexagram which was built from the bottom up. I was impressed that she knew the sixty-four hexagrams so well that she didn't even have to look it up in the book.

"I know this one. Twenty-four, it's about return. It's moving lines, which is about the future is eighteen, working on what's been spoiled."

"And what's that all about?"

"I think it's self-evident, don't you? You have unresolved issues back east, and you are never going to find peace until you go back and deal with them."

"If I decide I don't like the answer, can I ignore it and throw it again?"

"I wouldn't if I were you. That's disrespectful of the oracle. Just accept what insights it has offered you and carry on. Look at these two hexagrams again later when you get home and then tomorrow and then next week and then next month. Your understanding of these hexagrams will evolve the way your life evolves over the coming weeks."

I became pensive. A minute of silence ensued.

"Joe, you're going to blaze your own trail in this life apart from middle class convention. I don't know the details of that future, but spiritually someone on your team does."

"What do you mean?"

"You asked a question of the oracle. Who do you think is answering you back?"

"I don't know."

"Well, some spirit guide's got your back," she said. "How many copies of *The I Ching* do you have at home?"

"Two."

"Come to the store this week. We'll load you up with a few more."

"I will."

"Would you like a tour of the rest of the house?"

"Sure."

"Let me show you the bedroom."

It was a smaller room than her study. But it did have its own bathroom. A king size bed took up most of it. However, there was absolutely nothing on the walls.

"Why is your study so cluttered and your bedroom so stark?"

"Because there's only two things I do in this room."

"What's that?"

"Sleep and make love."

"I'm not very sleepy," I said.

"Me neither."

She took off her shoes, walked to the window and opened it wide. A cool breeze blew in. She removed her blouse and laid down on the bed, her head on the pillow. "Come here," she said.

"I waited a long time to make love to you."

"Yes, you have."

* * *

She drove me home after midnight. The next day I met Mike.

"You got home late last night," he said. "Who did you sleep with, Ruth or Iris?"

"I slept with Iris."

"How was she?"

"Better than Ruth. I didn't think that was possible."

"How was she better?"

"Our bodies were just a better fit. She's smaller than Ruth and a lot easier to roll around with."

"Rita says she studied the Kama Sutra."

"I got to buy a copy of that."

"Why?"

"I had three orgasms. I've never cum three times in one night in my whole life."

"She doesn't just fuck anybody," Mike said.

"What are you trying to say?

"Go slow, young prince."

As the winter progressed, I became a regular visitor at Iris's house. The conversation was wonderful. We could sit there talking for hours at a time. We smoked Ghani Purp, that loquacious weed. She'd drink chardonnay, but she was a petite thing, so she always added ice cubes to water it down. I'd drink Scotch. She taught me what she knew about the I Ching and Buddhism. I taught her what I knew about Homer and American politics. And then when we ran out of words, when language expressed everything we were thinking, we retired to her bedroom with its bare walls and finished our back and forth with physical intimacy.

One night I asked her the question that was bothering me most. "Jerome was the guy that tied you up and raped you, wasn't he?"

"Was he bragging about it?"

"No."

"Then how did you find out?"

"He has pictures. I found them hidden in his bookshelf. I didn't see your face, but I recognized your body."

"Yes, he was the one."

"What are we going to do about it?"

"What do you mean 'we'?"

"I mean we're involved now. And I hate the fucker for what he did."

"He didn't do it to you, he did it to me. We'll do nothing."

"What about the women he rapes in the future. You can prevent that."

"I've been in counseling ever since New Year's Eve at your house. Right now, that's all I'm concerned about."

"He's got to be punished. I'll take care of it myself if you want me to."

"I need a minute." She excused herself and walked to the bathroom. I knew that she sat on the toilet and stared at a Mandala hanging low on the wall right in front of her. Strategically placed, it helped her formulate answers to difficult questions.

Iris believed that the bathroom was the most spiritual room in the house. It's the place where you were often naked, most aware of your body with your guard down. She said in the bathroom, in quiet moments, she got her best revelations. When I started paying attention to the thoughts I had in my own bathroom, I realized she was right.

She flushed and returned to the table.

"We'll do nothing. I don't want to become the subject of lurid gossip. I don't want to go to the police or testify in court. Plus, I risk bodily harm to my person and my business. There's just no upside, Joe."

"What he did was wrong. Say it. Just say it once so I can hear it."

"What he did was wrong."

"I'm in business with Jerome. But I'll throw it all away to see him go down."

"Don't be silly. One more season of growing and you'll have enough money for your triumphant return home."

"I'm frying bigger fish than just money. You know that, right?"

"Yes, I know that. But I see his future, Joe. Don't soil yourself with Jerome. He'll pay for what he did."

We said everything there was to say about it, and in the process we drank more than we should have and smoked more than we should have. But the thrilling climax at the end of the evening was what we both lived for. And no amount of alcohol, THC or Jerome Mercuri could interfere.

The next morning, I broached the topic of our relationship. I thought it the right strategy considering that I was swooning over her in quiet moments. Perhaps it was the dimples in her cheeks when something I said made her laugh or the sage advice she offered when I sought to address an unresolved issue or the quiet contentment when we sat together in silence.

"What happens to couples like us?" I asked.

"As much as we both might long for a life like Rita and Mike, it's not in the cards."

"Why not?"

"Our love is not about romance or family. That's not what I want, and I know deep down it's not what you want either. It's about giving support to the other person so we can each move a little further along. Relationships like ours don't come around every day. Remember what the I Ching said about your future? Working on what's been spoiled. That lies back east. Until you resolve those issues you'll never be as emotionally present for me as I want you to be."

"Returning is not going to be easy."

"Why?"

"How am I going to integrate what I've learned in California back in Washington? Much of my brain is taken up with Homer and the I Ching and marijuana cultivation. It's like I found common ground between the natural and the supernatural worlds. It makes sense to me. But back there, where politics is everything, it's going to be awkward."

"You'll figure it out," she said.

"I need to get a clearer bead on this."

"You're entering undiscovered country."

"You've been my map."

Chapter 14

Our second year of growing began. Rex was gone and with him went a measure of our anxiety. We benefited from the previous year's experience and streamlined the operation. We also rented two farm properties in parts of the county as rural as Limerick Lane. Both had chicken coops. We turned them into gardens with grow lights substituting for the sun.

We were after the big bucks now. Cuttings from the ravine plants were kept alive over the winter in the basement with artificial light. When we planted them we knew they were girls. By the time spring came we were planting mature plants ready to thrive.

The three of us, Mike, Jerome, and I, formed a triangle with defined job descriptions. I was in charge of organizing a coterie of growers from around the county. I brought a dozen partners into the fold. Most were Rita's friends. We gave them cuttings from our strongest female plants and in some cases chipped in money for the grow lights and Rupert's Cannabis Candy.

Mike was the resident farmer. He visited their homes and schooled our associates about the virtues of chicken manure slurry and answered their questions about growing.

Since Jerome was captain of the team, no one worried about being robbed by him at the eleventh hour. He paid cash for everything we brought to him. After four months, we were deep in both buds and dollars.

Mike was now a family man. Rita put subtle pressure on him to mollify his behavior. She was worried about the safety of her man and their son. It changed his attitude about some things.

"Okay, ten plants are a felony. I'll plant nine," said Mike. The balance was more than made up for by the partners we had growing Ghani Purp.

We heard stories of giant warehouses with whole floors devoted to indoor pot growing. They used hydroponics, a method of using dissolved inorganic nutrients in water instead of soil. All were protected by sophisticated alarm systems.

By comparison we were just a nickel and dime operation. Even if we got caught, chances were our case wouldn't make it to court. Bigger busts would make us a low priority with the law, and we might be able to cop a plea. At least that's what our attorney had said. He was a hip Santa Rosa lawyer with a taste for Ghani Purp. For an ounce of our product he was put on retainer. He told us how to act.

"Carry the stuff in a locked valise in your trunk, and never have the key with you. If the cops get it open and bust you, we can beat the rap through the illegal search and seizure law. Don't say a word to them until I get there. Drive sober and safely. Be nice to them, and don't cop an attitude. There's no need to be unpleasant."

Our safety deposit box was filling up fast with cash. So we started spending it. We rented a storefront in Calistoga. Mike organized Rita and a coterie of her friends into a small guild and opened an art gallery a week before Easter. Rita's father owned the land her house was on. We paid three Mexicans to plant two acres of zinfandel grapes. Mike had this crazy theory that chicken manure slurry would make the red wine taste great. Ghani Purp Winery was launched.

In preparation for my return, I began taking courses at Sonoma State. I used my real name so I might rack up the college credits I had lost my last semester at American. I distinguished myself in my political science courses.

For many of my classmates, the federal government was a giant impersonal institution to be looked upon with awe. But at Harry's restaurant I had met the players, congressmen and senators, lobbyists and journalists too. I had walked the grounds of sacred Washington monuments and witnessed minor historical events. That I saw it all with my own two eyes gave my opinions an authority that set me above my classmates.

My favorite professor was a former Kansas legislator named Gary Hall. He was a tall, lean Midwesterner with a populist bent. He loved to bash conservative politicians and bask in the glow of such liberal deeds as extricating the US military from Vietnam and Richard Nixon from the White House.

One day in Hall's government class, we watched a documentary about Watergate. Hall was very excited about the film. It was narrated by A.J. Traub, a muckraking DC journalist who was one of Hall's political heroes. According to Hall, Traub was the voice of America's social conscience while standing up against Senator Joe McCarthy's Committee on Un-American Activities in the 1950s.

The movie was interesting enough. But what really got me excited were the film clips from Capitol Hill and Traub's narration of events as he walked the grounds of the Lincoln Memorial. It made me terribly homesick to watch and opened up a floodgate of nostalgic memories.

But I was in love with Iris Chan. There was an emotional presence in each other's company that led to fabulous conversation each night we spent together.

I was now able to surrender all my secrets to her supportive, non-judgmental gaze. To speak of my past, at long last, was an opportunity to reveal myself not only to her but at the same time to myself. The narration of my troubles made them easier to bear.

One evening, we drove out to Stoney Point to watch the sunset. It was an expansive setting. We sat staring out at the vast ocean that was met by an even vaster sky. The moon rose over our shoulders. Staring westward over smooth seas, white cotton puff clouds hovered at the shoreline casting kinetic shadows on the water.

"You have something on your mind," Iris said. "What is it?"

"The more I love you, the more I hate Jerome. I'm having a really hard time dealing with it."

"I'm not going to engage him, Joe. Not now. And you don't have a say in this."

"I know."

"You're finally ready to go home, aren't you?"

I was surprised at how perceptive she was. "Yes," I said, then I put my hand on her hand. "I wish you would come with me. We could both start over."

She shook her head. "This is a journey you have to do alone."

I read once that problems are like plutonium, they have a half-life. And over time their radioactivity decreases. And so it was with me. I figured out a few things on Limerick Lane. But for better or worse I couldn't shake the feeling that California was a way station, a roadside attraction, and that my real life was waiting for me back east. Despite Iris and Mike, I missed my dog. I missed Harry and Winn. I missed my DC life.

And then, a spontaneous image flashed before me— equanimity in a DC setting. I could see it. I could feel it too. I started to giggle because it felt like I was already on my way home.

Arnold Toynbee's historical essay "Withdraw and Return" gave me a framework with which to interpret my drama. But its only virtue was the second act. Hadn't Lenin returned to Russia after years of exile in Switzerland? Hadn't MacArthur returned to the Philippines? Hadn't Mohammed returned to Mecca? Hadn't Moses rejoined the Hebrews after his isolation on Mount Sinai?

Yes, it was time to go home.

Matelsky and I were clipping buds in my living room when I broke the news. "Mike, I'm leaving for Washington next week."

"You're what?"

"I'm leaving for Washington next week."

"Why isn't this good enough for you? Why do have to go back there?"

"You always knew I would. I promised you six months, and I've stayed for twenty-four. Maybe I want what you have, and I don't see me getting it anywhere but in DC. You're set here, you have money and a family and a future. But I think what I want is back there. Until I go and give it another try I'm never going to know for sure."

"Great! How am I ever going to find anyone to live in a house with seventy-five-thousand dollars-worth of marijuana on the property. I hope you know the rent I'm going to have to shell out is coming out of your share."

He cast his words in disapproving tones and focused on emotions that ran parallel with but never touched what he was really feeling. He understood. There was not as much room for me in his life now. Rita was pregnant with her second child, his child. Responsibility curbs spontaneity, it hurt Mike to admit that. Rita felt uneasy if I suggested a trip to the city when he already had plans to do something with her and Russell. I felt like I was playing Harry to Mike's Winn.

"I get everything you're saying," he said. "I just can't believe you're breaking up this partnership."

"Are you out of your mind? I'm not breaking up anything."

"What do you mean?"

"Mike, they've never seen pot like this on the east coast. Jerome now pays us fifteen hundred a pound for unclipped pot. How much do you think they'd pay for a pound of Ghani Purp in DC?"

"Holy shit. You're right."

"From now on consider me your east coast sales representative."

Mike finished grooming a big beautiful bud about eight inches long. He held it up at arms' length, turning it in the light and admiring his work. "You know, before he left, Rex told Rita we're going to hell for this."

"No way," I said. "We're going to be rewarded in heaven for introducing Washington politicos to Ghani Purp. It's going to make them more detached, way smarter and less full of shit."

So it was settled. I was going home. Truth is, that's also how I resolved my Jerome dilemma. I was going to sell Ghani Purp on the east coast and cut him out of the equation.

And so I was done with California. I discovered guiding principles in Sonoma County. Iris taught me about love and the I Ching, and Jerome taught me about Homer. Mark taught me about Carl Jung and Mike taught me about marijuana and friendship. Equipped with this new kit, I was ready to return to DC. Its hyperactive, competitive arena was going to test everything I held dear.

Chapter 15

When flying into Washington National Airport from the west, I request a window seat on the jet's port side. Over the years, airline flight paths have become familiar to me and from the left side seat you're treated to a panoramic view of the nation's capital.

"Give me an A seat please. And one as far from the wing as possible."

That's what I asked of the fair-haired ticket agent in the pressed blue uniform. She had a customer service smile and the winged logo of the airline pinned to her bosom. "Sightseeing?" she asked.

"No, I am going home."

"I didn't think anyone was actually from Washington," she said.

"I am," I answered.

Two years ago, I had taken a long, agonizing train ride to California to escape a bewildering predicament. Now I was flying home with a plan. I knew the drama would be fueled from seat A. More than anything else I wanted to feel a theatrical rush at first sight of the city. And even if the thrill was gone, if it aroused no more emotion than a black and white postcard, I'd pretend.

My reverie stopped when I noticed a young woman standing in the aisle. My first impression was that she was over dressed for the six-hour transcontinental flight. She wore a pressed white shirt closed at the collar with a gold pin that hid the top button. There were sheer stockings and a kelly-green skirt that fell to her knees. The sleeves of a matching cardigan sweater were folded back neatly at the wrist.

There was jewelry and makeup, actually too much makeup for such a pretty face. Her skin was smooth and creamy and was more alluring to the eye than the pale brown powder she covered it with. Her strong chin was framed by prominent lines of her jaw and two high cheekbones. She had big eyes, long lashes and a thin upper lip. In white tablecloth restaurants she was the kind of woman who turned heads and made conversation pause by merely walking by.

She had an auburn ponytail that reached to the middle of her back. She tossed it around with sudden motions of her head. Standing on her tip toes, she placed her bags in the overhead storage bin. The green skirt clung to her fine curves. She arranged her bags neatly and pulled some folders from one. When she was done with her rustling, she looked at the numbers and letters pasted above and sat herself in the aisle seat two feet away.

The jet sat ready for that long dash down the runway. The long awkward wings wobbled as it raced over sections of cement faster and faster. It built speed and the flaps moved. The jet arched its back and ascended. As it soared she closed her eyes and held her breath. When it leveled off she opened her eyes. She had a polite request. "Would you mind if I use this middle seat to put my work on?"

"No, not at all," I answered. Beside me she stacked folders and memorandums from work. One had the letterhead of an Indiana congressman. It looked official and important.

Damn, I came from the land of unwed mothers. She had nothing in common with them. When Mike and I were watching the Oakland Raiders play the last half of their football game, Rita would stick her head in periodically to get the score and drop off a beer. She'd sit down with us during the last five minutes of the game, grabbing Mike's knee with both hands and shrieking when Jim Plunkett threw a long bomb.

Somehow, I could never see this woman playing in that role. Was it beneath her dignity? Perhaps she'd think me a chauvinist forever contemplating her in that role. Yet Rita with her pottery, her son, and her man had a good life, didn't she?

We continued on in silence for the better part of two hours. I was reading a book when the flight attendant offered refreshments. When she ordered a glass of wine, I ordered a beer. We began a conversation. Her name was Elizabeth Ann Gilchrist.

"What do your friends call you?"

"They call me Elizabeth Ann," she said. "What are you reading?"

"*Symbols of Transformation.*"

"What's it about?"

"Analytical psychology."

"That sounds weird."

"It's not."

She worked for the American Sugar Consortium, a trade association located on K Street. Currently, her job focused on a piece of legislation intended to ban artificial sweeteners because they caused cancer. As a young man whose father had died of cancer, I took notice.

She had a degree in political science from USC and was considering law school. Her speech was well metered and spoken with conviction. But before I finished the beer I recognized how her opinions expressed a zero-sum mentality. If some foreign country was doing well, it could only be at the expense of the United States. If minority communities were improving, it could only be at the expense of white people.

"What were you doing in California?"

"I attended college, and I'm part owner of a small winery."

Of course it was a lie. But telling her I grew pot would never do.

"What kind of grapes do you grow?"

"Zinfandel."

"White or red?"

"Don't be silly," I said. "Red, of course."

I hid my rough, weather-beaten field hands behind the arm rest, embarrassed by the clipping callouses. My back straightened, and I became aware of my grammar. I feared that perhaps my purple shirt was too wrinkled, or my hair disheveled.

"You're not one of those pot-smoking Berkeley radicals, are you?"

"No, I attended Sonoma State."

"Good, I can't believe the way those people trash America."

"I try not get too worked up about it. Politics in America seems to alternate between egalitarian impulses and plutocratic impulses. First one, then the other, back and forth. It almost seems that they strike a balance and that's how, as a nation, we go forth."

"The business of America is business," she said. "Hard work is what matters most, and it sometimes seems that the egalitarian element of society sucks the life out of those who work so hard."

"I don't think it's as cut and dry as all that."

"Well I do," she said. "Conservative principles are important because they refresh American manhood."

I was so transfixed by the drama of my return that I forgot I was returning to Washington, DC where her archetype predominates. She was a career-oriented gal with a keen focus on the goals of her organization. In her mind anything that fell outside of its agenda was irrelevant. Political rhetoric is always trying to pass itself off as God's honest truth. Now I was stuck listening to it.

"How long have you been in Washington?" I asked.

"Six months."

"Six months? You talk like you own the place. I hate to tell you this, but there's a lot more to Washington than politics."

"Oh yeah, like what?"

"Like life."

Eye contact became self-conscious. The window seat suddenly made me feel claustrophobic. There was only one way out, and it was blocked by Elizabeth Ann, the corporate poster child. Excusing myself, I pointed my finger to the beer. She rose from her seat. In the aisle our bodies brushed up against each other as I walked to the toilet.

Once inside I locked the door. The light came on, and I breathed the odor of blue toilet disinfectant trapped in a small space. I saw myself in a mirror lit by bulbs encased in white plastic. The narrow sink allowed me to get close to my image. Every scarred pore, every blackhead, every blemish on my face glared back. I unclenched my sphincter and breathed a long, suppressed sigh. A paper towel sufficed to wipe the moisture from my face.

One-sidedness never doubts itself until it's too late. Suddenly, lazy afternoons, warm winters, illegal networks and Ghani Purp brought a sentimental smile. Then I imagined a city full of Elizabeth Anns. Young centurions of some master race blinding you with logic and flawless facades you never get to look behind. "Elizabeth Ann my ass!" I said to myself. "I'll bet her friends called her Betsy."

I guess I wasn't totally intimidated because when I sat back down I hit her with a little local color. "Have you ever eaten barbeque at Winnie's in Mount Pleasant, or driven out to Blobb's Park in Maryland for an evening of beer and polka dancing?"

She hadn't.

A few hours later the jet slowed its speed and descended. I looked out at thin, isolated clouds in the clear, azure sky. The sinking sun bathed the landscape in soft hues. County roads looked like the creases in freshly pressed pants. Plots of farmland dominated the landscape. It was spring and not until May would rich summer green cover the land. The suburban apartment buildings and tract housing reminded me of electronic circuit boards one sees inside radios and televisions.

The nearer we got to the Potomac River Valley the more the overturned land, mostly at construction sites, carried the red tinge of Indian clay. The pilot came on the intercom and mentioned that we'd be approaching National Airport via the river route.

National icons appeared. The Great Mormon Church at the Route 495 Beltway, looking like the Emerald City in the Wizard of Oz, was the first thing I recognized. Next came American University's campus and its tall public radio station tower that fraternities hung their banners upon. The National Cathedral was next. Standing high above the city in the western part of town, it's the biggest Gothic structure in North America.

Elizabeth Ann's interest grew, and when the stewardess wasn't looking she unhitched her seatbelt and slid over a seat to see what I was looking at. Cranes hovered above the city. Giant hooks on thick steel scaffolding were rebuilding old neighborhoods. From above, the wooden planked streets looked like the boardwalk at

Seaside Heights as men worked underneath connecting the new Metro subway system.

I could even see the precise seventh floor apartment window where my Uncle Harry lived. It's a wide apartment building near the corner of Columbia Road and Sixteenth Street. The building is easy to spot because it's situated beside three tall church spires that reach high above the neighborhood.

The way the Lincoln Memorial, the Washington Monument, and the Capitol Building line up perfectly on a surveyor's sight was perceptible when we looked down upon it from the south. It was spring. Cotton puff cherry blossoms surrounded the Tidal Basin.

At the spiritual center of it all is the Washington Monument. I've always thought the Washington Monument to be an honest confession. The monument to the father of our country is a giant boner. But then what else would it be?

The jet path followed the Potomac River. We peered right into the cars rolling across the 14th Street bridge. It seemed as if we were landing right on the river. But the tarmac appeared, seemingly from nowhere, wheels scorched the earth and then rolled. I was home.

To sit on this six-hour flight and miss what that porthole affords is like a sexual encounter that reaches no climax. For the only notable landmark seen from the starboard side is Arlington National Cemetery.

Elizabeth Ann and I disembarked from the plane and walked down the corridor together staring at the faces of the people rushing past us to catch their flights. It was Thursday evening, and the terminal was crowded.

My plan was to catch a cab downtown and rent a room in a cheap hotel around Dupont Circle. I thought I'd make a better appearance with a shave, shower, and a good night's sleep at a time when Harry wasn't busy at his restaurant.

I stood next to Elizabeth Ann at the baggage carousel. We were friends now. People from our flight were gathered for their bags. A tall young man with a beard and glasses interrupted our conversation. He wore blue shorts. The plastic cleats on the bottom of his shoes clacked on the floor as he walked along. His T-shirt had the printed name of a Trenton, New Jersey bar, "Al's Airport Inn."

The two of them were happy to see each other. I never asked her about a lover, yet he only kissed her on the cheek, so I thought that perhaps he was just a friend. He impatiently waited for our bags to come. She introduced me to him. John Anglund was his name. He shook my hand and though I said my name, it made little impression on him.

My bags came up first, and I grabbed them quickly because I had grown some of what was inside. In addition, there was a largesse of hundred-dollar bills. National Airport is in Virginia and Elizabeth Ann asked Anglund if he would mind dropping me across the river. He was a bit distracted and reluctantly agreed. There was something going on because they began whispering to each other.

It must have been something important because she became very animated. "Oh no... you're kidding... those fuckers!"

Those fuckers? That was pretty strong stuff coming from her lips. Her eyes narrowed, and she pursed her lips. Her heart was racing. Yes, she was back in Washington and had assumed the position.

It wasn't until I was seated in the back seat of John's Ford that I got the lowdown. The unfolding story was the kind of stuff she thrived on, a crisis requiring relentless, urgent attention. She was working herself into a temper. She pulled her shoulders back and pounded her lap with her fist.

I thought yes, this is a vicarious sign. Perhaps behind the professional facade was a passionate woman. I pondered the possibilities— heat and lust and Elizabeth Ann's firm body entwined with mine. The image of her naked and displaying sexually the same fervor she now showed for politics aroused me.

The story was pure Washington drama. Realizing that in me they had an audience, they revealed it. First one, then the other, in turn, in perfect rhythm, like two television newscasters sharing a story with the folks back home on their living room couch.

"John, and two of our other housemates work for Republican Congressman Neal Liston of Indiana," she said. "He's giving up his seat in the House to challenge Democratic Senator Bing Prewitt in November. Prewitt's a three-term liberal who is totally out of touch with the people of Indiana. Well, John made points last week with a press release he wrote about Liston's administrative assistant, Rockland McMorrow and another staffer going down to El Salvador on a fact-finding trip for the Congressman," she said. "Four newspapers ran the story."

"Prewitt is such a dove on defense that we figured we could make it a campaign issue in the November election," said Anglund, looking at me in the rearview mirror.

"Yes," added Elizabeth Ann, "it really put Prewitt on the defensive, and the big daily paper in Indianapolis printed an editorial condemning Prewitt for being soft on communism."

"When he spoke to the Indiana American Legion," said Anglund, "he was heckled by a bunch of World War Two veterans."

"Now, Prewitt's known Rock McMorrow for years, and he also knows that he's the star player on our office softball team," Elizabeth Ann said. "So when he is out of the country Prewitt challenges our office to a softball game. He says he is going to play and challenges Liston to represent his staff on the ball field too. Old Bing thinks he can get the moral high ground if his team kicks our butt."

"At first we thought it was a crackpot scheme," said Anglund. "But now all the newspapers from Indiana are going to be there to watch. They even got Federal Appeal Court Judge William Seton from Muncie to umpire the game. And Prewitt's office is calling it a preliminary to what the voters of the state can expect in November."

"What an asshole," said Elizabeth Ann.

"That fucker," added Anglund. "If they beat us tonight it is going to make me look stupid because I tipped our hand that Rock was out of town. I'm scheduled to leave for the Midwest in July to help manage the campaign. If we blow this one, I'll be answering constituent mail in a basement of the Rayburn Office Building for the rest of my life. Thank goodness your plane was on time. According to the rules we have to field at least three women, and if we don't we forfeit. Betsy here is our star pitcher."

"Betsy?"

She kicked him lightly in the shin. He recoiled and made a face at her.

"I'll bet this sounds silly to you," said Anglund in a lighter, less dramatic tone. "Unfortunately, it's these minor public relation scams that fuel a candidate's momentum. That was the first lesson I learned about American politics, it's 90 percent bluster."

The game was held on a baseball field situated in a triangular area between the Tidal Basin, the Bureau of Engraving and Printing and the Washington Monument just off Independence Avenue. There were campaign posters on the Prewitt side. Some were designed quite stylishly in red, white and blue. Another hand printed one read "Keep Bing Pitching for Indiana." Members of the press corps were there, a camera crew too. Prewitt's team wore T-shirts with American eagle emblems.

When John's Ford pulled up we were met by a small group of supporters. He stuck his head out the window and yelled, "The cavalry has arrived."

They were a man short. The congressman asked if I could play.

"I'm a pretty good shortstop."

"What's your name?"

"Joe Green."

"Nice to meet you, Joe. I'm Neal Liston," he said. "Meckler, you move to left field. Green, you take shortstop." He threw me a glove. I caught it with one hand and warmed up with Anglund.

The prize was two cases of Hoosier State beer, bottled in Bing's home town, not to mention bragging rights for the next few weeks in the newspapers.

I laughed at getting sucked into this situation my first hour back in DC.

What was really at stake here? In truth it was the aspirations of a dozen young people trying to hitch themselves to a rising political star. On one side was Neal Liston, a fiery redhead with freckles who was probably a pain in the ass to work for, yet obviously ambitious enough to risk his House seat to challenge a three-term Senate incumbent.

For the November winners there was more power, prestige and perhaps money, though money was not something young people in Washington cared about according to Elizabeth Ann… not yet anyway. They would occupy a position in an office with a higher profile and advance their careers. For a senator certainly carries more prestige than a congressman. And that's one clear thing about Washington, there's a pecking order that people swear by.

There was a photo opportunity at home plate. Liston and Prewett stood with mitts in hand. Standing between them was Judge Seton wearing an umpires mask. Prewitt had a big smile on his face. Liston wore a scowl. When the cameras stopped flashing Seton called out, "Play ball."

Before we took the field, Liston gathered his team. "Let us bow our heads and pray." The team obeyed. "Dear Lord, bless our team and the athletic effort we are about to embark upon. Make us strong and swift for your greater glory. In Jesus's name."

Now Jews usually don't implore God on such minor matters, so I thought it strange. But then I remembered the way Homeric heroes invoked the gods for nearly everything. So I bowed my head and closed my eyes too.

When Liston finished his prayer, he called out "Amen." The team responded with a unison "Amen."

Both teams played well. There was scoring in every inning. Liston stood on the third base line coaching with his scorebook in hand. He'd throw it on the ground in anger, or slap players on the butt with it for a good effort.

Prewitt pitched for his team. For a guy in his sixties he appeared quite vigorous. He was old enough to be Liston's father and perhaps his presence on the field was a strategy to counter any assertion that he was too old to continue. He was a good sport, even tempered and generous in his praise. His shortstop and second baseman had good gloves and accurate throwing arms. They covered balls hit up the middle that he was too slow to stop.

For a fill-in I was playing well. There was nothing on the line for me except to impress my newfound friends, which I was eager to do. In addition, it was a coed game and the quality of play was not as high as it might have been if both teams were fielding intense jocks.

I caught most of what was hit to me, threw a few guys out at first, snagged a couple of line drives, and turned a double play. But I made errors too. I overthrew first base once and had a grounder skip between my legs. I popped out with the bases loaded in the third inning but doubled twice, knocked in three runs and scored once.

If I rose to the occasion it was because I knew that Elizabeth Ann was watching. I too saw this contest as a metaphor but for a different campaign. Watching her gracefully deliver the ball to home plate made me quite vigilant. Once, with a man on first base, the batter hit a one hopper right back to her. She flicked her wrist and caught it in the palm of her glove. She turned around to get the lead runner at second base which I moved over to cover. It was just a split second; we looked into each other's eyes amid running and screaming and all sorts of kinetic action. For that split second there was no one else in the world but the two of us. Two stationary souls in a whirling maelstrom. She peppered the ball perfectly into my mitt, and I stepped on the bag to end the inning. As I walked past her to the bench I touched her shoulder and softly whispered, "Well done."

It was the bottom of the seventh inning, the last inning. We were down by just a run, twelve to eleven. Anglund led off. He hit a line drive in the alley between center and right field for a double. The next person popped out to the shortstop. Liston pinch hit for Sarah, a legislative aide from Mississippi who played catcher. This was interesting. Liston had watched the whole game from the third base line and now with victory on the line, he put the pressure on himself to produce.

He swung and missed the first two pitches Prewitt threw him. How funny if Liston himself blew the game for his own team. A noticeable sweat broke out on his forehead. I wondered what was going through his mind. Perhaps he had second thoughts about running against Bing Prewitt. He took a deep breath and got back in the batter's box, reared back the bat, fixed his eyes on the mound and grimaced.

Bing threw him a bad pitch, a ball, and then another. Now Liston was getting angry. Stepping out of the batter's box, he rubbed some dirt on his hands before stepping back in.

The pitch came, and the congressman slapped it on the ground between the third baseman and the shortstop for a single. The left fielder was so intent on preventing Anglund from scoring that he charged the ball and pegged a perfect strike to the catcher, backed up by Prewitt at home plate. Anglund was held at third base. But while that defensive drama was going on Liston snuck unnoticed to second base.

Triumphant, he brought Sarah back into the game as a pinch runner at second base. Putting one hand on her shoulder, finger pointing in her face with the other hand, he gave her stern instructions. She listened to him with a frightened look. He did the same thing to Anglund on third and then stayed at third base to coach.

In all the excitement I forgot that it was my turn to bat. I turned to the bench and there was Elizabeth Ann with a red aluminum bat in her hand. She thrust it to me the way a Greek maiden might have handed a sword to a Greek warrior off to fight the Persians at Marathon. She said nothing but then she didn't have to. I was already inspired.

Liston's chatter at third was a bit unnerving. Fortunately for me there was one out and with second and third occupied not much chance of a double play. I might disappoint the team, but I wouldn't kill its effort.

Prewitt laid a waist high meatball on the outside corner of the plate. I stepped into it and smacked it to the opposite field. The shot flew over the second baseman like a rocket. I thought I had broken the game wide open. Our bench rose to their feet. I took off running as fast as I could with one eye on the ball. But their speedy black center fielder had a mark on it. He seemed to run faster than the ball was flying. He sprinted after it. Liston screamed at the base runners. The outfielder leaped high in the air at the last possible moment and extended his left hand out straight. It was like watching ballet, so graceful was the motion of his body. He was three feet in the air when he trapped the bottom inches of the ball in the webbing of his glove. He came down hard and rolled on the grass and lay there flat. The crowd held its breath. Then he held his glove in the air with the top of the white ball visible. Prewitt's bench went wild, and I stood there in disbelief.

But Liston had a plan. He held his hands high in the air showing his palms. When the ball was caught he waved them vehemently for Sarah and Anglund to tag up. They raced for home plate. The outfielder, exhausted by his effort, got to his knees and tossed the ball underhand to the woman right fielder who came over to help. The first baseman ran to the outfield for the relay, but she made a bad throw, and it rolled to him.

Anglund scored and Sarah waddled around third and was heading home too. The first baseman turned and pegged it to the catcher. There was going to be a play at the plate, and it was going to be close.

The throw was wide of the mark. It hit Sarah right in the head as she raced down the third base line. The ball careened off her skull and bounced behind our bench. Her hands and legs jangled as she hit the ground. Blood and dirt soiled her brown hair. Her glasses went crooked on her face. She was out cold ten feet from home plate.

Meanwhile the third baseman scrambled in and out of our players trying to grab the ball and me, seeing the prostrate body of the young woman, grabbed her arms and began dragging her along the base path. But the more I pulled the harder it became. Her belt buckle acted like an anchor against the earth. Her face was scraping the ground, and I was afraid I'd break her glasses.

Liston appeared beside me. He grabbed her right hand. Now the two of us were dragging her body. "Damn, Sarah, you're a big girl," he groaned.

We glanced into each other's eyes and got the same idea. We flipped her over. Now it was her butt not the belt buckle scraping the ground. The third baseman, with ball in hand was running straight for us. We dropped Sarah's knuckle on home plate a full second before the tag.

Both benches emptied and gathered around home plate. Prewitt complained that she should be called out because we had pulled her along. And I got right in Seton's face screaming that the first baseman threw at her head purposefully and that she would have been safe if not for the beaning.

Prewitt nudged me aside with his big belly and went nose to nose with the judge arguing the opposite. The judge listened to both sides. After deliberating, Seton stepped back from the crowd and made his call. He extended his arms out straight and screamed, "Safe!"

We won.

The team went wild. I found myself screaming and hugging strangers. Sarah was carried from the field semi-conscious on their shoulders triumphantly. All the while her eyes were rolling somewhere in the back of her head.

"Put me down," she said. She vomited her dinner in the wire Department of Recreation litter basket as the team crowded around her and cheered every retch.

We sat right down and drank the two cases of beer with some fans. Prewitt's team was pretty dejected and didn't stick around. Old Bing was gracious enough to offer Liston his congratulations. But he was angry when the handshake was captured on camera because this time Liston was smiling, and Prewitt wore the scowl.

It was getting dark, and Liston decided that we should reconvene at the Tune Inn, a Capitol Hill bar, and continue the celebration. Since my bags were already in Anglund's car, I rode over with him while Elizabeth Ann and her girlfriends took Sarah home first.

"Take the scenic route to the Hill will you John?" He drove along the river and around the monuments which were now lit up in the dark. Washingtonians see these places daily and perhaps familiarity dulls their magic. But bring a stranger around and they'll go out of their way to promote their adopted city, if only the stranger will lend his enthusiasm to rekindle their own.

American society's memorials to its great forefathers, George Washington, Thomas Jefferson, and Abraham Lincoln, instilled a wave of piety in me that entering a church or synagogue never has. Perhaps it's because they are secular and suggest that any inspired man born of the republic can fire the imagination of his countrymen, achieve greatness, and one day stand with heroes.

"I take it from your T-shirt that you're from Jersey."

"Yes," John said. "I'm from Trenton. How about you?"

"I grew up in Jackson Township."

"I've been to the amusement park there."

"Great Adventure? That place put us on the map. Before that the only thing Jackson was known for was the mafia burial grounds on its chicken farms."

"I remember that story."

"How long have you been in DC?" I asked.

"Three years. I came to town right after college."

"I forgot how politics consumes everybody who lives here," I said. "I mean look at you. When I met you a few hours ago, your brazen press release almost got you shipped off to the Washington equivalent of Siberia. And now that the game is won, you're a hero."

"Believe me, I find it weird too," said Anglund. "It finally struck me after being here for a year that the people making the big decisions in town, decisions that affect millions of people are made by men with a grasp of events no greater than my own."

"This is the first time I've been in DC as an adult. The workings of the government were always something I studied in college classrooms. I'm getting a different feel for the city now."

The Tune Inn is located on Capitol Hill. Harry used to take me there. It's a well-loved watering hole for underpaid congressional staffers. "Mixed Drinks," a sign written in red neon script, catches the eye of people hustling down Pennsylvania Avenue Southeast. The yellow plastic clocks, one on each wall, date back to the early 1960s, a promotional item from Miller High Life beer. They show "bar time," accelerated by ten minutes to get drunken patrons out the door by two a.m. With National Bohemian on tap and its most expensive menu item at $3.95, it's a place where you can get a cheap beer and burger and feel comfortable wearing a three-piece suit or shorts and a T-shirt. With bowling trophies and taxidermy, it's the kind of place you'd expect to see in Duluth or Chattanooga, not four blocks from the US Capital.

The place was engulfed in a Thursday night rush, celebrating the near end of the work week. We had to push our way through the crowd to reach the team huddled around two booths in the back. Liston, pitcher in hand, was pouring beer to his staff. Anglund, the drama's catalyst, breathed a deep sigh of relief as Liston gave him an affectionate bear hug when they came face to face. Turning to me, he reached out his hand to shake mine.

"Joe, thanks for everything you did out there today," the congressman said. "The two of us pulling Sarah to home plate is a story I'll be telling for quite a while."

"You're welcome, sir," I answered.

Then Anglund and Liston walked to the corner of the bar and had a private conversation. The team was a friendly group. And though I was just a fill-in, they treated me as one of their own.

Each had a unique background from a different state of the union.

One had campaigned with Liston when he was a dark horse congressional candidate in 1972 and was rewarded with a job here. Another had gone to college in Washington and obtained an internship through a university program. Some were just in the right place at the right time; others had connections through friends and relatives. The one thing they had in common was a desire to participate in America's big political picture.

Elizabeth Ann arrived a few minutes later. I ignored her because my lustful feelings made me feel self-conscious in her company. I had stared at her from behind the entire game. There was something ethereal about the way her hair blew in the wind. I liked the way her shoulders moved when she delivered a pitch and how she stood stalwart facing the batter as he swung the bat. So I spoke to the others instead.

A woman named Rose Giotti sat upright in a chair and spoke to me. She was sitting on her hands. Her small nose had a cleft just above the nostrils. Her dark Italian eyes glowed as she presented herself as a future congressional candidate from a rural Pennsylvania district. She had played second base and was fresh out of law school. We discussed her district's ethnic makeup and their party allegiance.

She was, perhaps, a little full of herself but formidable. In her arsenal was a stern expression when challenged on a rhetorical point and a cynicism for ideas not her own. Her square jaw flexed forward at just the right time, and her eyes, looking right into mine, enlarged the effect.

John introduced me to his housemate, Calvin Merrick, a skinny kid from Connecticut. He had thick black glasses and pink gums. His hair was dense, dark and wavy. He laughed often and off key. He had graduated from Boston College with a degree in communication and marketing and had recently become Liston's press secretary. He wasn't a very good ballplayer. Liston platooned him with Sara at catcher and had him coach first. But I was told that he was good at his job. His pen could be devastatingly vindictive, and this fact compelled people to look past his appearance.

There was much beer drinking and then someone ordered a round of shooters. The bartender combined a sweet concoction of liquors to taste innocuously like ice tea. He poured out three fingers worth in a row of rocks glasses lined on the bar. The waitress carried it over on a brown cork tray. We toasted to an election victory in November. There were a few extras, so Anglund and I tossed them down.

Then I met Sven Peterson, a tall blonde Minnesotan. He returned from the bar with a beer, and we found ourselves standing next to each other.

"I hear this is your first day in town," he said. "How are you liking it?"

"I went to high school and college here. But I was gone almost two years. I'm really glad to be back."

"Yeah, it's all pretty amazing when you first get here," he said. "I look at you and I'm reminded how I felt when I first arrived."

"You sound as if you're sick of it."

"I guess I'm just a bit burnt-out. I'm beginning to think it's time to move on. That's a tough thing to admit. Years ago, I had fire in my guts. I was going to take this town by storm and become king of the mountain. It's a funny thing though, I've discovered that the real power lies back home and not here at all. A lifer in DC will only ever be a bureaucrat. Most opportunities lie in your home state, in judgeships, in congressional districts and in Senate seats.

"Washington is a good place to be when you're in your twenties," he said. "You get a strong dose of culture, get great experience, and meet people from all over the world. But when you get to your thirties and you want to marry, settle down and have kids, it's no place to be. Housing is way over-priced, the DC public schools are lousy, and you have to work too hard to keep up a decent standard of living. I'm thinking about moving back to Minnesota to be with my girlfriend."

"Just the thought of that cold weather gives me the shivers."

"Well, it's not so bad. Given my choice, I'll take a Minnesota winter over a Washington summer any day."

The bar emptied out. Anglund stood by the door with a group of people from his house. He had brought my bags from his car. He had no idea that one of them contained thirty thousand in cash.

"Well, this was an interesting first day back in Washington," I said with a touch of irony.

"I know what you're thinking," he said. "People here are full of shit. I get caught up in it myself, and sometimes it's hard for me to keep my perspective."

"Yeah? How do you manage?" I asked.

"I smoke a little pot, and it brings me back to earth."

"Me too."

"I live in a group house with Elizabeth Ann, Sarah, Cal and Sven. We are having a house party next week. Why don't you come by?"

"Thanks, I will."

"And we got another game on Wednesday night, same field, same time. Show up. We could use your glove."

We shook hands. As she was leaving, Elizabeth Ann slipped a piece of paper in my hand with the address, the time of the party and phone number of the house. "Please come," she said. I watched as she walked out the door to catch up with her friends.

I sat around finishing my drink. Then I grabbed my bags and walked out the door. They were heavy, but my head felt exhilaratingly light. Walking down the muggy street I could feel my pores opening to cool my body. It seemed like my whole being was opening too. The revelation that I was finally home sent shivers down the backs of my legs.

I flagged down a taxi and had him take me to a Dupont Circle hotel. The hotel's furnishings were old and worn, but I didn't care. The bathroom and bed sheets were clean. After a shower I got into bed. I was still reliving the day's events in my mind: the flight, the game, the sights and sounds of the city, Liston, Anglund, Peterson, Giotti and of course Elizabeth Ann.

Though it was past midnight I couldn't sleep. I was still on California time. So I pulled a book out of my suitcase and read till three a.m.

Chapter 16

Next morning, I walked out the hotel door and into the Washington, DC day. The first place I went was my old apartment. I wasn't sure what to expect when I knocked on the door. Jimmy Luther opened it. "Holy shit, the prodigal son." We shook hands. "Welcome home, Joe."

"Are you living here now, Jimmy?"

"No, but I stay here sometimes on weekends so I don't have to drive home late at night to Virginia."

Then, realizing that he was standing in the way of me entering my own apartment, he stepped aside. Almost two years had gone by and Harry let it be.

"Listen, Jimmy, I'm back to stay. But I don't know if Harry is going to want me to live here again."

"You mean he doesn't know you're back?"

"No, I just got in last night."

"Cool, I won't say a thing."

"How's business been in the upstairs apartments?"

"Harry shut that down when he had his troubles."

"That's too bad, I really liked the women who worked up there."

"Stop by the strip club. They're still around. I'm going to take off now," he said.

"Hey, Jimmy, I saw what you did in front of my apartment the day I went away. Thank you. Here, try this. I grew it myself." I handed him the Ghani Purp joint in my pocket.

"Thanks, Joe. Finding good pot in this city is nearly impossible sometimes." He took it and left.

Wow, did I really live here? The apartment seemed smaller than I remembered, especially when compared to the spaciousness of my California two-bedroom house with its wrap around porch as the last house on Limerick Lane. By comparison, this place was a sardine can. The sound of traffic on the street was louder than I remembered too. The direction of its windows did not allow for much sunlight. But the smell of it brought me comfort. My eyes got a little watery when I saw China's water bowl beside the refrigerator.

There on my bookshelf I found the signed copy of Robert Penn Warren's book *World Enough and Time*. I opened it and looked at the inscription. The author was right. There is world enough and time.

I walked to my closet. Tucked away in the corner was an orange metal container that held my stash. My green pipe and rolling papers were inside, but the pot was gone. That didn't surprise me. Myra, Galena and Minnie all knew it was there and probably smoked it the week I left. But my clothes were there and sixty dollars in cash was in my top drawer.

When I arrived at Harry's restaurant I saw Shameem, his head chef, sitting at a window table drinking his morning coffee. When he saw me crossing the street, he rose from his chair to unlock the door.

"Joseph! So good to see you," he said. "How long can you stay?"

"I'm back for good." With that he shook my hand.

He wore a white double-breasted cook's coat and a checkered pair of pants provided by the restaurant's linen service. His frame was straight and thin, his skin tone the color of a medium well steak. His straight black hair, which looked wet even when it wasn't, was parted on the side. A distinguished graying at the temples now added to his dignity. Planted in the middle of his front tooth was a brown nicotine stain.

In his breast pocket he carried a meat thermometer. A small spoon soldered to one of his wife's finger-sized hairpins was clipped beside it. He used it for tasting soups and sauces or for measuring amounts of saffron and cayenne. He looked a bit hung over and needed a shave. Despite being a Muslim, he loved bourbon.

The Pakistani immigrant had worked at the restaurant for ten years. He came to Harry the day he arrived in town and got a job as a dishwasher. From there he made it to line cook. Two years later he became head chef.

When Shameem brought his fiancée and mother to America, Harry sponsored them. It was more than loyalty that kept Shameem in the same job for over ten years, although loyalty played an important part of it. His job was part of his persona. It gave him an identity in the nation's capital. He held a major post at a minor DC institution—head chef at Harry's Bistro.

Everyone's heard of the place; Harry advertised in the *Post's Sunday Magazine* section. Thus, when people asked Shameem what he did for a living, he'd announce his title and company. People nodded in recognition. They knew the restaurant's reputation and rightly assumed it was his doing. Continuity reigned in Harry's kitchen under his tutelage, and that was a big reason for its success.

Shameem brought me a cup of coffee and sat down.

"Tell me about the place, Shameem."

"Business is good. We had our best March ever. All the big shots have discovered Harry's. They all come in to eat shiitake mushroom soup and Veal Shameem. *Washingtonian Magazine* rated us one of the city's best."

"Congratulations," I said.

"Did you hear about Winn?"

"Hear what?"

"He had a heart attack."

"Oh no, heart attack and a stroke?"

Just then the door swung open and in walked Harry. He looked better than the last time I saw him. He had cut about fifteen pounds, the red veins in his nose were gone and he had shed his polyester clothes for natural fibers. Shameen noticed my surprise and winked. "He's got a steady girlfriend too."

Harry stopped short when he saw me. "Well, look who's here. You lost young man?"

We were staring at each other in silence when the phone rang. He picked it up. "Harry's Bistro." Shameem excused himself.

Harry's stare softened into a smile as he smoked a cigarette in his usual way, no hands. He held the tip in place with his front teeth, frequently closing his lips around the end of a Camel straight. He pulled out the cigarette with the two long fingers of his right hand and exhaled smoke through cone shaped lips. With the same hand, he pulled a piece of tobacco from the tip of his tongue with his pinky and thumb.

My friends were always impressed by Harry's appearance. His thick build, stern gaze and reluctant smile were usually accompanied by a narrowing of the eyes, a contemptuous awning guarding the natural affection he felt for his friends.

"Joseph, I got Benny on the line. The Bullets are playing the Sonics in the big game. He wants me to bet. Who do you like?"

"Take the Bullets," I said.

"Okay, Benny give me five hundred on the Sonics."

Harry hung up the phone.

"Why do you bother to ask my opinion if you never take it?"

"Because you have a religious instinct for bad judgment. Being a businessman, I've learned to make money from it. You can get mad if you want, but when you say someone is going to win they inevitably lose. In the last five years I've probably won ten thousand betting against your advice. You're still a kid. When you become a real man, I'll know by the amount of money I lose betting against you."

Just then the kitchen door flew open. Shameem appeared with a silver tray. There were three champagne glasses on it and a green bottle of Perrier Champagne with painted flowers on it. He set it down and passed out the glasses. He smiled as he twisted the bottle and pulled out the cork.

"What the hell is this? That's an eighty-dollar bottle of champagne," said Harry.

Shameem smiled and said, "I know. I'm celebrating."

"What the hell are you celebrating?" asked Harry.

"Starting today, I no longer have to be your nephew."

After we clinked glasses and drank a toast, Shameem left us alone.

"So where's the key to the cellar door?"

"What?"

"Matelsky called last night. I had a party of six standing at the front door while he's bitching about you locking the hose in the cellar and running off with the key. He says they're so full of mud that he's afraid to carry them through his living room. So I say to him 'I thought he was out there with you' and he says, 'No, Joe's on his way home.' I waited around past midnight for you to show up."

"I remembered what Thursday nights are like," I said. I stayed at a hotel. Thought I'd get cleaned up and surprise you this morning."

"I was surprised you were even in town. Then I got pissed off when you didn't show. Then I began to worry. You been hanging out in the land of the lotus eaters for so long I thought maybe you forgot how to handle yourself in the old neighborhood."

"That's something I'll never forget."

"How's that idiot Matelsky doing anyway?"

"He hasn't changed a bit."

"I asked him what you were going to do when you got back here and you know what he said? 'He'll do whatever the fuck he wants, he's rich. We're the Benson and Hedges of Sonoma County pot growers.'"

"He didn't lie," I said.

"I knew you were up to something. When I found out where you were hiding I sent you a check for your birthday. It's never been cashed. I guess your uncle's money is no good now."

"I've got my own," I said.

"So what are you going to do?"

"Not sure yet. Is it okay if I move back into the old apartment?"

"Of course it's okay. I've been saving it for you."

"Shameem told me about Winn," I said. "Is he going to make it?"

"The bastard had a coronary. It figures though, the way he eats and drinks. Actually, I've always thought a heart attack the best way to go. Proof of a life well lived instead of wasting away with cancer like your father. Anyway, he's selling out and moving to Florida."

"What about my dog?"

"Good luck getting it back. Ruth has it. She loves that hound."

"Is she moving to Florida too?"

"No, they're going through a divorce. She's taking Winn for all his money."

"She told me about it when she came to California."

"Look, there's one more thing I have to say. When I was in jail I needed someone to take over the harem. You were gone, and I didn't trust anyone else. So I put Minnie Battle in charge."

"That seems like a good choice."

"Well, one thing led to another, and we've been living together for the last six months."

"The bad bitch? You're living with the bad bitch?"

"Watch your mouth!"

"Weren't you always the guy that said don't fall in love with the merchandise?"

"When you're in trouble you find out who your friends are. She stood by me the whole time. I've taken about as much shit as I'm going to take on the subject. So you better get along."

"Whatever you say, Harry."

"Minnie's always been good to you, and it's what I want for myself."

"I need a favor." I unzipped my backpack and pulled out a bag. I handed it to him. He looked inside. It was filled with hundred-dollar bills.

"Christ, a guy could get a hernia carrying this weight around."

"Got room in your safe?"

"Sure, and I can probably launder it for you in a week or so."

"I was hoping you could help."

"Listen, I'm not going to get all gooey about what happened to you because I suffered plenty. But what we did to you was not fair, and I'm sorry."

We walked to his office and after some rearranging inside, he found room in his safe for my money. Then he left for the hospital. I went back to the dining room and finished my champagne.

Minnie Battle as my aunt? I sat alone in the dining room and thought about it. It wasn't so hard for me to believe. But it was just one of those possibilities I'd never have considered. The flames of passion might be color blind, but not so the rest of the world. Miscegenation no longer carried legal penalties, but narrow-minded prejudice still stigmatized it. There weren't many places in America in the 1970s that would accept the melding of their two color-blind hearts without supercilious looks. But DC was certainly one of them.

I walked behind the bar with my champagne glass and poured some orange juice in it. After all, it was still morning. I walked to the kitchen and looked for Shameem. He was alone in the prep area.

"Why didn't you tell me he was living with Minnie Battle?" I asked.

"You've been gone a long time Joseph," said Shameem. "He's getting older and that bust took its toll on him. He threw his back out one afternoon and was unable to work for almost a week. Minnie walked into the place on a Monday and had everybody eating out of her hand by Wednesday."

"I like her too. But it's hard to imagine who's fucked more times, Minnie or Harry."

"Minnie's son Lloyd took it very bad," Shameem said. "He refuses to accept the fact that she's living with a white man. He chants all this black power stuff and causes his mother grief."

"I'm happy Harry found someone to love."

"You know, ever since Minnie there's been a rainbow over this place. Business is good. And we all know that it won't last forever."

Chapter 17

I played shortstop for Liston's softball team Wednesday evening. Though the congressman was absent, all the players from game one were there. We lost to a better team. It didn't matter because nothing as important was at stake. When people started to leave, Anglund suggested we reconvene at the Tune Inn again. But Elizabeth Ann looked at me and asked about a place I knew.

"Wasn't it called Winnie's? According to Joe Green the best ribs in town. How about going there?"

No one in the group knew of it. I hadn't been there in years either. But we piled into two cars and drove to the Mount Pleasant neighborhood. Anglund, Elizabeth Ann, Sarah, Rose, Cal, Sven and me.

Winnie's was an old grocery store converted into a ten-table restaurant. Despite the big picture window with the hand-lettered stencil and the black awning that shaded it, its real calling card was from its exhaust fan each morning when the ribs started cooking. The barbecue gave the neighborhood a sweet smell. It was also free advertising that circumvented modern communication media.

Most of its business was carry out. They had beer and wine licenses but no wait staff. You had to go up to a high counter to order your food and drinks. The ribs were thick and meaty, and they bragged about their special sauce which, according to Shameem, was no more than generic barbecue sauce doctored with oil, vinegar, and black and red pepper.

The man working behind the counter was a classmate of mine from Wilson High. Though his black face was familiar, it took me a full twenty seconds before I could recall his name.

"You're Bobby Smith from Harvard Street," I said.

"Yeah," he answered. "You're Gaston Collins' friend, right?"

"Yeah, Joe Green. Good to see you. Say, is that good looking sister of yours still breaking hearts?"

"These days she ain't breaking nothing but her old man's balls. She's married and got two kids. She's living out in Prince George's County. Say, I saw Gaston last month."

"Next time you do, tell him Joe Green's back in town, and I'm looking for him."

The group huddled around us. I didn't want to grandstand, but I did take pride in the fact that DC was my hometown and I had something to share with my new friends.

We pushed two tables together and crowded around. The political events of the day were debated loudly. The pitched polemics disrupted the good-natured banter and easy-going laughter of the regulars. The sound of our rhetoric bounced off the store window and rushed out the Mount Pleasant Street door whenever someone came in or went out.

It was Elizabeth Ann's turn to fetch the beer. She stood at the counter waiting for Bobby Smith to come out of the kitchen when a well-dressed black man came in to pick up a to-go order. He stared at her T-shirt and tight shorts. "Hey pretty lady," he said, "what are you doing in this neck of the woods?"

He leaned casually against the counter, tilted his head back and smiled a rakish grin. "Why don't you let me take you away from all this? Me and some of my friends are meeting at my crib for food, drink, and smoke. Why don't you come along? Pardon me, but I should introduce myself, I'm Malcolm Johnson, Mayor Marion Barry's administrative assistant. Some big people in this town are going to be there, and I know that they'd love to meet a sweet little honey like you."

"Sorry, I'm with them," she replied and nodded her head in the direction of our group.

By now I had abandoned the table conversation. My back straightened, and I tried to make out what he was saying to her. The others had yet to notice. Whatever he said she didn't like it. She pulled away from him and shouted, "I'm free, white, and twenty-one, and I can do whatever I want."

Heads turned at once. Silence hit the room. Elizabeth Ann glared at him with a tight jaw. Bobby Smith emerged in time to hear the exchange. We looked at each other with helpless expressions because we both felt responsible.

The softball team suddenly felt unsure of its surroundings. The awkwardness continued for over a minute. It wasn't so much what she said that riled the black man, it was what it implied—I'm free, white and twenty-one and you're not!

Bobby handed Malcolm his ribs. He paid and walked out muttering about tight ass white girls who didn't know how to fuck anyway and staying in your own goddamn neighborhood.

When Elizabeth Ann brought the beers to the table they were grabbed greedily and put to our mouths to alleviate the obligation to speak. Then our food came. The men were sheepish, fearful perhaps that we'd be called upon to defend a white woman's virtue from the battery of a black man on the make. The women were indignant that such a brash and clumsy pickup move should be foisted upon one of them.

Winnie's closed at ten. We were the last ones to leave. I collected the money and paid the bill with John while Cal and Elizabeth Ann waited for us outside. The others took the second car home. When Anglund and I emerged from Winnie's, we were talking about plans for their weekend house party. The car was around the corner and halfway down a tree-lined street.

A young black man stepped out of a doorway and pushed Cal and Elizabeth Ann against the side of a panel truck. He brandished a pistol and demanded money. He was aiming the gun at them when we came around the corner and surprised him. Now the gun was turned on us. He motioned us over. "All right you fuckers, get over here too, fast, c'mon."

The shock turned our blood to ice. He had a brown grocery bag, and he handed it to Cal. "Put all your stuff inside it," he ordered. We took what we had out of our pockets and put it in the bag as ordered. When the mugger reached for it, I recognized him. The pint size, the thin moustache over the lip, the tough street talk, it was Minnie's son. Under my breath, barely audible, I whispered, "Lloyd, you son of a bitch."

In the darkness he hadn't recognized me, but he did after I spoke his name. His mouth opened wide, and he took a step closer to make sure it was me.

"Are you going to shoot me, brother?"

"Oh fuck," he said out loud.

He looked to the left and then to the right and in his confusion Anglund lunged at him and they both hit the pavement. The gun was knocked from his hand as they wrestled on the sidewalk. Elizabeth and Cal didn't move. Reaching down I picked up the gun just as two black men started from across the street. Their guns were drawn. I took a deep breath, tensed my muscles and with two hands clasped aimed the gun at them. I took three steps forward. They stopped in the street and pointed their barrels at me. We were all terror-stricken. I wasn't game for a shootout, but there we were face to face and something was going to happen.

"John, let him go," I shouted. Instead, he rolled on top of Lloyd and started punching. "John, let him go."

With the gun in my hands, I swung to the right and hit Anglund on the side of the head. The blow knocked him off Lloyd and onto the pavement. Lloyd got up and ran to his friends. A siren in the distance was getting louder. "Let's get out of here!" Lloyd shouted.

I pointed the gun barrel to the sky with my palms up and my chest exposed. They stared into my eyes, and one of them nodded. Backing up, they started away, though every few steps they turned to make sure I hadn't lowered the barrel. Then they ran. Seconds later an ambulance rushed by on its way to another address. Our eyes were wide open, our breathing shallow and our hearts pumping.

"Sorry, John. Are you all right?"

He had a dazed look on his face and did not answer.

"Let's get out of here," said Cal.

"Wait, shouldn't we call the cops?" Elizabeth Ann asked.

"If I were you, I wouldn't want those guys to know your name or where you live," I said. "It's over, and we were lucky. Let's get out of here before they realize what happened and come back."

We grabbed our belongings from the bag. We didn't say good-bye. The three of them climbed into Anglund's car. He drove down the street with the lights off. I lived nearby and hurried home. But as I passed an alley I slid the gun on the ground like a bowling ball. It landed underneath a dumpster.

Up in my apartment I recounted the incident. I ran it through my mind a dozen times. Anglund had a bump on his head. He could say it was from a mugging he heroically broke up. But the fact that it came from a friend and not the mugger was embarrassing. I had thirty dollars and an old Timex watch in my possession, and I'm sure from the way Anglund rummaged through his pockets for his share of the check, he had even less. I recognized the robber and abetted his escape. I discouraged them from calling the police. That wouldn't go over well.

And then I got scared. What if Lloyd came here with his crew looking for the gun. I was defenseless. Would he believe that I slid it under a dumpster? It was past midnight, and it started to rain. I grabbed an umbrella and walked eight blocks to find it.

I searched on my hands and knees with the flashlight and finally found the gun wedged underneath a wheel. I stuck it in my pants and brought it home.

I thought the stories Shameem told about Lloyd were exaggerations. Now I knew it was serious. It might have been a gang initiation.

Lloyd had a nickname, *Little Taillight*. It was given to him by Gaston Collins and me when we were kids. He was always bringing up the rear on our forays around the neighborhood. We were older, could run faster and ride our bikes farther than he could. Trying to ditch him was one of our favorite games.

He was a goofy little kid. Snot was always running down his nose, his shoelaces untied, the whites of his pockets out. He never had a father and perhaps that is one reason he so ardently sought our friendship.

At the age of thirteen we declared Lloyd a man. We sent him down to the apartment business office to see Mrs. McEwan so he could apply for his masturbation papers. We had set him up. "Hey Lloyd. There's Chris Garvin. Go ask him how his sister dances."

So he walked up to Chris and asked the question. "Hey, Chris, how does your sister dance?"

Chris grabbed him by the throat. "My sister has polio, asshole."

She really didn't. But the look on Lloyd's face was funny to see. We filled a brown paper bag with dog shit and placed it in front of his door, rang the doorbell, lit it on fire and watched him stamp it out from behind the stairwell door.

When Lloyd got in trouble two men were ready from across the street. It was an old ploy. Get a youngster to do the dirty work and back him up. If the two men got busted it might mean a jail cell in Lorton Prison. If Lloyd got popped it was juvenile court. For his first offense he might walk free. He was still playing chump, a role I helped lock him into.

Did John harbor a grudge? I thought to call him on the phone. But matters like that are better done face to face. No telecommunication will ever replace the male epic of looking another man in the eye, speaking your mind and standing fast for his reply. So on Saturday night I was on my way to the house party that Elizabeth Ann, Anglund, Sven, Sarah and Cal were throwing. The address was located between Connecticut and Wisconsin Avenue in the Woodley Park neighborhood. It was a beautiful old two-story brick house with black trim on its window shutters. It had a front porch with two chairs. The small lawn was well kept, and azaleas were planted in front, three on each side of the sidewalk. The house was owned by Cal's father who worked for the State Department in Denmark.

I knocked on the door. When no one answered I walked in. Though it was an old house, it was in good condition. It seemed like a good party house too, spacious and elegant. The living room to the left of the front door had a fireplace, a big picture window and hardwood floors. Behind it was a dining room with a big oak table. There was an odd assortment of chairs pushed against the wall. Leading off the dining room was a kitchen. Behind that was a sun porch filled with plants and a big blue sofa that looked out on the backyard. The stairs leading to the second floor had a decorative wooden bannister. It faced the door when you entered.

Colored streamers hung from the ceiling. Dozens of candles were on mantels and end tables, to be lit when the sun went down. The dining room table was lined with plastic cups and soft drinks next to unopened bags of pretzels and potato chips. A stereo system sat on the mantel over the fireplace. Its tall, narrow speakers were positioned against the same wall in each corner.

I called out, but no one answered. Just then Anglund appeared from the basement stairwell at the back of the staircase carrying a large ice filled bucket big enough for the keg. The bucket was leaking a trail of water.

I felt a bit more at ease when he smiled. I ran toward him and grabbed one of the metal handles. We laid it beside the dining room table.

"You're going to lose all that ice by nine thirty," I said. "If you've got a plastic garbage bag it would make a lot more sense to put the ice and keg inside. At least it will retain the water to keep the keg cool."

"Damn, I didn't buy enough ice."

"Let's drive to my uncle's bistro. His ice machine should be brimming. We can take all we need."

"I'll tell the others we're leaving," he said.

He ran up the stairs reaching for two steps at a time with his long legs to get his car keys. We jumped into his Ford and drove over the Duke Ellington Bridge to Harry's Bistro.

"How's your head?"

"I've got a bit of a lump, thank you. Fortunately, my hair is thick enough so it isn't noticeable. But I didn't get shot and that makes me happy."

"Sorry I slugged you."

"We were up until two in the morning talking about it. It wasn't until about midnight that I heard the part about the two guys across the street. I looked at Cal and said, 'What guys?' Then he explained the stuff that went on while I was fighting. I said some pretty mean things about you. When I found out the rest of the story I cooled off."

"It was the only thing I could think of at the time."

"You didn't have to hit me so hard."

"I thought about that afterward."

"You knew that kid, didn't you?"

"Yes, we grew up together. Plus, his mom is living in sin with my uncle."

"Does your uncle know he tried to mug you?"

"No, and since no one lost anything I'm debating whether I even need to tell him. You know, no harm-no foul."

"That's not exactly true."

"Oh shit. What did he get?" I asked.

Anglund took one hand off the wheel and reached deep into his jeans' pocket. He pulled out an expensive gold watch, the spoils of his wrestling match. "Want to bet that Lloyd doesn't know what time it is?"

"I got his gun." And for the next block we laughed so hard we didn't speak. We walked through Harry's back door, grabbed the ice and drove back to his house.

It takes time to turn acquaintances into friends and the virtue of the party was that it was the third time we got to speak. We had a history to draw upon. It was the culture within their walls that interested me. Sara's Mississippi drawl, Anglund's New Jersey multiculturalism, Sven's Minnesota liberalism, Elizabeth Ann's plutocratic southern California values, and Cal's pseudo-aristocratic New England sarcasm created a blend distinctly American.

We put the keg in the plastic bag and filled it with ice. Anglund, a self-professed expert, tapped it. We poured ourselves a glass of beer.

Elizabeth Ann grabbed my right hand with both of hers and welcomed me. I think my entry with Anglund, carrying the ice, not to mention a bottle of Scotch I filched from the bar gave her the signal that it was okay to trust me.

"I've been thinking about you ever since the shooting," she said nervously. She still seemed a bit shaken by it because no shots were actually fired. We talked about the close call and people gathered around us to listen.

No one was surprised by Anglund's heroics. His reputation was that of a Jersey tough guy. It made many feel good that one of their own was as stalwart as a mugger. For though they acknowledged that black people were victims of social and economic oppression, they themselves felt oppressed by the thought of one day being the victim of street violence.

Elizabeth Ann excused herself when her boss from the American Sugar Consortium came through the door. "I've invited a lot of friends here tonight, and I'm afraid that I won't have much time to spend with you. But most of them will be leaving early so stick around."

By nine, the party was crowded. I stood in a noisy corner of the living room and had a broad view of it. It was easy to engage people in conversation and quite often what they had to say was interesting. But the ability to circulate at such affairs is the key to a good time, to make an acquaintance and then move on to the next person. You take inventory and then return to the more desirable ones later in the evening.

Thus, the ability to get out of a conversation as quickly as you got into it is an important skill. I learned this from a conversation with a tall bespectacled blonde man from Kentucky, who after chatting with me for a few minutes waited carefully for a pause, said "excuse me," pivoted on his toes and walked off before I had a chance to even say goodbye. I thought to myself, now there's a real pro.

People cleaved closely to their resumés. A man could have been an impotent lover, a pederast, a schizophrenic, or a deadbeat. It didn't matter in the fleeting cocktail conversation. What mattered more was his Master's Degree from Michigan State, or his JD from Georgetown University Law School. Those facts did the talking.

The women liked to talk about work and their lousy male chauvinist bosses. Surprisingly, they were less modest. As the forerunners of the women's movement, many of them were taking jobs previously reserved for men. Their success pleased them. Yet the Washington Monument still cast a long shadow upon the green plots of the Mall and their "struggle" at work was a common theme of their conversation.

Around DC there were thousands of anti-establishment bohemian types fighting for left-wing ideals and the rights of the less fortunate. They hadn't been invited. The people here were part of the establishment and in coming years would prosper in it.

When I went to get another beer, Anglund grabbed me by the arm and whispered, "We're meeting in my bedroom to smoke pot at ten thirty. Second door on the left at the top of the stairs. I'll be expecting you."

Near the beer keg stood a big man with short blonde hair. He was lecturing a small group of younger individuals; perhaps he was their boss. He spoke, and the small crowd nodded. As I held my cup beneath the beer keg's nozzle I listened in.

"The communists in Nicaragua are wreaking havoc on that country, and once they take over there it is only a matter of time until they take over El Salvador and Guatemala. I saw CIA reports of the Sandinista's plans for Central America. It's time to invoke the Monroe Doctrine in Central America and take action."

Cal was part of his audience. For some reason I just knew that this had to be Rock McMorrow, back from his fact-finding trip for Congressman Liston. He was tall, with a strong build and a Texas accent. His chin protruded out from underneath his mouth, and his big grey eyes reminded me of gunpowder.

"Aren't you afraid that we will be getting ourselves into another Vietnam?" I interjected.

"Hell, no! We're not talking about a small country ten thousand miles away. We're talking about our backyard. I was in Vietnam, it's not the same situation."

"I live in Adams-Morgan. Many of my neighbors are from that part of the world. If you ask them who they like better, the left wing or the right wing, they will tell you that they don't really give a damn about either one. All they want is a job and a chance to raise their families in peace. Down there, politics is a luxury reserved for young passionate men without children."

"That might be so, but they'll get a hell of a better shake under the American backed regime than they will under the communists," he said. "If I was President Carter I'd recognize the Sandinistas. I'd send them a hundred thousand Sears catalogues with charge cards and a monthly payment plan. Give Managua a team in the American League and let them play the Yankees and the Red Sox. Grant them a dozen McDonald's franchises. That will bring them into the American sphere of influence faster than attack helicopters and M-16s."

He hesitated and then realized it was a joke. As he laughed so did the rest of the group. He asked me my name, and when I told it to him he nodded. "I heard about you, Green. You're the guy who broke up the mugging and helped us win the softball game against Prewitt. You got some mad skills, boy."

I asked about his experience in Vietnam. He had been a company commander for an engineering unit stationed near Saigon and had been awarded the bronze star. After service he obtained a Master's degree through the G.I. Bill at the University of Virginia.

"John Anglund likes you, which is a recommendation," said Mc-Morrow. "He says you are new in town and are looking for work. Maybe I can help you. Send a resumé to my office and we'll see what we can do."

"I don't even have one," I said, "and if I did I'm not sure what I'd put on it."

"Do you have a college degree?"

"I'm a few credits short."

"Can you type, write or operate a computer?"

"No."

He threw his hands in the air and smiled. "Well hell, son, you might as well forget about working up on the Hill with these folks. You don't have a damn thing to offer anyone. If I were you I'd get myself enrolled in some college program because without a damn piece of sheepskin you're not going anywhere in this town. Hell, for most decent jobs you need a Master's just to get them to look at your cover letter."

"I'm kind of self-taught, auto-didactic so to speak."

He let out a big laugh. I don't think he knew what auto-didactic meant. But I don't think I realized what working on Capitol Hill meant.

A fresh group of young people walked through the front door and came up to McMorrow. They wanted to hear about his trip. Political questions were being asked of him, and he was glowing from the attention. In his right hand he grasped a beer. His two long fingers were stretched out away from the cup and held a burning filtered cigarette between his finger nails. His other hand was an extension of his voice, making a fist or pointing to an obedient face to add emphasis to his argument.

McMorrow was good at such assertiveness, and he had the credentials to back it up. A man of action who looked you straight in the eye and talked tough. And yet there was something about his rhetoric that didn't sit right with me.

"Is it my imagination or is there a disconnect between the American civil liberties you champion at home and those same liberties you trample upon in foreign countries?"

McMorrow and Cal stared at me and answered in unison. "It's your imagination."

Congressman Liston and his wife walked in. Anglund went to greet them. As he passed by he pointed to Lloyd's gold watch on his wrist and shook his head. He whispered. "Duty calls. We have to postpone the pot party."

As McMorrow continued his speech, I stared at him with a smirk. He heard me utter a soft sarcastic moan after one of his most assertive sentences. Everybody else heard it too. He looked at me with disdain. "What the hell are you looking at?"

That's when it came to me. "A man in handcuffs." I said it with a big grin. Everyone stared at me with a puzzled look. Then they turned their attention to his wrists which were bare. He suddenly remembered where we had met before. Harry's third floor apartment with Minnie Battle. "Piss off, Green," he said as he walked away.

A woman standing beside me was chuckling.

"He's a stubborn man to try and take on in debate. You'd have had an easier time debating a mule."

"Mules are usually Democrats," I said. Then I noticed to whom I was speaking. "You must be Mrs. Liston. My name is Joe Green." We shook hands. I was charmed by the ironic look on her face.

"Call me Darlene," she said. She had one of those peaches and cream complexions that you'd expect from a clean-cut, wholesome girl from the Midwest. Her black hair was wrapped in a bun at the back of her head. She had brown eyes and teeth like Chiclets. Her deep-set eyes were an interesting feature, and as we talked they seemed to signal the metaphor of her basic nature—eyes recoiling from the intrigue that her family's subsistence rested upon. She did not seem assertive, more the demure wife of a country lawyer who didn't enjoy confrontation. She was pregnant too.

"Actually, you did better than most do against him. When Rock and Neal get into it at my house the shouting is so loud they wake the kids and shake the rafters. One time our neighbor even called the cops. That he walked away instead of you says something in your favor."

"That's because he thinks I'm an idiot. I don't seem to have what it takes to be successful in political circles," I confessed.

"I did notice a certain detachment," she said. "For people who throw their whole beings into political affairs that attitude can be offensive."

"You seem to maintain a certain calm in all this. Being the wife of a senatorial candidate must really put you in the spotlight, and pregnant too."

"This is my third child so there haven't been many surprises. My husband is under most of the pressure."

"How do you feel about his running for the Senate? Aren't you nervous about him risking his congressional seat?"

"Actually, he's doing it for me. This business of running for re-election every two years is awfully hard. And each time Neal has had a tough reelection fight that just wears him down. He works hard and does right by his constituents. The idea of having to run again every two years just to affirm his good work drains him. If he wins he won't have to run again for six years, and if he loses he'll retire from public life and get to know his children while they're still young. Either way our lives will be better."

"He seems like a good man."

"Neal acts tough. That's not the way he was when I married him. He was just a small-town boy with big dreams. When he got here he changed. He had to. A congressman's life is run, run, run. And he was more than just a little intimidated by the high caliber of talent working in this town with their Ivy League diplomas and their long list of achievements."

Someone over my shoulder caught her eye. She waved her hand. "There's someone I'd like you to meet," Darlene said. She called across the room to a woman standing by herself drinking beer. Her pretty face had freckles. Her thick, curly red hair was cut short, and she had brown eyes.

"Joannie Quinn, I'd like you to meet Joe Green. Joannie is rather new in town and doesn't know many people. She is also very eligible."

Joannie gave Darlene a twisted look and whispered, "Shhh."

Just then Liston appeared and put his hand softly on his wife's shoulder. He shook my hand and teased me. "Green, are you poisoning my wife's mind?"

"Actually, I've been doing all the talking," she said. "The gentleman's very gracious."

"Darlene, come into the kitchen, there's a few people I'd like you to meet," he said. They left me alone with Joannie.

"Are you from Indiana too?" I asked.

"No, Elyria, Ohio. Darlene is my first cousin. I came to town for an interview with the State Department. I'm a nurse practitioner. On some of their smaller posts they've decided to employ us instead of doctors, so I applied for the job."

"How did your interview go?"

"Pretty well I think. Neal knows a few people who might be able to help me. But of course I won't know for a while. Even if I do get hired, they still have to do a security check on me and that can take months. Then I have to wait for an opening. I'm flying home tomorrow to get my car and then I'll be driving back. I'm also a midwife, and I'm going to deliver Darlene's baby and help her care for her kids while Neal's busy with the campaign."

"Midwives are kind of old fashioned, aren't they?"

"What's wrong with being old fashioned? I'm competent. I did my internship at Mayo Medical School in Minnesota and have delivered almost thirty babies. That's more than some doctors."

"But do you realize the moral implications of what you are doing? I mean the idea of bringing another Neal Liston into the world. Wow." I was teasing, and she picked right up on it.

"Well, you never know. The sins of the father are not necessarily the sins of the son."

"Are you interested in politics?" I asked.

"I've done volunteer work for Neal. During the summer I used to go to parades and hand out leaflets and bumper stickers. I'm not up on the issues, but I do like the contact with people, especially in Indiana where people are so friendly."

While she spoke her eyes focused on the collar of my blue Oxford shirt. She reached for the button on the left side and without missing a beat of her sentence, buttoned down the collar.

Anglund came along with Elizabeth Ann. "Joannie, I want you to meet my roommate."

As the two women spoke, I faded into the background and took the opportunity to talk to John. "Are you pleased with the turnout?"

"Yes," he said. "Almost everybody I invited showed up. I was surprised that Liston showed up. I invited him out of obligation never thinking he'd come."

"I had a little chat with his wife though. She seems pleasant enough."

"Oh, Darlene, she's a saint. Hates the public functions she's obliged to attend as the candidate's wife. I think she'll be happier if he loses."

"Oh, by the way," he continued, "I heard you met my boss, Rock McMorrow. I told him about you and how you were new in town looking for a job, and he said he'd give you an interview."

"Oh really, when?"

"It happened about twenty minutes ago, and you didn't do so good. He said the best place for you would be with the Executive Protection Agency. He thought you'd be in your element guarding the Russian embassy."

"Well, no love lost," I said.

Elizabeth Ann entered the dance floor with McMorrow, and I studied the couple carefully. I've certainly seen better dancers. She seemed to hop to the song a half beat out of step, and McMorrow was as bad. They camouflaged themselves in the middle of the dance floor. Every person has their foil, and that seemed to be the book on McMorrow and Elizabeth Ann—no rhythm. And it was "Saturday Night Fever" playing! A tune with a beat so good that only the deaf could miss it.

Just then Elizabeth Ann walked over to me and held out her hand. "Dance with me."

"I just had a talk with Rock," she said. "He said you and him had some words earlier this evening."

"Is that what he told you?"

"Actually, he called you a fucking asshole. But I told him you had spunk and smarts and that he would be a damn fool if he didn't find a place for you on his team."

"You told him all that?"

"Yes."

"Are you two involved or something?"

"God no. He is going through a sticky divorce with a real nasty wife. He's interested in me, but I've told him there's no way I'd even consider a dinner date until the divorce papers are signed. Call him. You can reach him at Congressman Liston's office. He wants to talk."

"Why are you going to all this trouble?"

"I kind of feel like I discovered you," she said, "and I'd like to see you do well."

"What makes you think I'd work for a guy like him?"

She pulled back and looked surprised. "What do you mean? He's a rising star in this town, and he's going to make his mark. You could go places with him."

"What he needs is a water boy. I'm free, white and twenty-one, and I won't do it."

She was insulted, especially since I was mimicking her own words of just a few nights ago. "I just groveled at McMorrow's feet in order to get you a chance. I stuck my neck out, risked my name and reputation and for what? So you could walk around in a huff because of your big male ego?"

Our hands had been clasped, and now she let go and stared at me. Her eyes had a glow like the mesquite coals in Matelsky's fireplace. "Your problem is that you just don't know how to play the game."

"Your problem is that you do."

With that she narrowed her eyes, exposed her bottom teeth, and huffed deeply for effect. Along with the carbon dioxide, she seemed to exhale any regard she had for me. Then she marched to the kitchen. I didn't want to, but I followed her with my eyes. She joined a group of people doing shots of tequila.

When Liston and Darlene walked out the door, I found Anglund. "Can we smoke now?"

"Sure, Sven has it. I'll go find him."

"Don't bother, I brought my own."

We retired to his room, picking up Sven and two friends along the way. We closed his door and sat around in a circle. I lit up the Ghani Purp.

After a few minutes, we put the joint down. We only smoked half. It was enough.

"Where did you find this stuff? It's fabulous," giggled Anglund.

"Actually, I grew it myself while I was living in California. It's called Ghani Purp." We talked and laughed for about fifteen minutes.

"Hey, me and Sven are hosting this party, and we should get back to it," John said.

"I should get going myself," I said. "I'll call you this week."

"We have a softball game on Thursday night. Same place. Show up. Afterwards we can go drinking."

"Thanks, I will."

"And Joe, bring some of this pot."

We all walked out of John's smoke-filled bedroom and closed the door behind us. Elizabeth Ann was standing in the hallway beside her bedroom door. "Were you going to leave without saying goodbye?"

"No, of course not. Thanks for a great party."

"I like your face," she said and rather artlessly threw her arms around my neck. She kissed me on the mouth.

I kissed her back. *At last, conquest*, I thought. Yet in the back of my mind I was thinking she must be really drunk. But she looked great in the dim light. The crush of her breasts against me, and her soft moist tongue flush against mine put all hesitation aside.

How many times had I fantasized about this? Ever since I saw her in the aisle of the airplane. Now I broke away from her mouth and led her through her bedroom door, closing it behind us. The room was illuminated by the moonlight cast through the sheer curtains. We laid down on her bed and I began kissing her.

I undressed her gently, and she gave a soft moan of accord. I liked the way her breasts fell together on her chest in alluring cleavage. She had big nipples in the middle of purple-brown areoles. Her waist had smooth curves, and she trimmed her pubic hairs short.

Suddenly, I realized she was out cold. I sat up in the bed and let out a cry of disbelief. "Are you kidding me?" Were she awake she would have taken offense at my tone. Perhaps getting really drunk was the only way she could allow herself to be seduced by me. But she lost sight of that fine line between reckless abandon and unconsciousness.

Why do men do what they do? The answer is simple. Women might be watching. That line came to me while I stared at her naked body. I thought about our meeting on the airplane. She had intimidated me on the flight home, but I got over it. At the softball game, she inspired me when she handed me that red aluminum bat at a critical time in the game. I remembered the frightened look on her face leaning up against a panel truck when Lloyd pulled his gun and how I was able to find a way out of that predicament.

Every time she was around I got to act brave. So of course I was infatuated with her. Men are inspired by beautiful women, and I was no different. But was this the outcome? A nine-inning game ending with a rainout?

I pulled her up so her head was securely on her pillow and covered her with the bedspread. I hung her bra from the light fixture to remind her that I was there. Then I tip-toed out of her bedroom, closed the door, walked down the stairs and out through the front door. In a car parked out front, Anglund and a brunette were locked in a front seat embrace. He didn't notice me, and I wasn't about to interrupt. Halfway down the hill a car stopped beside me. It was that Quinn woman.

"Do you need a ride somewhere?" she asked.

"Sure," I said and jumped into her car. I was loaded and not in the mood for small talk. I had her drive me down into the dark wooded valley of Rock Creek Park.

"Stop here," I said. She parked on a flat grassy spot between the woods and the road underneath a street light.

"You're going to get out here in the dark?" she asked.

"That's right. I got some thinking to do, and this is where I want to do it."

"It's pitch-dark out there."

"Thanks for the ride. Goodnight."

I walked straight into the darkness, stumbling over shrubs and tree roots. I still had the rest of that joint in my pocket, and I reached for it. To my annoyance, she got out of her car, slammed the door and came after me.

"Hey, I grew up in these woods, and I'll be perfectly all right."

"Well, if you want to sleep in the goddamn woods like an animal that's fine with me. But I have to get back to Alexandria, and I don't know where the hell I am and I don't feel like driving around all night lost in the dark."

I had already lit the joint, thinking that the next few hours would be spent alone. I took a deep puff on it, and when she finished bitching at me, I handed it to her. I sat down on a fallen log, and she sat next to me. We finished it off.

"What's the matter, Joe? Miss California wouldn't put out?"

"Putting out wasn't the problem," I said. "Passing out, that was the problem. She seemed willing, but unfortunately she doesn't hold her liquor very well."

"Well, after all those tequila shots I'm not surprised." She rolled her eyes. "I wouldn't worry much, she's not your type. Anybody with half a brain can see that."

"Oh really, and what types are we talking about?"

"I don't mean any offense. It's just that she's the kind of girl that would push you until you made it in society. You'd have a Tudor house in the suburbs, and you'd dress for dinner with the live-in maid serving. You'd have two perfect children and a host of friends from the country club. You'd collect art and travel to the capitals of Europe, and if you couldn't foot the bill her daddy would."

"Sounds like a nice life. What's wrong with that?"

"You'd be bored stiff."

"You're probably right," I said.

"I know I am."

"Well while we're on the subject, what type are you?"

"I'm the kind of gal that's easy to be around. I like people and the guy who gets me doesn't have to change his friends because I have four brothers, and I like male company. I'm a good hockey player and even better at racquetball. For vacation we'll ski Telluride in winter and hang out at my grandfather's cabin in northern Minnesota each summer. The guy who gets me is going to have his fun meter in the red zone all the time."

"And from the sound of all this I take it you're still available?"

"I am."

"Sounds promising. All right, let's get out of here. I'll lead you back to Memorial Bridge. It's easy to find Alexandria from there. You can drop me there, and I'll walk home."

As I finished the sentence a car pulled up behind hers. I heard the crisp retort of a police radio. The cherry light on the roof of the car came on, and it circled around the black forest like a luminous helicopter wing. A patrolman got out and examined her vehicle. Another cop, still inside, shined a spotlight in our direction. We ducked

behind the log. We leaned our heads against the trunk away from the
spotlight and stretched our legs out on brown leaves.

"Maybe I should go out there and talk to them," she whispered.

"With the number of drinks you've had, not to mention the smell
of marijuana on you, I wouldn't recommend it."

"But they might give me a ticket." she whispered.

"Don't worry, just tell them you ran out of gas. You don't have
any parking tickets in the city, do you?"

"No, I just got here last Thursday."

"That's funny, so did I."

The cops must have called dispatch to see if there were any out-
standing warrants on the plates because I could see them waiting for
a response. There was nothing to do but wait ourselves. One of them,
with a flashlight in hand, walked down the path we had tread. He
flashed his light amid the shrubs, and we held our breath.

Our shoulders touched. Then I rolled onto my side. She looked
at my lips and while we lay waiting, I kissed her lightly. The smell of
her hair, freshly washed with a scented shampoo, and the softness of
her freckled white skin made me feel more content than I'd been since
I returned. I unbuttoned her shirt and cupped her small breasts while
kissing her lips.

The crack of the police radio, the jingling handcuffs on the patrolman's belt, the clumping sound of his big black police boots, and
the whirling cherry light measuring time like a sweep second hand
were a stark contrast to the amorous embrace of Joannie Quinn. The
gulf separating us from a bust was a collection of laurel bushes, one
maple tree, and an old log stump.

We heard conversation between the two officers in the distance.
It created a minor fear that impelled us closer to each other. Soft
petting lead to heavy breathing, rising body temperature, soft sighs,
stronger hugs… love charms warding off the right angle forces of law
and order.

Suddenly, we heard the crackle of their police radio. The cops
jumped into the car and raced off to another location. We pulled away
from each other and giggled at our escape. With the danger gone, the

sobering consciousness of strangers returned. There was an awkward silence. We laid on our sides staring into each other's eyes. I stuck two of my fingers in her belt loop, gazing at her body.

"What's the matter, Joe, haven't you ever seen inverted nipples before?"

"Is that what's wrong with them?" I asked and then blushed at my poorly phrased response.

"You obviously haven't spent time with many red-headed women. It's a genetic trait. Don't worry, the nipples are in there. It just takes a connoisseur to make them appear. Some guys learn to like it like that. They compare it to owning a convertible."

"I looked, and I couldn't figure out what was different about them."

"Well don't fret, I'm sure your Elizabeth Ann's tits are quite normal."

"What made you say that?"

"When I spoke to her this evening, I asked about you, and she got defensive and implied that I should stay away."

"Oh really, and what prompted that conversation?"

She let out a laugh. "I mentioned that you had a nice butt."

We walked back to the car. A ticket was wedged inside the windshield wiper. She eyed it angrily. "Forty dollars for illegal parking and abandoning a vehicle. What nonsense! I'm not paying it."

"Don't worry about it. You can say the car broke down and you went to get help. It will cost you an evening in court but maybe you won't have to pay the fine. I'll go with you."

It struck me that I had just committed myself to a date with her. Most times I ponder and plan when asking a woman out. It takes all the deliberation of a chess move. But this all came so suddenly, so spontaneously, just like our tryst against the stump, that I was surprised by my own carefree attitude and the ease with which she accepted, as if we were friends instead of two people who had just met.

Back in her car, we turned south on Beach Drive and drove to Rock Creek Parkway. She was driving Liston's car, a sport's car made by General Motors. She drove it fast through the curving empty lanes of the smoothly paved road.

I stared at her profile. It was a nice face to look at. But I feared the minute I left her the small straight nose, the freckles, the rosy cheeks, and the big eyes framed in red curls would fade from memory. My gaze made her a bit self conscious, but she smiled, on purpose, so the image cast in my memory would be a warm one.

At a red light across from the Watergate, I told her I'd get out. It was a few miles to walk home but I wanted the time alone. I wrote down my phone number.

"It's a breeze to get to the Memorial Bridge from here," I said. "Across the river in Virginia you'll see signs for route 395. Call me when you get back in town. We can go to traffic court together, maybe even have some dinner if you like. "

"I'll be back in two weeks."

We were the first car at the light, and a few cars were lined up behind us. When the crossing traffic light turned yellow I knew ours would be green in a second. The pressure was on and I leaned over and planted a big kiss right on her mouth. As our lips met the car horn behind us sounded. I jumped out, and she sped off down the road.

It was several miles to my apartment. But the idea of walking home in the dark was comforting. The air was cool, and the stars were out. This had been a confusing night, and I needed to sort things out.

I walked east on Virginia Avenue past the Watergate complex all lit up in the dark. Its big round curves reminded me of a beached whale. "Well, there's McMorrow's monument to Republican virtue," I said to myself.

Walking on I came upon a statue of Simon Bolivar, the South American revolutionary. There was a park bench a few feet away, and so I sat down and rested. He was seated on a horse. There was no hat on his head, but there was a sword in his hand. His pose provoked a brief heroic fantasy in which I led a revolution against stupidity.

But truth is, I no longer believed in revolution. The French and Russian Revolutions had both turned into nightmares. Revolution in South America was just as fruitless. About the only revolution I believed in was the American Revolution, which after two hundred years was still working.

And yet no revolution was going to address my issues. They were too personal. I was searching for a new creed, a new gnostic ethos with which to go forth.

I felt a deep, prescient urge begging for articulation. And while the words weren't there yet, I was on its trail. To a political activist it might seem ridiculous, but I wasn't a political activist, and I recognized that standing in front of Bolivar. The revolution I aspired to wasn't about power or money or equality; it was about self knowledge and moral improvement. And I knew it would not come from politics, only from scholarship.

I thought about my father's last piece of advice—"Corporate lifestyle? Don't do it," he had said. And suddenly his words made sense because to fit into McMorrow's team I'd have to repudiate everything I aspired to. I didn't know what was going to happen to me. But whatever it was, it wouldn't be happening on Capitol Hill.

Then I thought about Elizabeth Ann and my aborted romantic foray. I had been so sensitive to the meaning of every word and action, carefully interpreting each nuance as a step toward consummating a relationship with her.

Compare that to the lack of effort that went into my tryst with Joannie Quinn. At first I thought to dismiss her as just an easy mark, someone anyone might have had at any time. But expanding on that idea, I pondered about how nice it was that in this complicated, self-conscious, scheming town, something so easy, so spontaneous and natural could still happen. And if for no other reason than that, I liked Joannie very much.

When I got home I did what any red blooded American boy in my situation would do— I masturbated. There in the steamy shower stall I beat off the tease of two women and watched my best efforts go right down the drain. Surprisingly, the mental image that sent me squirting was not the lean curvaceous body of Elizabeth Ann Gilchrist. It was the impish smile and inverted nips of Joannie Quinn laying on a soft bed of leaves.

Chapter 18

The day after he got out of the hospital, I went to see Winn. There was a sold sign from a real estate company on his front lawn. I startled when I saw it because I realized that one of the most life affirming rituals of my youth, Sabbath dinners here, would never be again. When he opened the front door he put his hands on my shoulders. "Joseph, it's good to have you back."

"Thanks," I said softly, and then I shook his hand.

"Come inside. I'll make you a cup of coffee." We walked to his kitchen, and he filled his coffee maker.

"Harry said you're moving to Florida."

"Yes, I'm making a new start. Yet I'm going to miss this house. I raised my daughter here. Ruth and I had wonderful dinner parties here with our friends."

Then there was an awkward silence while he looked around the room. "Look at me, Joseph. Not even sixty and I'm an old man."

"What about Ruth?" I asked.

"That whore?" Then he checked himself. "We're done. She never liked the life I led. After what happened to you, she had enough. She left me and that's that."

"Maybe it's good that you're making a new start in Florida."

"I got plenty of money, and there's so many women down there I'll be beating them away with a stick."

There was a sly look on his face. Despite his heart attack, that rakish self was still inside. I was happy for him. He was looking to the future. But then I changed the subject and said what I was so excited to tell him. "Winn, I learned how to read, I mean really read."

It felt so good to say it. Matelsky and Harry didn't see the virtue of my diligence. So I told him about my progress.

"Did you ever get around to reading *The Odyssey*?"

"It's been my bible for the last year. What it's taught me about being a man is incredible." With that I reached into my backpack and returned the copy he lent me the day I left. "You can have this back. I have my own copy now."

He opened it up and looked at his signature which he wrote on May 9th, 1955. Beneath it was my own signature, dated October 14th 1976. He smiled. Then I told him about reading Homer, Carl Jung and the *I Ching*. Such books were pushing me in a direction far away from the American mainstream. "I keep telling myself, stop reading this hocus-pocus and start reading history and the law," I said. "But I can't stop."

"Look at you, little Talmudic scholar. I'm proud of myself," he said.

"Why are you proud of yourself?"

"Because I put you on that path."

"Yes, you did," I said.

"Except maybe for sex, learning is the keenest of all human pleasures. It transcends every race and religion in the world. Ultimately, it's the yardstick by which I measure my friends."

"I understand that."

When the coffee was ready, we walked to his study and sat down on the two familiar chairs where so much good conversation had taken place. He smiled as I told him all my stories about Iris, Matelsky, Jerome and Ghani Purp.

"More coffee?"

"Sure," I said.

"Stay here, I'll get it."

I walked around his library realizing it might be the last time. It had been two years since I had studied his shelves. A little red book, a 1910 edition written by Thomas Carlyle entitled *Heroes and Hero Worship* caught my eye. It was in my hands when he returned.

"Care to play stump the scholar one more time?"

"Absolutely," I said.

"Give it here."

We returned to the chairs, and he opened it up to the date he read it. Then he thumbed through the pages to remind him of its contents. He placed it on the table between us.

"This is a good book for you," he said.

"Why's that?"

"Because you're young and when one is young, one is nothing. That's a quote from Goethe... he was a favorite of Carlyle. Don't be fooled by these wrinkles and bad heart. I was young once. When I think of myself, I'm still the twenty-year-old who went off to fight Hitler. But when you're young one question eats away at your guts. 'Am I good enough?'

"You're always measuring yourself against everybody else. You're not sure what path your life is going to take or what you're going to become. Unless you've got the balls to withstand the uncertainty, you'll throw your lot in with the first goofball that opens a door and lets you in."

I laughed out loud. "You just articulated my story. I feel like I'm drifting aimlessly, especially when so many decisive people are running around DC pretending to have all the answers."

"Those people like to pass themselves off as white knights out to save the world. Ha! Let me tell you something, the world doesn't want to be saved. The best thing a man can do is to save himself. If you read this book you'll find that Carlyle's heroes aren't bureaucrats, they're individuals who defy the status quo and blaze their own path, not someone else's."

Then he cast a glance at the beautiful bookshelves that defined his manhood.

"How are you going to get all these books to Florida?" I asked.

"I'm not. I'm selling my library. I look at those stacks, and I can trace my intellectual life."

"You don't hear much about scholarship anymore," I said. "It's all about entertainment with movies like *Star Wars*, and TV shows like *M*A*S*H*. Whenever I talk about what I'm reading people's eyes glaze over."

"Let them think you a snob. God loves a scholar."

"Can I buy them?"

"No, you can't buy them," he said and brushed the idea away as if swatting a fly. "A man's got to form his own library, little by little. You can't just buy someone else's."

"I don't want to read them, I want to sell them. I'm starting to see the advantage of owning a business instead of being someone else's flunky."

"Thinking about opening a used bookstore?"

"Yes, I'd like to champion the written word. It's under assault by rival media that aren't as interesting."

"Do you have any money?"

"Tons."

I'm not sure where the idea of opening a bookstore came from. It was a spontaneous idea that just burst out of me. But I liked the way it felt when I said it. Plus, if I was going to be the east coast sales representative for Ghani Purp, I was going to need a front. Doing it out of a congressman's office was out of the question.

A contented look came over Winn's face. He liked the idea of selling them to someone who held them in high esteem. Those Friday lectures listening to him wax poetic about individual books came back to him. Perhaps he saw it as a way of passing the baton on to the next generation. "Yes, it's time to get these books back in circulation," he said. "I've hoarded them for my own vanity long enough."

"They could be the mainstay of my store."

"All right, I'll have them appraised and let you know how much they are going to cost you."

"Can we shake on it?"

"Sure." He stood. I stood. He looked me in the eye, took my hand and we sealed the deal with a squeeze. Then he changed his expression. "Hey, I almost forgot. I got a surprise for you. Open that door and whistle. So I got up, opened the door to the back hall and whistled like I used to do for China. She suddenly appeared.

"Oh my God, China," I said, "did I ever miss you. Come here, girl."

My dog ran frantically around me in circles whining as she ran, letting out an occasional bark. When I went to pick her up she wiggled out of my grasp and wet Winn's carpet. Upon seeing that, I held her tight while she panted and began licking my face.

"It's good to see the two of you reunited."

"Look at her… she hasn't changed a bit," I said.

When I left him, with China on a leash walking beside me, I was excited because I had a plan, and my best friend was walking beside me.

The next day I saw Harry at the bistro. I was excited by my news. "I'm buying Winn's library. I'm going to open a used bookstore."

"Books? You're going into the book business? You'll starve."

"Not intellectually."

"There's no money in selling old books. You'll have people walking in the door spending fifty cents on a trashy paperback. How are you going to pay your bills with that kind of money?"

"When I find out I'll let you know."

"I wish you would have talked to me about it first."

"I've made my mind up."

"Rent is getting too high downtown because of the subway system. I think you should move uptown. I know a guy who's looking for a tenant on Columbia Road right near my apartment. The rent includes a one-bedroom apartment upstairs where you could live or rent out to help with your expenses. I'll call him this morning and set up an appointment."

The place was near the center of Adams-Morgan. Formerly, it had been an Asian grocery store. The smell of fish sauce still permeated the air. In the small two room apartment above the store was a kitchen, big enough for a table. The big windowed room overlooking Columbia Road was big enough for a bed, a desk and several chairs. It would be my living area. There was a small bathroom with a shower.

Perhaps the best feature was a small metal porch that stood atop the stairs off a private second floor entrance in the alley. It was supported by strong, black steel stilts attached to the building and the ground. It was big enough for two lawn chairs and a small table. It had a broad view of the sky. I signed a lease.

Two of Harry's Salvadorian busboys, Jose and Francisco, were carpenters back home. They welcomed the work I gave them. We built bookshelves, painted the walls and designed the space.

A big wooden sign hung perpendicular to the doorway. It was painted over with the name of my new business: "Tome's Greatest Hits." For a used bookstore I thought it was a pretty good name. Tomes, of course, are books and since the content of used bookstores are the best of what has been published in the last hundred years, it reminded me of the retrospective albums so popular in record stores like, *Frank Sinatra's Greatest Hits*, *Elvis Presley's Greatest Hits*, and *The Beatles Greatest Hits*.

I painted the name of the store in green letters on the picture window and beneath it wrote, "Book Searches." I had framed photos of Ralph Waldo Emerson and Thomas Jefferson hanging near the front door, a bulletin board with notices of upcoming literary events and a small shelf of recommended books for those who hadn't the time to mill through the shelves.

I needed a company car to get me around town so for fun I bought an old Checker Cab. I had it towed to a New York Avenue garage. The new transmission and fuel pump cost me plenty, but the car was unique, and it was what I wanted. I drove it two doors down to a body shop and had it painted sky blue with the name of the store painted stylishly on the side in yellow.

Though Winn's library was the mainstay of my stock, it wasn't nearly enough to fill the store. He put me in contact with a wholesale bookseller in Farmville, Virginia. I hooked a U-Haul trailer to the Checker and brought three thousand books back to DC.

One Wednesday morning I crawled out of bed and hung a small red sign on the door that read "Open." There was no fanfare or hoopla, no streamers or brass bands. I merely opened the door and waited for money. A dozen people came in to look around, and a few of them even bought something. But all in all, it was anti-climactic. Much of my time was spent taking books off bookshelves and arranging them alphabetically. At the end of my first day I took in $49.86.

The second day a bookish looking old man came into the store. Through the course of a half hour, he looked at almost every book I had. He was short and wrinkled and clasped his hands behind his back as he squinted through his eye glasses. We didn't speak. There was a hearing aid in his left ear, and he had a slight wheeze when he breathed. But his gait was formidable, and from the way he studied the bookstore it was evident that he had a firm mind.

I'd seen that face before but couldn't recall where. From the way he carried himself, it seemed that even if he wasn't someone important himself, he was at least a peer in important company. He had a pipe in his mouth and even though it was unlit, it filled the store with its aroma.

After examining all my wares, he headed for the door. Before he passed through it, he turned to me and said, "You know, Washington is a place where people care about the written word. So I assure you that if you get your hands on good books you'll find yourself a loyal following. Since the way you acquire your books is neither uniform nor institutionalized, people are relying on your literary taste. So allow me to be frank. Your store is a mess. You have very good titles but they're disorganized. Titles that belong in the economics section are stuck in the political section, books on international relations are in the history section, political topics are in three different areas. That might seem like a moot point to you, but to a reader it's annoying, especially since one has so little time to browse these days. I realize that you are probably new at all this, but you can't be a bookman until you learn about books, can you? Make a map so people know where things are. And one more thing, your prices are out of line with the market, raise them. Your customers won't balk."

My body tensed up when I realized I was being lectured by A.J. Traub, Professor Hall's hero at Sonoma State. I knew his fault-finding was correct, and I wasn't offended because someone was taking me seriously.

When he finished speaking, the best I could offer was a weak "Thank you." He was already out the door. But his words stayed with me all day. It challenged me because I realized that what I was doing required greater diligence.

Chapter 19

A letter came from Matelsky. Inside was a photo of him and Rita standing next to a giant Ghani Purp plant. He had a joint stuck in his teeth and a pitchfork in his hand. She stood beside him. Her big belly suggested that she'd give birth soon. Their pose was a takeoff on Winslow Homer's painting, *American Gothic*. On the back he wrote, "Wouldn't you rather be in Sonoma County?"

I was musing about how nice it would be to live in a dry climate, out of the humid city, clipping and carefree when John Anglund walked through the door. He browsed through the shelves as I closed up the shop and counted the day's receipts. We walked upstairs and in the cool night air sat on my porch, drank beer and smoked Ghani Purp.

"I'm leaving for Indiana next week," he said. "Things on the Hill are slowing down and a summer intern is going to help with my work load. I'll be there until November."

"I thought you weren't traveling for another month. What's changed?" I asked.

"Liston's turned into a whirlwind on the fundraising trail. He's been blowing the anti-communist horn and people are throwing money at him. Prewitt is a big supporter of Detente and the Salt Two Treaty. Liston has been hammering away at him for his naive stand toward the Russians. He's making points too. A new statewide poll shows us closing the gap on Prewitt. The whole campaign plan has been accelerated."

"Sounds exciting," I said.

"If things go the way we expect, I'll be back in five months with a better job and more responsibility. Kind of sorry you never took that job from McMorrow. I'm dealing with a lot of disagreeable people, and it would help to have a confidante on the team."

"I envy you for the interesting stuff you do, but I've just opened the bookstore, and I'm committed to seeing it succeed."

"So how's it going?" he asked.

"Something interesting happened. A.J. Traub came in."

"No kidding. Did you talk to him?"

"Well, not exactly. He lectured me for about sixty seconds on how disorganized my store was. He left without buying anything. I wasn't sure it was him at first, and I was too bashful to ask because I was afraid I'd be wrong."

"You should have taken the chance. Traub is really cool," said Anglund. "He was friends with Che Guevara and FDR. He interviewed Nikita Khrushchev, Ho Chi Minh and Gandhi. I ran into him by Dupont Circle last year. I introduced myself. He looked me over and asked what I did in Washington. When I told him I worked on the Hill, he pointed up Connecticut Avenue and said, 'I'm walking this way for a doctor's appointment. Why don't you join me?'

"I walked with him for about twenty minutes. He asked a lot of questions and let me do most of the talking. Then we shook hands. I found myself a mile out of my way, sweating from the walk, and late for my appointment. But hell, I didn't care. How many times do you get to talk to a legend?"

"He certainly fired me up," I said. "He made me feel like what I was doing mattered. I really was proud afterward which was good because before that I was feeling a little lonely."

"I can fix that," said Anglund.

"How?"

He reached into his pocket, pulled out a card and handed it to me.

"What's this?"

"It's an invitation to a hundred-dollar-per-person fundraiser at the Folger Shakespeare Library. Open bar and tons of food. All the media has been invited. Unfortunately, we've only sold a hundred tickets so far, and if the cameras show up and see a small gathering it's going to make us look stupid. So I've got your name on a guest list at the door. Bring a friend if you like. The more people that show up the better it will be for the campaign. I've invited a lot of friends, so it might be fun, and even if it's not, we can get drunk for free and go somewhere else afterwards to play."

I almost asked if Elizabeth Ann would be there. I hadn't seen her since the night of the house party. I was a bit embarrassed by the way it had ended. I'm sure she was a bit embarrassed by it too, if indeed she had any memory of it at all.

"I have a guy from the *Washington Tribune* coming to interview me about my new store. I'll come right after that," I said.

"So you're going to make the papers?"

"They'll probably send some hack who hasn't read a book in years. But hell, it's free press so I'm not going to knock it."

Chapter 20

My shoes were shined. My gray suit and black tie were laid out on the bed upstairs. My plan was to give the reporter a quick rap about the virtues of used books and be out the door.

I was more excited about the fund-raiser than the interview so when six thirty came and he didn't show I was just as glad. I eagerly watched the clock inch to seven so I could turn out the lights, lock the door, get dressed and drive downtown.

I was straightening out my desk when I spied a big black man enter the store. His face swooped over the counter in a swift motion that startled me. We were eye to eye. In a loud, brash ghetto voice he called out, "Hey man, where the fuck books?"

Before I could even answer he broke into big smile and when he took off his glasses, I pointed to the bottom shelf. "Try that red book. Pictures of your mama are on page three." It was Gaston Collins. "And look at you, you still got those rashy cheeks. Still shaving with tweezers?"

He recoiled his head slightly. "They still take a shit with the door open at your house?"

I was about to fire another shot when he interrupted. "Be easy now. I got a big surprise for you. I'm here to interview you about your new bookstore for the *Washington Tribune*. So you better be nice to me or I'll portray you as a pornographer subverting the morals of white children."

"I can't believe I'm about to be defined for the reading public by a functional illiterate."

He was trying to hold back the giggles and was doing a lousy job of it.

"Tell me you're joking," I said.

The best he could do was press his lips together and shake his head. No, he wasn't joking. He broke out into a deep resonating laughter. He composed himself a few seconds later. "When did you get back?"

"About a month ago."

"Where the fuck were you?"

"I was living out in California with Matelsky growing that good herb. Made lots of money. But I was homesick for DC. So I'm back."

"With money too? Good. You can advertise with us, because if you don't buy an ad I won't write anything good about you."

"Last thing I heard about you Gaston, you were going to school at UDC."

"I graduated with a journalism degree. Now I'm managing editor of the paper. It's just a weekly, but it's fun. When I heard about a new bookstore run by a guy named Joe Green, I assigned myself the story. Do you realize that the fate of your business is in these hands?"

"I made plans for tonight, but I've got an hour. Let me go upstairs and change and we can go down to Millie and Al's for a beer."

Gaston walked China in the alley while I changed. I came downstairs in a short sleeve shirt with my jacket and tie slung over my shoulder. It was a warm evening, and I didn't want to wilt before I got to the event.

Millie and Al's was just a half a block down 18th Street. The place was known for their cheap happy hour prices and their double shot drinks. We found two seats at the bar.

"So what do you write about?"

"The city council, the mayor and urban development stuff," he said. "But never mind me, I'm supposed to be interviewing you. What's it like owning a bookstore?"

"I can see where it is going to be a grind, especially since I can't afford to pay anyone to sit at the front desk for me. Own a bar and you can drink good liquor and fantasize about the women who frequent your place. But there is no great excitement in owning a bookstore. You're appealing to individuals less animated, less sensual than the people laying down dollars at places like Harry's Bistro. Of course I'm my own boss, and I get to read. I like that part of it."

"Hey, I'm writing an article here!" said Gaston. "Asked how he likes owning a bookstore, Green said, 'It's kind of a grind and I'd rather be checking out the busty babes at my uncle's restaurant.' What are you nuts? If I write that shit it's going to make you look stupid. Christ, this is going to be more work than I thought."

With that he proceeded to ask the questions and give the correct answers as well. This public relations stuff was new to me. I thought being honest and straightforward was the correct thing to do. I was unaware of the smoke you have to blow up people's asses to succeed. Gaston was teaching me some valuable lessons, and I paid close attention. In the course of thirty minutes he had all he needed to write the story.

"I'm going to a reception down at the Folger Shakespeare Library for a senatorial candidate from Indiana. Why don't you come along? All you'd need is a tie, and I have a spare in my apartment."

"No way," said Gaston. "I leave that tripe to the *Washington Post*. I cover the local community exclusively. I don't care about the feds, they ain't shit to me. But I'm driving down that way, why don't I drop you off? It will give us more time to talk."

We jumped into his station wagon and drove downtown through Rock Creek Park. Its shaded roads were cooler, and the dense foliage made the air smell delicious.

"So what are you doing hanging out with a lot of Capitol Hill stiffs?"

"I met them the first day I returned. Some of them are dopes, but there are also some really cool guys in the crowd."

"Democrats or Republicans?"

"Professionals," I said. "They don't care so much for the partisanship as much as they do the success of their candidate and their own careers."

"Mercenaries."

"Why don't you come in and judge them for yourself?"

"No thanks, I want to get home before my boy goes to sleep. Maybe another time."

"Do you still smoke pot?" I asked.

"Oh yes."

"Then I'm your new best friend. I got more pot than you can shake your dick at." I reached into my pocket and handed him a big joint of Ghani Purp.

"Well look at this," he said. "You still remember how to roll a fatty."

"It's always been my specialty."

"I want to see what passes for good dope with white boys these days."

"I think you might like it."

Gaston dropped me off in front of the Folger Shakespeare Library. The elegant building was located behind the Library of Congress. They put on the plays of Shakespeare, and noted writers gave readings in their Globe Theater.

Tonight, culture was not on the menu. Politics however, was. Neal Liston was holding his fundraiser in their Great Hall. Perhaps he hoped the nobility of the place would lend some dignity to his campaign.

I was late. A woman sat behind a desk at the front door with a paper name tag. "Tammy." She was well dressed and gracious, the perfect first impression. She had a guest list typed out on three pages before her. When I announced my name, she found it and said, "Yes Mr. Green, go right in, we have a name tag already made out for you."

I grabbed the name tag and had put it on when I heard a commanding voice say, "No, no, no. Come on, Green. I can tell you're new at this sort of thing. Put it on the left side of your breast, not the right. This way when you shake someone's hand they'll have a clear view of your name and you'll be able to introduce yourself better."

Rock McMorrow peeled off my name tag and put it on my other side. "Glad you could come," he said. "We've got a great turnout, and the candidate is going to make a speech in just a few minutes. The food's great, and the bar is in the back. Help yourself."

"Thanks," I said.

"And by the way, congratulations on your new business. Guess you'll be voting Republican with us from now on."

I saw Anglund across the room, and he waved me over.

"Christ, what's happened to McMorrow?" I asked. "He was nice to me."

"He's had a good week. His divorce went through, and this event is a success."

"Lucky guy."

A few minutes later I spied Elizabeth Ann from across the room. Her sleeveless white dress had a lace front and a modest neckline. It looked good against her tanned skin. She wore pearls around her neck and diamond earrings.

I was crossing the room to greet her when Rose Giotti stepped in my path. "Hey Joe, a bunch of us are going down to the Tune Inn. Want to come with?"

"No thanks, Rose, I just got here. I'm going to stick around. Maybe me and John can catch up with you later."

I continued in the direction of Elizabeth Ann. But when I caught sight of her again she was standing close to McMorrow. Their hands were hanging down at their side, and his hand was clutching hers. I took a deep breath and stopped short in my tracks. I pivoted on my left foot and headed off in the direction of the bar.

Joannie was standing there. She was leaning up against the bar with her left hand holding her right elbow. In her right hand she held a cocktail. Her legs were crossed, and her head was tilted back.

She saw the whole thing. An ironic smile came to her lips as if my embarrassment was staged for her amusement. I walked to the bar and ordered a Scotch.

"Disappointed?"

I thought to act naive and pretend I didn't know what she was talking about, but I didn't. "Sometimes I think those two were made for each other. It's a funny coincidence though, every time I strike out with her you seem to be right there."

"Some people don't believe in coincidence." She turned her body away from me and grabbed a handful of pretzels. "Those two have been on the gossip circuit for the last week," Joannie said. "Elizabeth Ann got sick the night of the party. McMorrow was upstairs using the bathroom. When he heard noises coming from her room, he opened the door to find her naked and sitting upright in bed, vomiting all over her sheets and blanket. She had it in her hair, on her legs, up her nose, everywhere. It was a big mess. There were still people downstairs, and she was mortified."

As Joannie told the story my mind returned to Elizabeth Ann's bedroom. I remembered her stretched out naked on her bed. The soft moans accompanying her exhaled alcohol breath, the way she licked her lips and rubbed her knees together as she nestled into the sheets was an image locked in my mind. I thought I was being moral by leaving her alone that night. In retrospect I should have hung around to make sure she was all right.

"By the time McMorrow got her cleaned up, changed her sheets and put her back to bed it was almost three in the morning," Joannie said. "He was too drunk to drive home himself, so he slept that night on a chair in her room. They went out for breakfast together the next morning and have been an item ever since. Darlene is thrilled. Rock's a lot easier to work with, which makes her husband much easier to live with. It's worked out great for everyone. Well, almost everyone."

"Are you back here for a while?" I asked.

"Yes. I'm staying with the Liston's right now. Darlene is due any day now, and I'll be there until after the baby is born. All my belongings are in boxes in their basement. I have another interview with the State Department next week. How have you been?"

"I'm good."

"You know I still have this little problem to take care of thanks to you." She reached into a narrow pocket on her hip and pulled out a pink parking ticket. "Remember this? You were going to help me explain it to a judge."

"I suppose I owe you an apology for that."

"You were a jerk, at least at first. I have a court date on Monday night. Will you come with?"

"Sure. My uncle's restaurant is nearby. Let's meet there for dinner. Then we can ride over to the court."

McMorrow's voice was on a microphone. He asked for the crowd's attention. He was standing in the corner of the long rectangular hall. He asked that the people gather round. When the television cameras came on, the tightly bunched group seemed bigger than it was. The acoustics were good too, so that when Liston stepped to the microphone, the TV-like applause was as loud and boisterous as a game show.

"I'd like to thank all of you for coming tonight," Liston said. "Tomorrow we are going to take our message back to the people of Indiana and tell them that American resolve is back and ready to assert itself again. That we have the strength of character, the strength of will to break out of the national malaise that Jimmy Carter had spoken about, and he ought to know all about it too since he and the members of his party are the cause of it all." The crowd laughed.

Standing in the crush of the crowd my body leaned into Joannie's. I was about five inches taller, and the familiar aroma of that shampoo perfuming her thick red curls reminded me of our interlude in Rock Creek Park. When Liston finished, I touched her on the small of her back and whispered. "Let's take a walk."

We strolled around the Capitol building. It was dimly lit, but the moon was full. A strong breeze straightened the flags hoisted around it. Tourists milled about.

It seemed ironic that I knew Joannie intimately, relatively speaking anyway, but knew little else about her. We had skipped step one and two and gone directly to three. We didn't even know if we liked each other. But there I was by her side. She suggested we sit on the House steps.

"No, let's be optimistic tonight and sit on the Senate side," I said. We walked across the front and sat down on the well-worn marble steps that led to the upper chamber.

"What made you become a midwife?"

"I watched my mother have a miscarriage when I was a kid. She delivered the fetus in the toilet."

"That must have been tough to watch."

"It was. I don't ever want to feel that helpless again."

"Do you like the work?"

"I love it. I'm with the moms the whole time. I tell them just what to do. Sometimes, it gets real dramatic, and you think it's never going to end and then these beautiful little babies slide out and you put them on their momma's belly and everybody's happy."

"That's cool."

"Say, I heard Neal and Rock talking about you the other day. They're impressed by your quick thinking during the robbery and the softball game. They said you were bright and despite an attitude problem, which they thought you might outgrow, you'd be useful."

"They were wrong. I won't be outgrowing it."

"Why not? You might do well working on the Hill."

There was an earnest look on her face, as if she were trying to connect me to my true destiny. But she was wrong.

"I don't care for the partisanship. I like people. I like ideas. The notion of sticking fast to a political agenda at the expense of truth goes against my grain. The Hill might be right for some people, but its wrong for me. Besides, I don't really give a damn about politics."

"You have to give a damn. This is America. If bright people don't participate in government the country will go right down the drain," she said.

"There's no shortage of good people in America."

"Then why do you live here?" She said it with a sarcastic tone.

"Joannie, can I be honest with you? I like you way better as a midwife than I do as a politico."

"Oh, was I getting strident?"

"A little bit."

"Sorry, I suppose it's from listening to Neal."

"Washington is my home. It's where I went to high school and college. I know people here, and I now own a business. It's better for me than working for your cousin. Want to know why? Because long after he's been defeated on election day and is back home sulking over lost glory, I'm still going to be here selling books."

"So why books?"

"My reasons are similar to yours. When I was a kid my father contracted cancer. It was a slow, painful, ugly death. The worst part is that he lost his faith in God, in life and family. It made a mark on me. So I decided to commit my life to learning and wisdom so that when I become fifty-two and get the same prognosis, I'll be in a better place and maybe go out with a little more grace."

"Are you in love with Elizabeth Ann Gilchrist?"

"That came out of the blue."

"Sorry, I need to know."

"No, I'm not," I said. "But I did have a crush on her. I met her the day I returned to Washington, and she was the one who introduced me to Anglund, the congressman and all the rest."

"Did you sleep with her?"

"Hey, what's it to you? And be careful, you're starting to make me mad." I rose to my feet. "I think we better head back."

She remained on the marble step staring at her feet. She was grasping for the right reply, and I think she was mad at herself for playing her hand so clumsily.

"I liked what happened that Saturday night," she said. "I'm just a little worried that if you sleep with Elizabeth Ann you'll fall in love with her."

"You mean instead of you? I think it's kind of a moot point now that she's with McMorrow. Don't you think?"

"So you're not going to try and get her back?"

"No."

Now she stood up and and started down the steps. She never turned to see if I was following her. Nor did she feel the need to make any more conversation.

The fund-raiser had cleared out and those left were mostly Liston's staff. The bartender was breaking down the bar, and servers were collecting glasses. Joannie went off to find Darlene while I stood near Anglund waiting for him to finish a conversation.

Elizabeth Ann walked by on her way back from the bathroom. I was startled when I saw her, and she seemed equally startled to happen upon me. "Looks like another success for the Liston campaign," I said.

"Yes," she replied. "Camera crews from *Good Morning America* and *The Today Show* taped segments for tomorrow morning's broadcast. Getting them here was a real coup. How are you doing?"

"I'm doing well. It's been a while since I've seen you," I said.

"Yes" she said. "I…"

McMorrow came up from behind me and interrupted. "Elizabeth, we've been invited to go out with the Listons and a few others. They want to leave right now. Here's your purse." He nodded his head to Darlene and Neal who were walking toward the door. "Sorry we can't chat now Green, but we're in a hurry. Another time perhaps."

"It was nice seeing you," I said.

"Yes, it was," she answered.

McMorrow whisked her away with a lot of poise. It just seemed so natural. The candidate demanded their presence. They couldn't keep him waiting. But as McMorrow led her gently away, he turned his head back and shot me a contemptuous glance.

Anglund walked over. "I hate to ditch you like this," he said, "but Liston's taking us out. I've got to go. I'll call you tomorrow."

"Thanks for the invite."

Joannie walked toward me. I knew she was invited too. I was suddenly accosted by a lurid thought. What if she invites me to come along? The very idea had a nightmarish quality. For I'd have to contend with Liston's reserve lest I challenge his politics, McMorrow's suspicion that I wanted his new girlfriend, Joannie's suspicion that I really wanted Elizabeth Ann instead of her, Anglund's fear that I might say something embarrassing in front of his boss and Elizabeth Ann's curiosity of why I was sitting with Joannie.

I nipped it in the bud.

"Listen, I've got to go. I'll meet you at Harry's Bistro at seven on Monday night. We'll have some dinner and then go to the traffic court."

"Okay," she answered.

I rushed out into the Washington night and took a deep breath of fresh air.

Chapter 21

I was talking to Shameem in the bistro's kitchen when Harry announced that a young woman at the front door was asking for me.

"By the way, Lloyd came by to see me today. He says you have his gun."

"Did he tell you how it came into my possession?"

"Yeah, he tried to stick you up. But all he got for his trouble was a lump over his eye that's still swollen."

"He deserves a lot more than a lump."

"Give it back to him."

"No."

"Drop it off here. I'll be responsible for any consequences."

"You're being foolish. He's going to get himself in more trouble."

"Don't call me foolish. I'm a hell of a lot smarter than you give me credit for. It was a gang initiation and he fucked it up. So there's still hope for him. But without a gun he's an easy mark. I'm trying to bring him back into the fold, and I'm not going to succeed until he trusts me. So bring that gun down here tomorrow. If things work out, I'll have him cooking here by September."

"He can't even mug a party of four. What makes you think he can cook for them?"

"I don't. But his mother does. If you won't to do it for me, do it for Minnie."

"Okay."

Joannie and I sat at a table beside the window and ordered drinks. Liz, a waitress who was one of Harry's original employees, plied Joannie with stories of my youth. Joannie ordered a New York strip steak, medium rare. I ordered the Veal Shameem. A bottle of Bordeaux came with the dinner, compliments of the chef. We started with deep-fried artichoke hearts with a hollandaise sauce.

Joannie was modestly dressed in a white cotton top and a black skirt, a prim and proper look with which to face a traffic court judge. She was excited by the bistro and seemed to be enjoying herself. When Minnie walked in she came over and sat down.

Joannie looked surprised when Harry joined us and gave his black girlfriend a kiss. Harry noticed, and he didn't like it.

Liz came by to ask if Minnie and Harry would have dinner.

"What's the special of the day, Liz?" asked Minnie.

"We've got sautéed mahi-mahi."

"What's mahi-mahi?" asked Minnie.

"It's dolphin fish," said Liz.

"Oh Harry, you're not serving those smart sea mammals for dinner, are you?"

"No, you got it all wrong," said Harry. "It's a fish. It only swims with the dolphins... it's not like Flipper."

"Are you sure? Those animals are very smart. I won't eat anything that's smarter than me," said Minnie.

"Give her the fish, Liz. I'll take the veal," said Harry.

When Liz walked away Minnie shrugged her shoulders and repeated in a softer voice, "I won't eat anything that's smarter than me."

Joannie's face lit up. "Is that why the Jews don't eat pork?"

She was proud of her little joke. But when she saw Harry's grimace, she recoiled. Trying to make up for her faux pas, Joannie told Harry his place looked beautiful. He reacted as if he were being patronized. "It ought to, it cost me a fortune."

Minnie asked about Joannie's family back home. I could see the contempt on Harry's face as she told about her Ohio hometown. Her father was in charge of the high school marching band that played at city parades and high school football games.

Things got easier when the women discovered they were both Methodists. But when Joannie mentioned her cousin, Darlene, was married to Neal Liston, a congressman challenging Bing Prewitt for his Indiana senate seat, Harry exploded. "Prewitt is one of the best men in the Senate. The idea that he might be thrown out by that punk makes my blood boil."

Joannie sat lower in her seat. Minnie must have kicked Harry under the table because his body jolted unexpectedly.

Liz brought our dinners on beautifully decorated plates. Harry and Minnie's dinners were a few minutes away. When Joannie cut into her steak it was obvious to both Harry and I that it was over-cooked. She noticed it too and decided to say nothing.

"How's your steak?" Harry asked.

"Oh, it's delicious," she replied.

Harry slapped the table top as if he were being patronized again. "You ordered it medium rare. Does that look medium rare to you? They burnt it. Admit it… it's burnt."

"It's not my fault," said Joannie, with a horrified look. Harry stood up and grabbed her plate and marched to the kitchen. Minnie got up and followed after him. They started arguing before they made it through the kitchen door. "Goddamn it, Harry, you're acting like a child," she said.

"I'm sorry Joannie, he's not always like this," I said. "Here, take some of my veal." I put a portion on her bread plate and poured her some wine.

"I'm sorry he doesn't like me," she said.

Harry and Minnie returned ten minutes later. Harry laid a new plate in front of Joannie and said, "Here, I cooked it myself."

She cut into it. The perfect medium rare. Then Liz brought out their dinners too. Harry, under Minnie's watchful eye, made an effort to be nice.

"Well, how is everything in the book business?" Harry asked.

"It started off great guns, but it seems that business is slowing down with summer."

"I don't know how you can expect to make a decent living sell-ing used books. The successful book sellers in town are published writers like Doris Grumbach and Larry McMurtry. They don't have to rely on their stores to support themselves."

"True, but I have other business interests too."

"I think what Joe's doing is important," said Joannie. That line surprised even me. Minnie gave her an affirmative glance.

"He's got his great grandfather's genes," Harry said. "He was a rabbi in Kiev in the 1880s. He was known in all the Jewish communities of the Ukraine for his learning. During a pogrom he got hit on the head with a shovel. The blow caused a brain injury that took away all his learning and wisdom. He died two months later. It made my father a bitter man. He had nothing but contempt for learning even though he made his living translating Russian documents for the government during World War II. That contempt made an impression on me. But not on Joseph."

"I never heard that story before," I said.

"Your father never told you?"

"He mentioned that my great grandfather was killed in a pogrom, but he never said anything else about it. What was his name?"

"Moishe, or in English, Moses," Harry said.

"I always wondered where I got the scholarly gene. Neither you nor my dad ever showed it."

"Well, now you know. It came from Moishe."

"There's a word for it," I said. "I looked it up once. It's called atavistic. It's when a family trait skips several generations and suddenly appears seemingly out of the blue."

"See that," Minnie said, "you learn something every day."

"Do you have any pictures of him?" I asked.

"Sure," Harry said.

"Good, I think I'll frame it and hang it on the bookstore wall."

Joannie's beeper sounded. She silenced it. "Darlene is in labor," she said. "I've got to run."

"What about traffic court?" I asked.

"This is way more important," she answered.

"Do you need a ride to the hospital?" Minnie asked.

"No, I don't want to take you away from this. I'll grab a cab. Thanks for dinner."

***

The next day Harry stopped by the bookstore with an eight by ten photo of Moses Green. He had a long face covered by a white beard. A black yarmulke was on his head, and a prayer shawl was over his shoulders. His eyes were as big as an owl's.

That night, I walked to the corner drugstore and bought a picture frame. I put the photo inside it and hung it by the door. Never mind that he was family, the tight grip he had on the book was a metaphor for the kind of passionate scholarship I longed for. I hung it beside the photo of Thomas Jefferson and Walt Whitman. The three pictures looked good side by side. The three of them had one thing in common—they were my heroes.

I went to sleep at ten thirty. An hour later, there was a quiet knock on the back door. China barked and woke me up. I opened it to see a worn out looking Joannie, a bit drunk, holding out a cigar.

"Ah a boy."

"Yep, and he's a stubborn little brat. Didn't want to come out. We finally delivered him at about three thirty this afternoon. He was breech, and I had to call in a doctor. We almost did a C-section. Neal is happy as hell. He took me out to a bar. I hope you don't mind me coming over like this."

"No, not at all."

"I wanted to finish our date."

"That was yesterday."

"I know. I'm exhausted. Can I sleep over?"

"Sure. Come on in."

"I didn't know you had a dog. What's her name?"

"China."

China sat perfectly still, wagging her tail. Joannie got down on one knee and stroked her fur. Then she undressed. I saw her naked for the first time. She walked to the bathroom, sat down on the toilet and peed. Then she crawled into my bed with her eyes half closed, nearly unconscious.

"I am so tired."

"What did they name him?' I asked.

"Nathaniel. He'll be a beautiful boy. But not as beautiful as ours."

She was asleep a second later.

***

Next morning, we sat at the counter of the Uptown Grill and ordered breakfast. I had bacon and eggs. Joannie had a hamburger and fries.

"A letter came yesterday," said Joannie. "I've been accepted by the State Department. There's a slot in Panama.I'm scheduled to leave in February."

"Congratulations."

I purposely kept a carefree attitude. In the hierarchy of DC values, a foreign posting for the State Department made what I had to offer her paltry. She was very cool about it too.

"Graham Greene has a book entitled *Getting to Know the General*," I said. "I think it's about a military strongman ruling Panama. Maybe you should read it. It might give you a feel for where you are going."

"Maybe if the book business isn't going to fly here, you should move to Panama with me," she said.

I shook my head. "I've got to go next door to open up. Finish your sandwich, and meet me next door."

She jumped out of her seat two seconds after I did and followed me out the door. That was one thing I liked about Joannie Quinn. She was the only woman I ever met who ate as fast as I did.

Chapter 22

Joannie stopped by the store while I sat at the bookstore counter reading. It was almost closing time. "I haven't seen you in a few nights. You haven't found a new girlfriend, have you?"

"No, just working," I answered. "How's Liston's baby?"

"He's great. They brought him home to Indiana and aren't coming back for two weeks," she said. "I'm staying in that big house all by myself."

"Really? If I come over can we screw in their bed?"

"Sure, how about tonight?"

"Can't. I have an appointment at the home of a rich Washington widow. She's selling her dead husband's library. Come with me. You can charm the old girl while I sort through her books."

The eight o'clock appointment was at the home of Mrs. Irwin McLaughlin. Their house was a Tudor style mansion on Foxhall Road on the western edge of the city. It was surrounded by a high brick wall. The black iron gate across the circular driveway was open for us. We drove to the front door and parked the blue Checker beside an old black Mercedes.

Mrs. McLaughlin answered the door herself. She was in her sixties with short, brownish-gray hair. She was a tall, buxom woman who held her head up high and her lips pursed. Her narrowing eyes seemed suspect of everything.

"Good evening, Mrs. McLaughlin. My name is Joe Green. We spoke on the phone."

"Yes, Mr. Green, thank you for being on time."

"This is my friend Joannie Quinn."

"Good evening, Miss," she said.

Behind the front door was a grand foyer with a crystal chandelier hanging down from the second-floor ceiling. A regal staircase with a polished mahogany banister stood before us. Windows were every-where, giving the interior so much sunlight that everything gleamed. Joannie's eyes grew wide at the sight of it.

"God, what a fantastic house," said Joannie, as she walked a few steps inside. "My grandmother has the same Hoosier cupboard back in Dayton."

"Oh, are you from Ohio?" the older woman asked.

"Yes, ma'am. My family is from Elyria."

Joannie took a few steps inside and stared at a portrait on the wall. "Is that your late husband?"

"Yes, that's Irwin. He was quite a man. Military officer, US Senator and later Ambassador to Italy."

"God, is he ever handsome."

She examined Joannie closely. "You know, I've always thought that women from the Midwest had more class than women from the east or west coasts. Of course, I suppose that's a personal bias."

"I agree 100 percent," Joannie said.

"I'm from Illinois myself, and I'll be moving back next month."

To an east coast boy all the Midwest nationalism seemed quaint. However, I did notice a certain resemblance in their perspective styles that pivoted upon clean-cut looks lacking the hint of libido and a stoic gaze in the face of effrontery.

"Could I have a tour of your home?" Joannie asked.

"Certainly, my dear."

The lady of the house lost interest in me. She pointed to the top of the stairs, preferring to attend to her young guest. As I walked toward her husband's study, I noticed that something resembling a mutual admiration society was developing between the two women.

The second-floor study had oak book shelves from floor to ceil-ing on three walls, all empty. Their contents were in dozens of unsealed boxes around the room. All the books were carefully packed and arranged by topic, which saved me hours of work. A huge desk stood in the middle of the room facing the door. I'll bet that sitting behind it, McLaughlin was a commanding presence.

Several boxes were filled with foreign language books written in Italian and French. Some of these titles were easy to figure out because I recognized the names of such authors as Dante, Cellini, Flaubert and Balzac. Others offered me no clue.

I got excited when I opened up several boxes filled with American novels, the kind I wanted on my shelves. Most of them were first editions. He had several books by Henry James. Being from the prairie I was not surprised to see that the old man had a copy of Willa Cather's *O, Pioneers!* and *My Antonia*. In addition, there were books by James Jones, Edgar Lee Masters, Carl Sandburg, Ernest Hemingway and William Faulkner.

The history boxes were most impressive. They included rare tomes about ancient civilizations written by a host of Oxford dons. In addition to the more obscure titles there was the regular stuff popular in McLaughlin's time like Symonds' multi-volume study of the Italian Renaissance, Gibbon's *Rise and Fall of the Roman Empire* and Matthew Arnold's *Essays in Criticism*.

Two sealed boxes tucked away in the open closet looked as if they had come straight from the publisher. I hesitated, wondering if I had the right to open them. I picked up one of the heavy boxes and shook it. There obviously were books inside. I took out my pen knife and sliced it open. What I found was fifty copies of a book I'd never seen before… *Force and Freedom*, by A.J. Traub, publication date 1952.

I opened the second box only to find fifty more copies of the same book. The covers were stuck to the pages, and it was obvious that these virgins had been locked away for over thirty-six years. A hundred copies of a Traub book? Talk about a bookseller's albatross!

I separated the books into two piles, the ones I was willing to buy and the ones I wasn't. I figured I could sell many of them quickly and at a great profit. And even if some stayed on my shelves for a while that was okay too. They looked so elegant that their presence might attract serious book collectors. The rest, I feared, would lay around forever so I had no use for them, especially one hundred copies of Traub's, *Force and Freedom*. Although I did take one for John Anglund.

"I'll buy about sixteen hundred of them and give you a good price," I said to the widow. "The remaining ones are good, but I don't really have a market for that many books in Italian and French. I'm afraid it would take me too long to sell them."

"I'm sorry, that just won't do," said Mrs. McLaughlin. "I'm not going to have you take the wheat and leave me with the chaff. Take all or none. I'm moving my belongings to Illinois, and I won't get stuck paying freight for boxes of books. I had a big fight with another bookseller last week. He came in with boxes, loaded them and started taking them out the door. He said he'd give me fifty cents apiece. He actually had the nerve to tell me he was doing me a favor."

"You have one rare volume up there that I'm charging twenty dollars for in my shop. So I know they are worth considerably more than fifty cents apiece. The value of the library stems, in part, from the complete works he has of many writers. I'm not talking about collections published by Reader's Digest either. From what I can tell, your late husband collected books one at a time and has every poetry book Sarah Teasdale published in first edition. He has Rimbaud and James in first editions too, not to mention Nietzche's *Thus Sprach Zaruthrustra* in English, Italian and in French. However, you've got to understand that they are only valuable if I can find someone to buy them. As you probably found when you put your house on the market, you can ask any price you want. The trick is finding someone to pay. Plus, you've got to realize, ma'am, that you have one hundred copies of the same book up there. What am I supposed to do with—?"

"Which book is that?"

"*Force and Freedom*, by A.J. Traub."

The comers of her mouth pulled downward, and she then seemed to suffer a slight tremor. Her eyes narrowed and a faraway look came to her face. She exhaled a deep breath and said softly,

"My, that takes me back." And then she paused as if trying to find just the right words to explain.

"Irwin and A.J. met back in the thirties. They were friends for over twenty years. Both embraced Progressive Era ideals and came to Washington with Roosevelt as New Dealers. Irwin even underwrote the publishing costs and owned the copyright of *Force and Freedom*. But when Traub was indicted by Senator Joe McCarthy's committee on un-American activities, all of Traub's friends ran for cover, unfortunately even my husband. He was up for reelection in Illinois. You might have noticed that A.J. dedicated the book to him. We feared that if Traub was convicted, the dedication would be a scandal. So Irwin made sure the book was never distributed. Ironically, Traub stood up to the committee and was exonerated and my husband lost the election anyway. But Traub never forgave him. I guess Irwin forgot about those copies, and they've been laying there ever since."

She bit her lip and sighed. "I want all those boxes out of my house, especially that one. So you see, my friend, it is all or nothing."

I asked for a day to arrange the financing, and I think because of her fondness for Joannie, she agreed. I wrote her a two hundred dollar down payment and left the house without the books.

"I'm going to hate myself for doing this," I said while driving back to the store.

"Will they be hard to sell?"

"Not sure. Maybe I'll call the French and Italian embassies and see if they know anyone who might be interested in the foreign language ones. They probably have libraries there too, so maybe they'll buy them. I guess the only thing bothering me is that Traub book. What am I going do with one hundred copies of *Force and Freedom*? I just violated the first cardinal rule of bookselling—don't buy books you can't resell."

Next morning, Joannie and I were sitting at the bookstore counter with China beside us. A package came from the UPS man. It was a big brown box addressed to me from Anna Donaldson of Cotati, California.

Joannie was curious. "Is she an old lover?"

"I never heard of her."

"Then why is she sending you a package from California?"

"I have no idea."

I cut the box open. Peering inside I started giggling when I realized that inside was about two pounds of Ghani Purp and a wad of cash. "Business must be good in California."

Joannie got wide eyed at the sight of it. "Aren't you afraid of getting caught?"

"Are you going to turn me in?"

"No."

"Then I'm not afraid of getting caught."

Chapter 23

That afternoon I began unpacking the books I had purchased from Adeline McLaughlin. The novels were great; they'd help with my cash flow. But when I opened the box filled with Traub's *Force and Freedom*, I felt like a knucklehead because those books were never going to sell.

But I reached for one and began reading the book of essays. One was about his experience interviewing Jews at the Bergen-Belsen concentration camp after World War Two. In another, he told the tale of how he ran the British blockade and smuggled himself into Palestine with dozens of other Jewish refugees in 1947. There was an essay about his trip to India to interview Mahatma Gandhi and another about Franklin Delano Roosevelt. The coolest one was a bohemian account about riding the rails with hobos during the Great Depression. I put three in the bookstore window as a sort of advertisement.

The next day Traub walked past the bookstore. When he saw the titles in my window, he stormed inside. "Where did you get that book?"

"Adeline McLaughlin… she sold me her late husband's library."

"You have no right to sell that book!"

"I have every right. I paid for them."

"It was not hers to sell."

"Maybe you should call the cops."

"McLaughlin was just a damn coward! He owned the book rights and never released it. He was too scared of Joe McCarthy

and his gang of hoodlums. When he lost reelection it was just
what he deserved."

"I have about a hundred copies. Will you sign them for me?"

"Sign them? Are you out of your mind? No, I won't sign them."

He surveyed my empty store with a contemptuous expression
and asked, "So what's a guy like you doing here all alone?"

"My name is Joe Green," I said and reached out my hand for his.
"I own the place."

He never extended his hand. "A young man like you shouldn't
be sitting behind a cash register. Why aren't you up on Capitol Hill
competing with other young men trying to make this damn country a
better place."

"Sorry, I like the culture of Washington way better than the politics."

"Look at you, sitting here while other people do the hard work
of democracy for you," he said. "That's all it takes you know. Good
men sitting home on their asses while narrow minded demagogues
take power."

"Get used to it. I have friends working for Neal Liston, the Indiana congressman challenging Bing Prewitt. Their politics suck, but
that's the tide that's coming."

"The hell it is." He looked me straight in the eyes trying to
browbeat me into submission. But he was an old man and despite
his aggressive pose, he hadn't the muscle to back it up. Suddenly, he
came aware of something wrong. His nose was bleeding. Sticking out
his tongue he caught a red drop just as it fell off his top lip. He lost his
fire and recoiled from the fight. Reaching into his pocket he pulled out
a handkerchief and put it to his nostril. His color grew pale, and after
some hesitation he said, "I need to sit down."

I led him to my chair, and he slumped into it with his head tilted back. He sat there with his mouth open. His handkerchief was
saturated, and I ran up the stairs to get him some Kleenex from my
apartment. An awful obituary popped into my mind—*Muckraking
Journalist Bleeds to Death in DC Bookstore*.

I ran back downstairs to find him in the exact spot. He had buttoned the top button of his shirt for warmth and upon seeing that, I grabbed a sweater I had hanging on a hook and laid it across his chest. His top lip pushed his bottom lip forward. His brow was down over his eyes. I knew he was still worked up over our words and had much more to say. But his body lacked the physical deportment to pursue what was still so keen in his mind. We sat silently in the empty store.

I reached for one of the books in the window and handed it to Traub. "Here. Take it."

He opened it to the dedication he wrote to his then good friend Senator Irwin McLaughlin. His teeth grinded at the sight of it. When he noticed the price, it added insult to injury. He whispered. "Two dollars?"

He removed the tissue and touched his nostril several times to make sure the bleeding had stopped. And then, as dignified as possible, he rose and returned the sweater to the hook. He grabbed the book and headed for the door. "You'll be hearing from my attorney," he said.

Chapter 24

Next time Gaston Collins visited the store, he was already a fan of the Limerick Lane brand. His reaction was all business. "The brothers don't usually spend so much money on a bag of boo. But I can pay you twenty-two hundred dollars a pound for this pot."

"I have two pounds I can sell you right now."

"I'll take it. Can you get more?"

"Lots more."

"I'll take three more pounds this month. More next month if it sells. But tell that honky Matelsky that if he shorts me in weight or quality I'll fly out to California and personally kick his ass."

I laughed out loud. "I don't think you can do it. But don't worry. I'll personally guarantee every transaction."

"You're doing DC a favor, Joe," Gaston said. "The bullshit is so deep in this town that I'm convinced that only good weed can save America from the clutches of white honkies."

"We're probably the only two men in town who see the virtue of marijuana and aren't afraid to say it. I recognize that it isn't for everybody, and I'm not sure it can heal the collective consciousness, but hell, it's a step in the right direction."

On election night the phone rang after midnight. "Joe, it's John. How's it going? I'm calling from Indiana. It's over. We won. I'm flying back tomorrow evening. There's a party at Liston's house in Alexandria on Saturday night. Be there, okay? It starts around eight."

"Sounds like fun, I will."

"Liston's promised me a job... chief of staff."

"What happened to McMorrow?"

"The Republican National Committee offered him a better position."

I could feel his excitement radiating over the phone line. His enthusiasm even infected me. Somehow the campaign and the victory Anglund experienced seemed so heroic. And there it was again, the irresistible pull of the macrocosm, to belong to the establishment and bask in the community it offered. Hanging up the phone, I felt a little jealous. But deep down I knew it wasn't for me.

When I asserted myself, I was hoping for some better civic enterprise than a partisan political agenda. And I was ready to play tortoise until I figured how to do that. Harry's description of Moses Green, wonder rabbi from the old country, gave me a role model. That I might be actualizing the same Talmudic gifts as my great grandfather gave me the resolve to stay the course. It was my hope that the genius running through him might somehow achieve its purpose through me.

Chapter 25

The next day the phone rang. "Tomes Greatest Hits," I said.

"I'm looking for a book," said the caller, who couldn't have been more than three. "Matelsky's Sure Fire Pot Production... book." When he got it right his parents cheered.

"I think it's out of print, Russell. But how are you?"

"Good."

"Is your daddy there or did you call all by yourself?"

"Daddy."

"Can I talk to him?" The kid handed the phone to Mike. He was chewing something.

"What are you chewing on?" I asked.

"An onion bagel toasted medium well with cream cheese."

"That's good nosh."

"You don't have to tell me. I'm eating it."

"How's Rita?"

"She swallowed a beach ball."

"How much longer does she have?"

"About three weeks."

"Your boy talks pretty good."

"He's like me," Mike said. "Once he starts talking, it's hard to shut him up. But you should see him clip pot. He's a machine. Sometimes me and him spend the whole day clipping together. He's not ready for the Yippie Rats but his Don King buds look a little bit better than yours."

"Good thing you have an assistant. You're going to be busy. I just got an order for three pounds."

"From who?"

"Gaston Collins."

"The big black guy?"

"Yeah. His brother, Ronnie, sells pot on Chapin Street. It's an open-air pot market next to Malcolm X Park. The cops don't fuck with him. I sold him the two pounds you sent me. He paid twenty-two hundred a pound and wants three pounds as soon as possible. After that, if he likes it, he thinks he'll be good for five pounds a month. His guys break it up into nickel bags and sell the hell out of it. They're making six hundred an ounce."

"Damn, that's seven hundred dollars more a pound than Jerome pays," Mike said.

"They've never seen pot as good as ours."

"This year's crop is going to be even better."

"I had a conversation with Jimmy Luther. His friends want in. But it gets a little complicated because he works for Harry, and I'm not sure Harry wants him selling pot from the strip club. We'll have to wait and see with him."

"Good work, Joe."

"I'll only be selling to people I trust and only by the pound."

"I'll ship the weight to the bookstore this week."

"Just make sure it's wrapped good."

"We bought this vacuum sealer that takes all the air out of the bag, and there's literally no smell at all."

"The last batch was perfect."

"The network we set up here is cranking it out, and Jerome's buying everything."

"I don't want Jerome to know about this," I said. "This is about me and you and has nothing to do with him."

"How's life in DC?"

"Stumbling forward."

"Have you made any friends?"

"I fell in with this group who work on Capitol Hill."

"Big shots?"

"Low level munchkins."

"You like them?"

"Some. But a lot of them hide behind the American flag and a shallow notion of Jesus Christ. Sometimes I just shake my head at the stupid things they say."

"Remember, you can always come back to Sonoma County."

"I know."

"Call me when the package arrives so I don't worry."

***

Later that week I delivered a California package to the *Washington Tribune* office after everyone had gone home. As promised, Gaston paid me in hundred-dollar bills.

Later, as I had promised, Gaston and I sat together and designed a display ad for my store. He seemed right in his element. From a book of graphic images, he pasted up a picture of Abraham Lincoln sitting in his majestic memorial throne. A book was in Abe's hand. It was the new logo for my store—Abe Lincoln focused on a book he bought at "Tomes Greatest Hits Bookstore," which was written in bold block letters below the picture. On top he wrote "Make Friends with a Book Today."

"Don't you think the image is a little sacrilegious?"

"Maybe," said Gaston.

Satisfied with his work, I agreed to run it every week for a year.

"I think I'm about to have a problem with the law," I said.

"The cops find out about Ghani Purp?"

"No, it's not about pot, it's about books."

"How?"

"A.J. Traub wants to sue me."

"Yeah, yeah, yeah," said Gaston sarcastically. "I know him. He's one of them big-head mother fuckers. He spoke to our journalism class at UDC. I thought he was arrogant."

"Yeah, maybe a little."

"Someone in class asked him what his initials stood for. Do you know?"

"No," I said.

"Adolph Joseph. The great American liberal, named after the two biggest tyrants of the twentieth century—Hitler and Stalin. Ha, ha, ha. That's funny."

"No wonder he calls himself A.J.," I said. "Man, you should have heard him hollering at me."

"Why was he doing that?"

"I have a hundred copies of a book he wrote back in the 1950s called *Force and Freedom*. It was supposed to be published by this small press owned by the late Senator Irwin McLaughlin. Traub even dedicated the book to him. Just before it was to appear, Traub got hauled before Senator Joe McCarthy's senate committee for alleged Communist activity. McLaughlin was up for reelection in Illinois, so he quashed the entire edition. But thirty-six years later I found two boxes of them when McLaughlin's widow went to sell the dead man's library."

"Whoa." Gaston sat up straight in his chair. He started flexing his nose and sniffing in an exaggerated style. "I smell a story coming on." And then he started rubbing his hands together greedily. "Tell me everything."

"Can you believe it? They tried to ban his book. It's too bad… his essays are really interesting. But he says I have no right to sell them. He's consulting a lawyer. And then when he discovered that his precious manuscript was on sale for two dollars, I thought he was going to cry. But what the hell? I'm trying to get rid of a hundred copies."

"Damn, that would make a great feature article."

"He's really articulate. What's even better is that he's been around DC since the New Deal, and his essays put everything into an historical perspective. You know, I was thinking I should sponsor a lecture by him and sell the book as a souvenir."

"So why don't you?" Gaston said. "I'll bet I could convince the publisher to co-sponsor it. Tomes Greatest Hits and the *Washington Tribune* working together. It might work."

"How do you promote a gig like that?"

"I can handle the publicity," Gaston said.

"I'm willing if you are."

"What we need is a gimmick," said Gaston. "And I think I've got one. The *Tribune's* publisher wrote an editorial urging the city to reopen the New York Avenue library. If you'll donate the proceeds to the DC Library Fund, you could write the whole thing off on next year's taxes, you'll get rid of the books and your bookstore would get some great publicity."

"I wonder if Traub would go for it?" I asked.

"What else does he got to do with his life?"

Chapter 26

Traub's address was in the phone book. I went looking for him. He lived in a two-story brick house in a quiet residential neighborhood off Military Road. There were no bare spots in the lawn. There were chairs on the front porch. The trim was freshly painted. Upon seeing his home, I realized he was a middle-class journalist and certainly no left-wing insurectionalist.

His wife, Delores, answered the door. She was a short, thin woman with silver hair and glasses. A pronounced Brooklyn accent was the first thing I noticed about her voice. "He's out on one of his walks, and there's no telling when he might return," she said. Though I decided not to wait, I did explain the reason for my visit. Her enthusiasm for it was genuine.

"That would be a godsend," she said. "He's outlived most of his friends, and he's lonely. This would get him back in the ring. I promise to speak to him about it when he returns."

Traub called the next day and agreed to do it. Two weeks later Gaston's feature article on the lost book made the *Washington Tribune's* front page. The article continued on page two and included a formidable photo of Traub holding the book tightly to his breast. The transformation I saw in his face was remarkable. His eyes glowed behind his thick lenses, and his expression was resolute. He bore no traces of the old man with the bloody nose at my bookstore.

I was part of the story too. I gave cogent answers to questions that Gaston never asked. He referred to my false quotes as poetic licenses. At the end of the article he listed the scheduled date of Traub's lecture, the night of January 21st at the Ward Circle Building on the campus of American University at seven o'clock. It was easy to book the hall. Traub was a recent writer in residence there, and the university's dean was his friend.

Gaston sent a carefully worded press release to every journalist in town. The article was widely read, and I had several inquiries about the event at the store. Washington based journalists were covering it for their home papers and requested press tickets.

One night, after several beers and some Ghani Purp, Gaston and I sat in his office and designed a poster announcing the event. "If we're going to get a good turnout we have to make people take notice," he said, "which means putting the lecture in their faces as many times as possible."

We made a hundred copies on the office copy machine, and that night we drove around DC in the blue Checker. Gaston jumped out at every red light and with a staple gun attached the notice to telephone poles in Adams-Morgan, Mount Pleasant, Dupont Circle, Georgetown and Capitol Hill. We sought conspicuous places that would be seen by thousands of people every hour.

When the posters were gone, Gaston pulled a can of red spray paint from a brown paper bag. "Now here's a medium that ought to get the hippies really excited," he said. In Georgetown we found a nice wall belonging to the Riggs Bank, and upon it we wrote "Force and Freedom." At the Adams-Morgan McDonald's, while pretending to wait for the L2 bus, Gaston scribbled "A.J. Lives." On the sidewalk next to the Dupont Circle fountain we printed, "Free speech shouts down McCarthy reaction."

WMAL radio did a little piece on Traub for their Monday morning show and Channel 9 news told the story of how I had found the book in McLaughlin's library.

***

A crowd was gathered outside when we arrived at six o'clock. We set up a table near the door to collect the admission fee. Another table at the back of the hall was where Traub would sell and sign *Force and Freedom* for ten bucks. All book proceeds went to the Friends of the DC Public Library.

Joannie volunteered to collect money at the door while Gaston and I pulled a lectern to the middle of the stage and set up the microphone. When we opened the door there was a long line that reached the sidewalk at Nebraska Avenue. The temperature outside was below freezing and it wasn't until people found a seat inside and shed their hats and coats that we determined who was in attendance.

Young bohemian types had come to hear A.J.'s story. Lawyers, bureaucrats and college professors were well represented too. Many of them were of Traub's generation. When he arrived and studied the crowd, they were the first people he noticed.

"I see the New Dealers turned out tonight," he said. And though he said it calmly, I could tell he was proud of the fact that his peers had braved the cold to hear him speak.

Traub arrived with the poet George Luft, who had won the Pulitzer Prize. He was a former Poetry Consultant at The Library of Congress and had been blacklisted in the fifties. I was unfamiliar with Luft's poetry. But I did read his only novel, a bittersweet story of Jewish immigrant life on New York's lower east side in the early years of the twentieth century.

His appearance was one of the evening's surprises. Traub proudly informed me that the poet would be introducing him to the crowd. That was a job I wanted myself. I had even practiced a short speech. Though I was disappointed at missing my debut as a public person, I knew Luft was the right choice.

John Anglund arrived.

"Did you come right from work?" I asked. It was a logical assumption since he was dressed in a grey three-piece suit and had a nametag on his breast he had forgotten to remove.

"Me and Liston went to a reception in Georgetown. He just dropped me off," John said.

"You should have invited him in."

"Actually, I did. I told him you were sponsoring it. He knows all about Traub, even read his essays in college."

"So why didn't he come?" I asked.

"He said that he and Traub stand for different things, and if word got out that he attended the lecture it might send out the wrong signal."

"Oh baloney."

"Don't be that way. You know how the game is played." Then he turned his eyes to the crowd. "It looks like a really great turnout tonight."

"Yeah there's going to be standing room only. I just hope A.J. can pull off his end of the deal."

Sven, Elizabeth and Cal entered the hall. They spotted us. Sven and Elizabeth Ann were friendly, but Cal was aloof and scanned the crowd suspiciously.

"Rock is meeting us here," said Elizabeth Ann. "I hope he gets here soon. The place is filling up,"

"You're right," said John. "Maybe we should find a place to sit." As they moved to find seats, John stayed behind and whispered, "Rock hates everything Traub stands for. Is there going to be a question and answer period following his speech?"

"That's the plan," I said.

"I sure hope he doesn't try and make a scene," said John. "He was bragging that he'd like to debate Traub. He said he'd cut him a new asshole."

"I'll warn Traub not to call on him if he raises his hand," I said. "What's with Cal? He's got a look on his face that I recognize... the high school wallflower preparing a stink bomb for the junior prom."

"I'm not sure. Tell Traub to watch out for *him* too."

"Thanks, I will."

Traub was standing backstage with Joannie. He didn't look nervous, more determined to make this night a success since it was an opportunity to settle an old score and reinvigorate his reputation. He still felt the need to be useful, to play the role of the wise political pundit in a city consumed with such matters. He now had a bully pulpit with a sympathetic audience and the media in attendance. All he had to do was make a showing.

During his life he must have had dozens of opportunities to contribute to the body politic. But he didn't have many years left. When he died, these very people would help define his place. This might be his last chance to impress them with what he had contributed over the past five decades. So he had to be good tonight.

I studied him, his lips pressed together, his narrowed eyes, his squared shoulders. He started pacing the floor backstage organizing his thoughts. He was ready to go.

Joannie opened her purse and reached for a handkerchief. "Just in case your nose starts bleeding," she said meekly.

As she pulled it out, a Liston campaign button fell from her purse. It rolled on its rim in circles around and around and around, grinding against the floor and landing face up beside his black shoes. Traub reared back. "Bing Prewitt is an old friend of mine," he said. "Why the hell are you carrying around a Liston button?"

"He married my cousin Darlene."

Traub deliberated. "That's a good reason."

I saved two seats in the front row for Minnie and Harry, who were late. When Harry arrived and surveyed the crowd, he tried to act unimpressed. "What are you giving away here?"

When I pointed to Traub, a small smile came to his face. He massaged the inside of his left cheek with the tip of his tongue. "Him? Dry sherry on the rocks."

"You recognize him?"

"Sure, he's been in my place plenty of times."

Minnie wore high heels, red lipstick and was dressed in a full-length mink coat. Just three seats away sat Delores Traub. Ironically, she was wearing the same mink coat. The ladies eyed each other's fur, and when their eyes met both were slightly startled. They acknowledged each other with a nod and turned their heads stiffly to the stage.

Just before Traub went on, Adeline McLaughlin walked in the door with an older gentleman at her side. He looked like her attorney. Perhaps the old girl was here to protect her husband from slander. Joannie grabbed her by the elbow. "Adeline, it's wonderful to see you. I saved you a great seat."

She marched her right up to the front row where Traub's wife sat. Adeline was trying to resist gracefully but Joannie wasn't paying attention.

"Holy shit," I gasped from the stage. "Don't do that."

It was too late. With Adeline on her arm, Joannie walked right up to Delores's front row seat and said, "Delores, look who's here."

Even from a distance I could see Delores's mouth drop. And there was an awkward silence that Joannie chose to ignore. She beamed because she had brought two old friends together. Both women stared uneasily at each other and then looked at Joannie's broad smile. Adeline's hard features softened, tears welled in her eyes and she said, "Oh Delores we're so sorry. Can you ever forgive us?"

Delores stood and hugged Adeline. They kissed each other on the cheek and both sobbed out loud. When Traub saw the reunion, he was thrilled. He came down from the stage and gave them both a big kiss on the lips. A photographer nearby snapped pictures.

When Joannie saw me staring, she wrinkled up her nose at me as if to say, "Look what I did!"

Staring at the scene, I began to muse about Adeline's idea about "Midwest class." Perhaps it stems from naiveté, the failure to realize that the world is an awful place. If you could get through life with that attitude and not get mugged by reality, well then maybe that's what class is really all about.

When Traub returned backstage I stood beside him. We were joined by Luft and Gaston.

"Are you nervous A.J.?" asked Gaston.

"Don't let the glasses fool you. Those people want me to do well, and I'm not going to let them down."

I looked out upon a crowd of smiling faces. Anglund saw me and nodded his head in the direction of Rock when he entered the auditorium. He took the seat Elizabeth Ann had saved for him.

"Not everyone out there is going to be rooting for you," I said. "In fact, there's a guy out there who might make trouble. His name is Rockland McMorrow. He's wearing a red sweater. He hates your politics and says he'd like to cut you a new asshole."

"Maybe he should have gone into proctology. With my colon he might have been useful," Traub said. "There was an article in the *Post* not long ago about a guy named McMorrow who took a job with the Republican National Committee. Is that him?"

"Yes."

"All right, I'll be careful," Traub said.

There was polite applause for Luft and his short introduction. But when Traub took center stage with a formidable stride, the crowd went wild with hand clapping and cheers.

He stood behind the podium and basked in the crowd's adulation, slowly turning his head until he saw every impassioned face. The applause went on and on, and Traub stood there showing no trace of self-consciousness or modesty. His public persona was a stark contrast from the woes of the private man. Here was his true element. How strong and invincible he seemed, and he had yet to speak. From their seats, the audience never saw the hearing aid, the thick lenses over his eyes or his small frame. It was all overshadowed by the Traub aura. When the noise died down and people settled down in their seats he admonished the crowd in a serious tone.

"The story regarding my book, *Force and Freedom*, is a painful one for me to tell because it brings back memories of very difficult days. It is the story of dishonorable men whose view of America was characterized by arrogance, intolerance and an unforgiving moral absolutism. It is also the story of honest men who hadn't enough faith in their own ideals to defend them. It created an American inquisition where the integrity of all men was suspect.

"*Force and Freedom* was the most ambitious thing I had written up to that time. Coming at the end of the second world war, the intent of the essays was a probe into the very essence of democracy and what actions were needed in order to avoid another conflagration like the one that had engulfed the world in Asia and Europe in the nineteen forties.

"How ironic that in making the world safe for democracy, America's own ideals were betrayed by demagogues whose narrow moral parameters trampled the ideals of the Founding Fathers. The virtual ease with which they carried out their ploys made me question what it meant to be an American.

"And now at long last, I've been given this public forum to vent my spleen at the reactionary era that suppressed my work and the work of so many other talented, loyal Americans like George Luft. Ironically, I now feel no anger. For the men that perpetrated those wrongs are dead and buried, and to speak ill of the dead is not honorable. I am alive to tell this tale and they are gone, and in my heart that simple fact mollifies the rage that was once so strong in my heart. All that's left is the wisdom one gains from an emotional trial that's now been resolved.

"I could slander my late publisher and friend Irwin McLaughlin, even as his wife sits next to mine here in the front row. But that is not the real story… the real story is about being intimidated by the rule of reactionaries and not doing what is right. For too many years McCarthyism was associated with Americanism. It was not the Americanism of the Founding Fathers, of FDR's New Deal, or the progressive attitude that has melded this nation of nations together. No, it was the Americanism of mean spirited men who accosted our constitutional rights with witch hunts, loyalty oaths, and black lists.

"In all my years as a journalist none were so heroic as those days in the early fifties when Senator Joseph McCarthy started his campaign against alleged subversives. I say heroic because it tested the mettle of constitutional principles. And despite some inglorious moments the constitution won.

"I was running my own small newsletter at the time, and because I was critical of his methods I was brought up before that committee and slandered for alleged communist sympathy. Sympathy.

"Ladies and gentlemen, it will not be the Russian or Chinese Communists who bring down the America we know and love. It will be small men wrapping themselves with the mantle of such righteous American icons as the American flag and manipulating what it stands for to suit their mean-spirited souls."

A.J. held the audience. Every eye in the place was on him. I walked to the back of the hall and began laying copies of *Force and*

Freedom on a long, flat table. I made sure there was a pen so he could autograph the book and a pad of paper in case he needed it.

At the end of an hour, I could hear A.J.'s voice starting to crack.

His pitched polemic reached a high point, and after one very emotional sentence that he shouted out loud, he stopped… just stopped unexpectedly. There was a stunned silence from the crowd who never thought the old man could deliver such zealous hellfire.

One could almost hear a collective sigh as people reminded themselves to breathe. And then, realizing it was over, they burst into wild applause. I saw Traub wipe the sweat from his brow and take a long deep breath of his own. He looked relieved that it was over and he had done well. Joannie walked shyly out on stage and handed him a glass of water.

When the applause died down he asked for questions from the audience. A dozen hands shot up. He called upon a young woman, dressed in a long sleeved, tie-dyed T-shirt. She stood up and asked, "What are the problems that disturb you most about America today, and what should young people do to help solve them?"

"What did you say?" asked Traub. He came out from behind the podium to the edge of the stage and cupped his palm against his ear in an effort to amplify the women's voice.

All eyes were upon her. She was self-conscious about asking her question a second time, but she did so and then sat down. Traub still couldn't make out what she had asked. I could see his concern. Delores suddenly jumped up from her seat and with hands at her mouth acting like a megaphone, shouted in her best Brooklyn accent, "She wants to know what you think the major problems facing America are today and what young people should do to try and solve them."

"Oh, that's what I thought she said." The crowd laughed. He motioned for Delores to come up on stage.

"My biggest concern is that people no longer read books. I know of individuals who will watch a hundred movies this year but will only read two books. There is no replacement for books. It is the only true way to transmit culture from one generation to the next. The fact that intelligent people no longer read scares me. It is impossible to maintain a strong and flourishing culture through the medium of pretty moving pictures and music that is television. We are as a nation competent enough to solve all the problems of the world, but only so long as we educate ourselves to the way the world really is."

The crowd applauded. As a bookseller, my hands clapped the loudest. Traub then looked right at McMorrow, who was standing with his arm raised and called on him. I didn't know if he had done it on purpose or by accident. He had already shown that his ears were weak… perhaps his eyes were worse. I felt a feeling of dread. Since McMorrow resented Traub's politics and my friendship with Elizabeth Ann, I feared he was about to stink up the place.

"I thought your speech pushed all the right buttons to bring out the crowd's liberal sympathies," McMorrow shouted. "But the crucial question that you have failed to answer is this—were you a communist sympathizer, and was the McCarthy committee indictment of you justified?"

Delores was startled by the question, and as she began to repeat it he put up his left hand and bid her to stop. He had heard it. The room went silent.

"No one will ever be able to justify the activities of McCarthy to me," said Traub. "For one, he never convicted anyone of being a communist. All he did was ruin the lives of good men and women. The only man who benefited from that witchhunt was McCarthy himself. He held up the communist bugaboo before the American people, exaggerated the threat it posed to a free society and claimed to be the only man with the guts to stand up to the red menace. That was a big lie, and the bastard got just what he deserved—an eternal place on the American scrap heap of history."

The crowd clapped politely. McMorrow continued standing. "But isn't it true that as a young journalist you published articles in left wing journals edited by card-carrying communists and that you collaborated with Leon Trotsky?"

"I was never a member of the communist party, but I am a Jew, and in the 1930s communism drew my interest because it was the only force in Europe capable of standing up to the Nazis. Knowing how some men speak in moral absolutes, where even sympathy taints you, I confess to not being morally pure. But by the 1940s I, and many others of my generation, realized the truth about Russian communism and repudiated it."

But McMorrow was not done. He wanted to respond before Traub even finished. Gaston joined me at the back of the hall.

"Should we go beat the shit out of that guy?" Gaston whispered.

"Wouldn't that be fun."

Gaston nodded to a can of Coke on the floor against the wall. "I'll bet I can hit him in the head and not get a drop of it on his girlfriend."

"Let the old man handle it," I said.

There was some back and forth between them. When Traub questioned his righteous zeal, Rock shouted back. "Zealousness in the pursuit of liberty is no crime, sir!"

"Tell me, Mr. McMorrow," and Rock was a little embarrassed and a little gratified that the old man knew his name, "is that zeal more important than the first ten amendments to the US Constitution or what we commonly call the Bill of Rights?"

Now someone else was asking the questions and McMorrow lost his advantage. When a few seconds went by Traub said, "I suggest you sit down. Raise your hand when you figure it out."

The crowd cheered when he took his seat. The next person Traub called on was Cal, sitting three seats away.

"I am very concerned about the Russian invasion of Afghanistan," Cal said. "Don't you think that it requires a bolder response than the one President Carter has proposed?"

"No, I think the Russian invasion of Afghanistan will work to our advantage. We suffered the insolence of the whole world when we invaded Vietnam to prop up an unpopular regime. Obviously, the Russians learned nothing from our mistake. But there is another reason, and to understand it you have to know a little about Russian history. The only way social progress comes in Russia is when they go to war and lose.

"In the 1850s they fought a war in the Crimean against the British and lost. The Russian establishment was discredited, and it led to the freeing of the serfs. In 1877 they lost a war to the Turks, and the result was the Stolypin Land Reforms which gave land to the peasants. In 1905 they lost the Russo-Japanese war, and a parliament was created. They lost World War One, and the czar was overthrown. I predict that they will become involved in a prolonged war in Afghanistan and that the present communist regime will be so discredited that they will have to reform, and any reform in the Soviet Union can only benefit us."

He took three more questions and ended it. He mentioned that copies of the book were for sale and that all the proceeds were going to the Friends of the DC Library. As he walked off stage, arm and arm with Delores, he received thunderous applause. He sat down on a chair behind the table and signed every book until they sold out.

I was standing by the door watching the faces of people as they left the hall. There was good cheer among them. An older man looked me right in the face and giggled. "Boy, he really gave it to them tonight, didn't he?"

"He sure did," I answered.

After Traub had autographed all the books, he spent time with members of the press, who asked him questions about his life as an American journalist. It was more than just an interview; it was an audience. Traub spent half the time haranguing the writers about their responsibilities as members of the Fourth Estate and the other half regaling them with stories about famous men and women he'd known.

Then he was interviewed by a National Public Radio reporter. He was a short man with straight black hair and a well-groomed beard. When he finished he clicked off his tape recorder and put on his coat. "The speech is going to be broadcast at the noon hour tomorrow in its entirety," he said.

When the last of the audience was gone, Minnie made an announcement. "Harry's invited us to the bistro for drinks and a late dinner. Come on, let's go... all of us."

Chapter 27

We sat at a big round table in the center of the restaurant. There was Traub flanked by Delores on one side and Harry on the other. Then came Minnie, Gaston, George Luft, Joannie and me. We spent the dinner reliving the evening from everybody's viewpoint and between the eight pairs of eyes captured almost every nuance.

"I was pretty impressed old man," said Gaston. "You gave a good speech tonight. That afternoon you spoke to our journalism class, you didn't make half as good an impression."

"And why was that?" I asked.

Gaston hesitated a bit and then found the courage to tell the truth. "Because people thought he was condescending and that he didn't like blacks."

A.J. wasn't the least put out by Gaston's comment. He looked at Delores sitting next to him and raised one eyebrow as if the two of them were going to share a secret.

"It's true. I don't like blacks," said A.J. "I don't like Jews or Germans or Wasps or rednecks or Italians or Irish or any other group for that matter. But I do like you Gaston." And as he said it, he pointed his finger right at him. "And I like Harry and Joannie and Joe. I like most individuals. But an ethnic group packed together brings out their worst qualities."

"Carl Jung once said 'the bigger the group, the lower the IQ,'" I added.

"I've always believed the American melting pot is not just a fact, it's an ideal," Traub said.

"That kind of thinking has been used to alibi a lot of racial discrimination," said Gaston. "I've worked really hard to make my way in the world, but I'm revolted by some of the behavior required to make it in white, middle-class society. Black men have big hearts, we're emotional, we trust our feelings, and to make ourselves acceptable it sometimes seems like we have to suppress all that comes natural to us."

"That might be true," said Traub. "But what bothered me the night I spoke to your class was the lethargy I saw in the eyes of your classmates. The American ideal is a meritocracy where the best and the brightest rule. When I was young, there was discrimination against Jews. We recognized that if we were going to be equals in American society we had to be better. That's how we made it. The black community is going to have to do it too. It's already happened in sports and entertainment. It's just a matter of time before it happens in every other sphere of society too."

There was a momentary pause, and Harry decided to get into the act. "Listen Gaston, let me give you some advice."

"Oh wait, I know this one," Gaston said playfully. "Never show your dick or your money, never start a home improvement project when the hardware store is closed and never play poker with a guy named Doc. Right, Harry?"

"That's one of my favorites," I said.

There was laughter around the table. Harry lowered his eyebrows sternly. "That's not what I was going to say."

I watched Delores look around at her new friends. The glint in her eye revealed the young woman that Traub had fallen in love with. She noticed me staring, and she smiled back. Turning to her her husband she said, "Ajela, say a few words to honor the evening."

He nodded his head, pushed back his chair and cleared his throat. Picking up his glass of dry sherry, he began.

"I'd like to make a toast to Joe Green. By some grace of God, he uncovered a secret that haunted my past. The way he put this evening together and the great success that it's been has helped heal something that's been eating at me for years. So I'd like to thank him. How lucky I am to have found a friend in the baby-boomer generation who shares the same ideals that I do. Here's to you, Joe."

They all tipped their glasses in my direction and drank. Harry raised his eyebrows and gave me a smirk, mocking the testimonial. From the lascivious wink Joannie gave me, I knew our celebration would not end with dinner.

Just before the group went home I gathered up A.J., Gaston and Joannie. Grabbing the camera Harry had behind the bar, I had Minnie take a picture of us. Another picture of the eight of us was taken by Shameem.

The next day a story about Traub's speech graced the front page of the *Washington Post* style section. It was broadcast at noon on National Public Radio. China and I listened carefully to it in my store as I priced books.

Chapter 28

Anglund called the next night. "We're going to the movies tomorrow night. Want to come along?"

"Sure," I said.

Four of us went to the Biograph Theater in Georgetown—John, Sven, Cal and me. No one mentioned what film was showing. I was enjoying their company so much that I never thought to ask. It wasn't until I saw the marquee out front that I realized what we were in for. It was a Ronald Reagan double feature—*Bonzo Goes to College* and *The Santa Fe Trail*.

These movies were attracting interest since the star of the show was making a serious bid for the presidency. No one desired to sit through two whole movies, so we caught the tail end of the Bonzo movie and settled in for *The Santa Fe Trail*.

Cal knew that Bonzo jokes would be thrown at him because he had a Reagan bumper sticker on his car. Cynical liberals in the audience teased Reagan's character throughout the film by imitating the voice of Bonzo, which, though done in poor taste, made everyone laugh.

What struck me most about Reagan's college professor character was how likable he was. It was a different impression from the one Reagan was making in the liberal press which portrayed him as the bane of all enlightenment.

In the second movie, *The Santa Fe Trail*, Reagan played straight man to Errol Flynn. Like most Flynn films he got the girl, Olivia De Havilland. No great feat there, he'd done it at least seven other times.

I've never watched any actor who was better at swashbuckling than Flynn. And charming? He's the best. To Reagan's credit he didn't look too bad standing beside him.

In *The Santa Fe Trail*, Reagan played George Armstrong Custer while Flynn played Jeb Stuart. The two of them were buddies at West Point and later rode together in Kansas against the radical abolitionist John Brown, who was played by Raymond Massey. Jefferson Davis, Robert E. Lee and several other Civil War generals like Phil Sheridan were also portrayed. It was a good "shoot 'em up western" that all of us enjoyed. The crowd laughed when Flynn reminded Reagan they were soldiers and not politicians and hence, were not supposed to think.

Despite the compelling script, which more than held our interest, I knew that all four of us were making mental notes for the inevitable debate that would follow the movie.

Sven "harrumphed" more than once when Reagan said something in the movie out of character with his political persona. Cal was making mental notes to defend Reagan from Sven's onslaught. Anglund just seemed to be enjoying the gun play. We walked to a bar called "Poor Roberts" when it ended.

"Can you believe that a guy like Reagan might be our fortieth president?" asked Sven.

"Actually, he is a pretty likable character," I said.

"Baloney," said Sven, "he's just an actor."

"Why is it okay for a peanut farmer to be president but not an actor?" asked Cal.

"Because Jimmy Carter really was a farmer. He didn't pretend for the benefit of a camera and a contrived plot," said Sven.

"Reagan served two terms running the biggest state in the union, California. Its budget is bigger than most of the countries of the world. But that carries no weight. I swear, guys like you think the world would be a better place if people just shed their designer jeans."

"That's right, I do," said Sven. "I think it's the hallmark of the coming age—style over substance."

"Hey, you're getting out of the game anyway, so your opinion no longer matters," said Cal.

Anglund and I looked at each other and smiled, neither one of us wanting to get caught up in their debate. But there was a stalemate between the two of them, and they were looking to us to break the deadlock.

"I think Reagan's got a great chance to win," said Anglund. "Look at it from a campaign manager's point of view. He's got great name identification. Everybody's known him for years, and the opinion they have of him is based on films in which he plays the self-effacing good guy. Not bad I'd say. All he has to do is prove that he can handle the rigors of the campaign and he's a contender."

"Spoken like a true political hack," said Sven.

"What I found interesting about the film is the way they portrayed John Brown," said Anglund. "I don't know that much about Brown, but they really made you hate him even though he had an honorable cause—freeing the slaves. What's ironic is that Reagan went gunning for liberals in the movie, just like he's gunning for liberals today."

"I always worry when Hollywood writes history," I said. "I found it a little too convenient that Custer, Stuart, Jefferson Davis, Robert E. Lee, Phil Sheridan, and John Brown should just happen to be hanging around waiting to get involved in an historical drama. I have a selection of Civil War books back at my store, and I can't wait to get back and see how accurate the facts are."

"I think you're on to something when you're talking about history," said Anglund. "The movie was done in 1940. It was a time when the world was preparing for world war. What it portrayed was the life of a legendary hero from the Old South and another from the North, putting their politics aside in order to fight together for America. Maybe that sentiment needed cultivation in 1940. It's just unfortunate that the villain should be someone fighting for racial equality. But if it helped unite the nation for the fight against fascism then perhaps it's understandable."

"But your judgment's an anachronism," said Cal. "The movie was made in 1940 long before the Civil Rights movement. You can't expect a movie made forty years ago to express 1980 values."

"I thought Reagan was real believable leading the cavalry charge," I said. "If he becomes president and a crisis erupts he'd basically have to do the same thing—get in front of a camera and act tough. I don't think there's any doubt that he can do that."

"Oh Jesus, I can't believe I'm listening to this," said Sven. "Green of all people. I can't believe that you'd vote for that reactionary."

"I never said I'd vote for him. I just don't hate him the way you do. My father told me to vote for the guy who will promote my interests. Reagan made his name in film... that's my rival medium. If he gets elected and promotes movie culture, people will stop reading. Call it enlightened self-interest. I just can't vote for a film star."

I managed to pull Sven aside at one point and I asked him, "What's this about you getting out of the game?"

"I'm going to marry my college sweetheart and move back to St. Paul. I've been offered a job doing research for the Democratic Farmer-Labor Party. It's not a great job, but at least it's a foot in the hometown door. Kristin just graduated law school and has a job lobbying for a Minnesota trade association. In Minnesota, what she's earning is big bucks. She wants to support me until I get settled, buy a house, raise a family, the whole nine yards."

"Are you sure that's what you want?"

"I've invested a lot of time here, so I hate to leave. But all I'll ever be in DC is someone else's lackey. Me and Kristin have been talking about this for a long time. If I really want to do anything in politics, back home is where I have to start. It's one of the most liberal areas of the country, so I'll fit in well there."

"What did she do to persuade you?" I asked.

"Fucked my legs off and then cried a lot."

"I guess you never had a chance."

"Actually, I've seen it coming for some time," he said. "The opportunity to do it painlessly is here so I'm going."

Cal and Sven both had meetings the next morning and walked home together after their second beer. John and I ordered another round.

"Peterson told me he's leaving. I'm sorry to see him go."

"Me too," said John. "But he's been unhappy for some time, and he's not as much fun as he used to be. Besides, him and Cal are always at each other's throat."

"I can't say as I blame Sven. I look at what's going on, and I feel like an outsider myself."

"I used to feel the same way," said John. "But it's no longer a matter of ideals for me. It's a job that I'm trying to be good at."

"Well, it doesn't sound too bad for Sven," I said. "He's got a girlfriend and a job to go back to."

"Speaking of girlfriends, what's the story with you and Joannie?"

"We're friends."

"Come on, tell. Are you guys going steady? Are you sleeping together? What are your intentions?"

"Who wants to know?"

Those question weren't part of the usual Anglund discourse. Between us it was strictly culture and politics. He was pulling for answers that I really didn't think he was interested in. Plus, he was blushing.

"Okay, Liston asked me to find out," he confessed. "But don't tell Joannie. Her parents are coming to DC. They heard she had a Jewish boyfriend and is getting cold feet about the State Department job. They're concerned. They asked Liston about your relationship. He was embarrassed to say he didn't really know. So he asked me to inquire, discreetly."

"Tell him I love her," I said.

"Really? You don't have to say—"

"Tell him."

I got back home around midnight, but I wasn't very sleepy. That movie was on my mind. Were Custer and Stuart really the heroes they were portrayed as? I decided to check my shelves.

I found that most everything the movie portrayed was indeed true. Jeb Stuart did graduate from West Point in 1854, and John Brown was the religious zealot Raymond Massey portrayed him as.

Robert E. Lee and Jeb Stuart were leading the forces that captured John Brown at Harper's Ferry, Virginia.

Apparently, Ronald Reagan's character, George Armstrong Custer, was the only part of the movie that was fake. He didn't graduate West Point in 1854. It was 1861. He never wooed Jefferson Davis's daughter at a plush Washington ball and never led a charge against John Brown.

Well, so much for cinematic history. I was sure Hollywood would justify it as poetic license. But I wondered if skewed facts like these would be the hallmark of a Reagan presidency.

Chapter 29

Delores Traub called me the next day. "He's dead, Joe." There was a tone of disbelief in her voice. "I don't understand it. He just died."

"Oh God, Delores, I'm so sorry. What happened?"

"Neither one of us could sleep last night, so I made us both a glass of warm milk. We talked for a while about the speech and all the new projects he had planned. Then he went to his study. He used to get up at six o'clock every morning and bring me coffee. When he didn't come I went looking for him. He was slumped over his desk."

With that she started sobbing.

Adolph Joseph Traub made headlines in the *Washington Post* twice in one week. The first was the speech, the second his obituary. For me it was a shock. And the hurt I felt brought back forgotten memories of my father.

Gaston wrote an emotional first-person piece on his short, but meaningful relationship with the old man in his newspaper.

The funeral was at a Jewish cemetery in Maryland. It was near the end of January, but warm weather from the south raised temperatures into the forties. Joannie and I got there early to say our goodbyes in private, but before we even reached the gravesite her beeper went off.

"Oh Gosh. Sorry, I've got to go."

"Take the Checker, I'll get a ride home."

There was something very meaningful about that. While one person was being buried, another was being born. That's the way life is supposed to be. I walked over to George Luft to express my condolences. How different he was from his best friend. Luft was a shy introvert. His handshake was cold and clammy, and that disappointed me when we had first met. But his quiet sober voice drew me in. You had to listen attentively to hear what he was saying, and it was always worth the effort.

"It was good that before he died he had one more chance to get up and rail against the establishment," said Luft. "He has you to thank for that."

"I could have learned so much from him. Now I feel cheated."

"Delores asked me to be his literary executor. I told her you should do it instead," said Luft.

"You'd be a much better choice."

"That's true, I would be a better choice. Unfortunately, I've been diagnosed with cancer. I'm about to begin chemotherapy, and I'm afraid that I won't have the time to order my own work, let alone his."

"Oh God, not you too, George. I'm losing all my role models."

"Joe, it's time for you to pick up the baton."

"I don't know how."

"You know, in my day most publishing houses started out as used bookstores."

"Maybe, but that's years away."

"But you have the years."

I laughed. "Yes, world enough and time."

"This might be an inappropriate time to mention it, but my new book will be published in March. I was wondering if you could arrange a reading for me like you did for A.J."

"Sorry, I only sell old books. Your new book won't be available in my store for two years."

He looked embarrassed to have even asked.

To my surprise I watched Rock McMorrow get out of his car. George and I stood shoulder to shoulder as he came toward us.

"Do you suppose he's here to get the last word?"

"Can you believe the nerve of this guy," I said.

McMorrow was dressed in a black suit. He had his hands folded behind his back. I didn't want to talk to him. So I turned to Luft and looked for something to say.

"Listen George, I have an idea. How about if I sponsor a reading for you in April. By then I could collect a large number of your earlier books and sell them at the reading. I think it would be more interesting to stress your lifetime achievement. I learned a lot from the Traub gig. I think I can do better this time."

"That would be wonderful. How about if we meet for lunch next week to discuss it?"

McMorrow interrupted us. He had a small bouquet of white mums in his right hand, and that seemed to alleviate any obligation to shake. "Gentlemen, I just want to express my sadness at the loss of your good friend."

I did not respond. The best I could do was raise my eyebrows. He walked past. He repeated the sentiment to Delores and handed her the flowers.

Anglund was twenty steps behind. "What the fuck is he doing here?" I asked.

"Blood is thicker than water," Anglund said.

"What do you mean?"

"When Liston found out what McMorrow did at your reading, he was furious. He considers you family now. He ordered McMorrow to come and apologize."

***

That night after I closed the bookstore, I sat at the desk and took a few tokes of Ghani Purp. I turned the phone off and lowered the lights. China slept at my feet. I stared at the photo of our victory party. Four of us were in it—Joannie, Gaston, A.J. and me. Big smiles were on all of our faces, and our arms were wrapped around each other. I never noticed the boyish dimples in Traub's cheeks before. I found a hammer and nail and hung the photo near the front door beside pictures of Thomas Jefferson, Walt Whitman and Moses Green.

I thought to shed tears, but sobbing is beyond my ability. For some reason I only cry when I'm happy. However, I did sneeze... a loud "achoo" that shook my bones. Alone in my store, there was no one to say, "God bless you, Joseph." It didn't matter... I was already blessed.

So I got good and drunk and later, in the wee hours of a silent night, I lit a candle and chanted a solemn prayer for Traub, my father, my great grandfather and a million other men who are lost and searching for a way home.

The End

About the Author

Bob Gilbert grew up in Jackson Township, New Jersey. He attended American University and later moved to Minneapolis where he worked as a newspaper reporter and a waiter. His passions include backpacking and the study of old books. Currently, he splits his time between Washington, D.C. and the Philippines where he is working on his fourth novel.